11.75

1/75 mc

STEPHEN ARCHER

AND OTHER TALES

PHOSY.

STEPHEN ARCHER

AND OTHER TALES

BY

GEORGE MACDONALD

Short Story Index Reprint Series

BOOKS FOR LIBRARIES PRESS
FREEPORT, NEW YORK

First Published 1888 ?
Reprinted 1971

INTERNATIONAL STANDARD BOOK NUMBER:
0-8369-3805-4

LIBRARY OF CONGRESS CATALOG CARD NUMBER:
79-152946

PRINTED IN THE UNITED STATES OF AMERICA

CONTENTS.

STEPHEN ARCHER.

STEPHEN ARCHER was a stationer, bookseller,
and newsmonger in one of the suburbs of
London. The newspapers hung in a sort
of rack at his door, as if for the convenience
of the public to help themselves in passing.
On his counter lay penny weeklies and books
coming out in parts, amongst which the
Family Herald was in force, and the *London
Journal* not to be found. I had occasion once
to try the extent of his stock, for I required
a good many copies of one of Shakspere's
plays—at a penny, if I could find such. He
shook his head, and told me he could not
encourage the sale of such productions. This
pleased me; for, although it was of little
consequence what he thought concerning
Shakspere, it was of the utmost import that
he should prefer principle to pence. So I
loitered in the shop, looking for something
to buy; but there was nothing in the way
of literature: his whole stock, as far as I
could see, consisted of little religious volumes
of gay binding and inferior print; he had

nothing even from the Halifax press. He was a good-looking fellow, about thirty, with dark eyes, overhanging brows that indicated thought, mouth of character, and no smile. I was interested in him.

I asked if he would mind getting the plays I wanted. He said he would rather not. I bade him good morning.

More than a year after, I saw him again. I had passed his shop many times, but this morning, I forget why, I went in. I could hardly recall the former appearance of the man, so was it swallowed up in a new expression. His face was alive, and his behaviour courteous. A similar change had passed upon his stock. There was *Punch* and *Fun* amongst the papers, and tenpenny Shaksperes on the counter, printed on straw-paper, with ugly wood-cuts. The former class of publications had not vanished, but was mingled with cheap editions of some worthy of being called books.

"I see you have changed your mind since I saw you last," I said.

"You have the advantage of me, sir," he returned. "I did not know you were a customer."

"Not much of that," I replied; "only in intention. I wanted you to get me some penny Shaksperes, and you would not take the order."

"Oh! I think I remember," he answered, with just a trace of confusion; adding, with a smile, "I'm married now;" and I fancied I could read a sort of triumph over his former self.

I laughed, of course—the best expression of sympathy at hand—and, after a little talk, left the shop, resolved to look in again soon. Before a month was over, I had made the acquaintance of his wife too, and between them learned so much of their history as to be able to give the following particulars concerning it.

Stephen Archer was one of the deacons, rather a young one perhaps, of a dissenting congregation. The chapel was one of the oldest in the neighbourhood, quite triumphant in ugliness, but possessed of a history which gave it high rank with those who frequented it. The sacred odour of the names of pastors who had occupied its pulpit, lingered about its walls—names unknown beyond its precincts, but starry in the eyes of those whose world lay within its tabernacle. People generally do not know what a power some of these small *conventicles* are in the education of the world. If only as an outlet for the energies of men of lowly education and position, who in connexion with most of the churches of the Establishment would find no employment, they are of inestimable value.

To Stephen Archer, for instance, when I saw him first, his chapel was the sole door out of the common world into the infinite. When he entered, as certainly did the awe and the hush of the sacred place overshadow his spirit as if it had been a gorgeous cathedral-house borne aloft upon the joined palms of its Gothic arches. The Master is truer than men think, and the power of His presence, as Browning has so well set forth in his " Christmas Eve," is where two or three are gathered in His name. And inasmuch as Stephen was not a man of imagination, he had the greater need of the undefined influences of the place.

He had been chief in establishing a small mission amongst the poor in the neighbourhood, with the working of which he occupied the greater part of his spare time. I will not venture to assert that his mind was pure from the ambition of gathering from these to swell the flock at the little chapel ; nay, I will not even assert that there never arose a suggestion of the enemy that the pence of these rescued brands might alleviate the burden upon the heads and shoulders of the poorly prosperous caryatids of his church ; but I do say that Stephen was an honest man in the main, ever ready to grow honester : and who can demand more ?

One evening, as he was putting up the shutters of his window, his attention was arrested by a shuffling behind him. Glancing round, he set down the shutter, and the next instant boxed a boy's ears, who ran away howling and mildly excavating his eyeballs, while a young, pale-faced woman, with the largest black eyes he had ever seen, expostulated with him on the proceeding.

"Oh, sir!" she said, "he wasn't troubling you." There was a touch of indignation in the tone.

"I'm sorry I can't return the compliment," said Stephen, rather illogically. "If I'd ha' known you liked to have your shins kicked, I might ha' let the young rascal alone. But you see I didn't know it."

"He's my brother," said the young woman, conclusively.

"The more shame to him," returned Stephen. "If he'd been your husband, now, there might ha' been more harm than good in interferin', 'cause he'd only give it you the worse after; but brothers! Well, I'm sure it's a pity I interfered."

"I don't see the difference," she retorted, still with offence.

"I beg your pardon, then," said Stephen. "I promise you I won't interfere next time."

So saying, he turned, took up his shutter, and proceeded to close his shop. The young woman walked on.

Stephen gave an inward growl or two at the depravity of human nature, and set out to make his usual visits; but before he reached the place, he had begun to doubt whether the old Adam had not overcome him in the matter of boxing the boy's ears; and the following interviews appeared in consequence less satisfactory than usual. Disappointed with himself, he could not be so hopeful about others.

As he was descending a stair so narrow that it was only just possible for two people to pass, he met the same young woman ascending. Glad of the opportunity, he stepped aside with his best manners and said :

" I am sorry I offended you this evening. I did not know that the boy was your brother."

" Oh, sir ! " she returned—for to one in her position, Stephen Archer was a gentleman : had he not a shop of his own ?—" you didn't hurt him much ; only I'm so anxious to save him."

" To be sure," returned Stephen, " that is the one thing needful."

" Yes, sir," she rejoined. " I try hard, but boys will be boys."

" There is but one way, you know," said Stephen, following the words with a certain formula which I will not repeat.

The girl stared. " I don't know about that," she said. " What I want is to keep him out of prison. Sometimes I think I shan't be able long. Oh, sir ! if you be the gentleman that goes about here, couldn't you help me ? I can't get anything for him to do, and I can't be at home to look after him."

" What is he about all day, then ? "

" The streets," she answered. " I don't know as he's ever done anything he oughtn't

to, but he came home once in a fright, and
that breathless with running, that I thought
he'd ha' fainted. If I only could get him
into a place!"

"Do you live here?" he asked.

"Yes, sir; I do."

At the moment a half-bestial sound below,
accompanied by uncertain footsteps, announced the arrival of a drunken bricklayer.

"There's Joe Bradley," she said, in some
alarm. "Come into my room, sir, till he's
gone up; there's no harm in him when he's
sober, but he ain't been sober for a week
now."

Stephen obeyed; and she, taking a key
from her pocket, and unlocking a door on the
landing, led him into a room to which his
back-parlour was a paradise. She offered
him the only chair in the room, and took
her place on the edge of the bed, which
showed a clean but much-worn patchwork
quilt. Charley slept on the bed, and she on
a shake-down in the corner. The room was
not untidy, though the walls and floor were
not clean; indeed there were not in it articles
enough to make it untidy withal.

"Where do you go on Sundays?" asked
Stephen.

"Nowheres. I ain't got nobody," she
added, with a smile, "to take me nowheres."

"What do you do then?"

"I've plenty to do mending of Charley's
trousers. You see they're only shoddy, and

as fast as I patch 'em in one place they're out in another."

" But you oughtn't to work Sundays."

" I have heard tell of people as say you oughtn't to work of a Sunday ; but where's the differ when you've got a brother to look after ?   He ain't got no mother."

" But you're breaking the fourth commandment; and you know where people go that do that.   You believe in hell, I suppose."

" I always thought that was a bad word."

" To be sure !   But it's where you'll go if you break the Sabbath."

" Oh, sir !" she said, bursting into tears, " I don't care what become of me if I could only save that boy."

" What do you mean by *saving* him ? "

" Keep him out of prison, to be sure.   I shouldn't mind the workus myself, if I could get him into a place."

A place was her heaven, a prison her hell.

Stephen looked at her more attentively. No one who merely glanced at her could help seeing her eyes first, and no one who regarded them could help thinking her nice-looking at least, all in a shabby cotton dress and black shawl as she was.   It was only the " penury and pine " that kept her from being beautiful. Her features were both regular and delicate, with an anxious mystery about the thin tremulous lips, and a beseeching look, like that of an animal, in her fine eyes, hazy with the trouble that haunted her mouth.   Stephen had the good sense not to press the Sabbath question, and by degrees drew her story from her.

Her father had been a watchmaker, but, giving way to drink, had been, as far back as she could remember, entirely dependent on her mother, who by charing and jobbing managed to keep the family alive. Sara was then the only child, but, within a few months after her father's death, her mother died in giving birth to the boy. With her last breath she had commended him to his sister. Sara had brought him up—how she hardly knew. He had been everything to her. The child that her mother had given her was all her thought. Those who start with the idea " that people with nought are naughty," whose eyes are offended by rags, whose ears cannot distinguish between vulgarity and wickedness, and who think the first duty is care for self, must be excused from believing that Sara Coulter passed through all that had been *decreed* for her without losing her simplicity and purity. But God is in the back slums as certainly as —perhaps to some eyes more evidently than —in Belgravia. That which was the burden of her life—namely, the care of her brother— was her salvation. After hearing her story, which he had to draw from her, because she had no impulse to talk about herself, Stephen went home to turn the matter over in his mind.

The next Sunday, after he had had his

dinner, he went out into the same region, and found himself at Sara's door. She was busy over a garment of Charley's, who was sitting on the bed with half a loaf in his hand. When he recognized Stephen he jumped down, and would have rushed from the room; but changing his mind, possibly because of the condition of his lower limbs, he turned, and springing into the bed, scrambled under the counterpane, and drew it over his head.

"I am sorry to see you working on Sunday," Stephen said, with an emphasis that referred to their previous conversation.

"You would not have the boy go naked?" she returned, with again a touch of indignation. She had been thinking how easily a man of Stephen's social position could get him a place if he would. Then recollecting her manners, she added, "I should get him better clothes if he had a place. Wouldn't you like to get a place now, Charley?"

"Yes," said Charley, from under the counterpane, and began to peep at the visitor.

He was not an ill-looking boy — only roguish to a degree. His eyes, as black as his sister's, but only half as big, danced and twinkled with mischief. Archer would have taken him off to his ragged class, but even of rags he had not at the moment the complement necessary for admittance. He left them, therefore, with a few commonplaces of

religious phrase, falling utterly meaningless.
But he was not one to confine his ministra-
tions to words : he was an honest man.
Before the next Sunday it was clear to him
that he could do nothing for the soul of
Sara until he had taken the weight of her
brother off it.

When he called the next Sunday the same
vision precisely met his view. She might
have been sitting there ever since, with those
wonderfully-patched trousers in her hands,
and the boy beside her, gnawing at his lump
of bread. But many a long seam had passed
through her fingers since then, for she
worked at a clothes-shop all the week with
the sewing-machine, whence arose the possibility of patching Charley's clothes, for the
overseer granted her a cutting or two now
and then.

After a little chat, Stephen put the question :

" If I find a place for Charley, will you
go to Providence Chapel next Sunday ? "

" I will go *anywhere* you please, Mr.
Archer," she answered, looking up quickly
with a flushed face. She would have accompanied him to any casino in London just
as readily : her sole thought was to keep
Charley out of prison. Her father had been
in prison once ; to keep her mother's child
out of prison was the grand object of her life.

" Well," he resumed, with some hesitation,
for he had arrived at the resolution through

difficulties, whose fogs yet lingered about him, "if he will be an honest, careful boy, I will take him myself."

"Charley! Charley!" cried Sara, utterly neglectful of the source of the benefaction; and rising, she went to the bed and hugged him.

"Don't, Sara!" said Charley, petulantly. "I don't want girls to squash me. Leave go, I say. You mend my trousers, and *I'*ll take care of *my*self."

"The little wretch!" thought Stephen.

Sara returned to her seat, and her needle went almost as fast as her sewing-machine. A glow had arisen now, and rested on her pale cheek: Stephen found himself staring at a kind of transfiguration, back from the ghostly to the human. His admiration extended itself to her deft and slender fingers and there brooded until his conscience informed him that he was actually admiring the breaking of the Sabbath; whereupon he rose. But all the time he was about amongst the rest of his people, his thoughts kept wandering back to the desolate room, the thankless boy, and the ministering woman. Before leaving, however, he had arranged with Sara that she should bring her brother to the shop the next day.

The awe with which she entered it was not shared by Charley, who was never ripe for anything but frolic. Had not Stephen been influenced by a desire to do good, and

possibly by another feeling too embryonic
for detection, he would never have dreamed
of making an errand boy of a will-o'-the-
wisp. As such, however, he was installed,
and from that moment an anxiety unknown
before took possession of Stephen's bosom.
He was never at ease, for he never knew
what the boy might be about. He would
have parted with him the first fortnight, but
the idea of the prison had passed from Sara's
heart into his, and he saw that to turn the
boy away from his first place would be to
accelerate his gravitation thitherward. He
had all the tricks of a newspaper boy in-
digenous in him. Repeated were the complaints brought to the shop. One time the
paper was thrown down the area, and
brought into the breakfast-room defiled with
wet. At another it was found on the door-
step, without the bell having been rung,
which could hardly have been from forget-
fulness, for Charley's delight was to set the
bell ringing furiously, and then wait till the
cook appeared, taking good care however to
leave space between them for a start. Sometimes the paper was not delivered at all, and
Stephen could not help suspecting that he
had sold it in the street. Yet both for his
sake and Sara's he endured, and did not
even box his ears. The boy hardly seemed
to be wicked: the spirit that possessed him
was rather a *poltèr-geist*, as the Germans
would call it, than a demon.

Meantime, the Sunday after Charley's appointment, Archer, seated in his pew, searched all the chapel for the fulfilment of Sara's part of the agreement, namely, her presence. But he could see her nowhere. The fact was, her promise was so easy that she had scarcely thought of it after, not suspecting that Stephen laid any stress upon its fulfilment, and, indeed, not knowing where the chapel was. She had managed to buy a bit of something of the shoddy species, and while Stephen was looking for her in the chapel, she was making a jacket for Charley. Greatly disappointed, and chiefly, I do believe, that she had not kept her word, Stephen went in the afternoon to call upon her.

He found her working away as before, and saving time by taking her dinner while she worked, for a piece of bread lay on the table by her elbow, and beside it a little brown sugar to make the bread go down. The sight went to Stephen's heart, for he had just made his dinner off baked mutton and potatoes, washed down with his half-pint of stout.

"Sara!" he said solemnly, "you promised to come to our chapel, and you have not kept your word." He never thought that "our chapel" was not the landmark of the region.

"Oh, Mr. Archer," she answered, "I didn't know as you cared about it. But," she went on, rising and pushing her bread on one side to make room for her work, "I'll put on my bonnet directly." Then she checked herself, and added, "Oh! I beg your pardon, sir— I'm so shabby! You couldn't be seen with the likes of me."

It touched Stephen's chivalry—and something deeper than chivalry. He had had no intention of walking with her.

"There's no chapel in the afternoon," he said; "but I'll come and fetch you in the evening."

Thus it came about that Sara was seated in Stephen's pew, next to Stephen himself, and Stephen felt a strange pleasure unknown before, like that of the shepherd who having brought the stray back to the fold cares little that its wool is torn by the bushes, and it looks a ragged and disreputable sheep. It was only Sara's wool that might seem disreputable, for she was a very good-faced sheep. He found the hymns for her, and they shared the same book. He did not know then that Sara could not read a word of them.

The gathered people, the stillness, the gaslights, the solemn ascent of the minister into the pulpit, the hearty singing of the congregation, doubtless had their effect upon Sara, for she had never been to a chapel and hardly to any place of assembly before. From all amusements, the burden of Charley and her own retiring nature had kept her back.

But she could make nothing of the sermon.

She confessed afterwards that she did not know she had anything to do with it. Like "the Northern Farmer," she took it all for the clergyman's business, which she amongst the rest had to see done. She did not even wonder why Stephen should have wanted to bring her there. She sat when other people sat, pretended to kneel when other people pretended to kneel, and stood up when other people stood up—still brooding upon Charley's jacket.

But Archer's feelings were not those he had expected. He had brought her, intending her to be done good to; but before the sermon was over he wished he had not brought her. He resisted the feeling for a long time, but at length yielded to it entirely; the object of his solicitude all the while conscious only of the lighted stillness and the new barrier between Charley and Newgate. The fact with regard to Stephen was that a certain hard *pan*, occasioned by continual ploughings to the same depth and no deeper, in the soil of his mind, began this night to be broken up from within, and that through the presence of a young woman who did not for herself put together two words of the whole discourse.

The pastor was preaching upon the saying of St. Paul, that he could wish himself accursed from Christ for his brethren. Great part of his sermon was an attempt to prove that he could not have meant what his words implied. For the preacher's mind was so filled with the supposed paramount duty of saving his own soul, that the enthusiasm of the Apostle was simply incredible. Listening with that woman by his side, Stephen for the first time grew doubtful of the wisdom of his pastor. Nor could he endure that such should be the first doctrine Sara heard from his lips. Thus was he already and grandly repaid for his kindness; for the presence of a woman who without any conscious religion was to herself a law of love, brought him so far into sympathy with the mighty soul of St. Paul, that from that moment the blessing of doubt was at work in his, undermining prison walls.

He walked home with Sara almost in silence, for he found it impossible to impress upon her those parts of the sermon with which he had no fault to find, lest she should retort upon that one point. The arrows which Sara escaped, however, could from her ignorance have struck her only with their feather end.

Things proceeded in much the same fashion for a while. Charley went home at night to his sister's lodging, generally more than two hours after leaving the shop, but gave her no new ground of complaint. Every Sunday evening Sara went to the chapel, taking Charley with her when she could persuade him to go; and, in obedience with the supposed wish of Stephen, sat in his pew. He

C

did not go home with her any more for a while, and indeed visited her but seldom, anxious to avoid scandal, more especially as he was a deacon.

But now that Charley was so far safe, Sara's cheek began to generate a little of that celestial rosy red which is the blossom of the woman-plant, although after all it hardly equalled the heart of the blush rose. She grew a little rounder in form too, for she lived rather better now,—buying herself a rasher of bacon twice a week. Hence she began to be in more danger, as any one acquainted with her surroundings will easily comprehend. But what seemed at first the ruin of her hopes dissipated this danger.

One evening, when she returned from her work, she found Stephen in her room. She made him the submissive grateful salutation, half courtesy, half bow, with which she always greeted him, and awaited his will.

"I am very sorry to have to tell you, Sara, that your brother—— "

She turned white as a shroud, and her great black eyes grew greater and blacker as she stared in agonized expectancy while Stephen hesitated in search of a better form of communication. Finding none, he blurted out the fact—

"—has robbed me, and run away."

"Don't send him to prison, Mr. Archer," shrieked Sara, and laid herself on the floor at his feet with a grovelling motion, as if

striving with her mother earth for comfort.
There was not a film of art in this. She had
never been to a theatre. The natural urging
of life gave the truest shape to her entreaty.
Her posture was the result of the same feeling
which made the nations of old bring their
sacrifices to the altar of a deity who, possibly
benevolent in the main, had yet cause to be
inimical to them. From the prostrate living
sacrifice arose the one prayer, " Don't send
him to prison; don't send him to prison!"

Stephen gazed at her in bewildered admiration, half divine and all human. A certain
consciousness of power had, I confess, a part
in his silence, but the only definite shape this
consciousness took was of beneficence. At-
tributing his silence to unwillingness, Sara
got half-way from the ground—that is, to
her knees—and lifted a face of utter entreaty
to the sight of Stephen. I will not say
words fail me to describe the intensity of its
prayer, for words fail me to describe the
commonest phenomenon of nature : all I can
is to say, that it made Stephen's heart too
large for its confining walls. " Mr. Archer,"
she said, in a voice hollow with emotion, " I
will do *anything* you like. I will be your
slave. Don't send Charley to prison."

The words were spoken with a certain
strange dignity of self-abnegation. It is not
alone the country people of Cumberland or
of Scotland, who in their highest moments
are capable of poetic utterance.

An indescribable thrill of conscious delight shot through the frame of Stephen as the woman spoke the words. But the gentleman in him triumphed. I would have said *the Christian*, for whatever there was in Stephen of the *gentle* was there in virtue of the *Christian*, only he failed in one point : instead of saying at once, that he had no intention of prosecuting the boy, he pretended, I believe from the satanic delight in power that possesses every man of us, that he would turn it over in his mind. It might have been more dangerous, but it would have been more divine, if he had lifted the kneeling woman to his heart, and told her that not for the wealth of an imagination would he proceed against her brother. The divinity, however, was taking its course, both rough-hewing and shaping the ends of the two.

She rose from the ground, sat on the one chair, with her face to the wall, and wept helplessly, with the added sting, perhaps, of a faint personal disappointment. Stephen failed to attract her notice, and left the room. She started up when she heard the door close, and flew to open it, but was only in time to hear the outer door. She sat down and cried again.

Stephen had gone to find the boy if he might, and bring him to his sister. He ought to have said so, for to permit suffering for the sake of a joyful surprise is not good. Going home first, he was hardly seated in

his room, to turn over not the matter but the
means, when a knock came to the shop-door,
the sole entrance, and there were two policemen bringing the deserter in a cab. He had
been run over in the very act of decamping
with the contents of the till, had lain all but
insensible at the hospital while his broken
leg was being set, but, as soon as he came
to himself, had gone into such a fury of
determination to return to his master, that
the house-surgeon saw that the only chance
for the ungovernable creature was to yield.
Perhaps he had some dim idea of restoring
the money ere his master should have discovered its loss. As he was very little,
they made a couch for him in the cab, and
so sent him.

It would appear that the suffering and the
faintness had given his conscience a chance
of being heard. The accident was to Charley
what the sight of the mountain-peak was
to the boy Wordsworth. He was delirious
when he arrived, and instead of showing any
contrition towards his master, only testified
an extravagant joy at finding him again.
Stephen had him taken into the back room,
and laid upon his own bed. One of the
policemen fetched the charwoman, and when
she arrived, Stephen went to find Sara.

She was sitting almost as he had left her,
with a dull, hopeless look.

"I am sorry to say Charley has had an
accident," he said.

She started up and clasped her hands.

"He is not in prison?" she panted in a husky voice.

"No; he is at my house. Come and see him. I don't think he is in any danger, but his leg is broken."

A gleam of joy crossed Sara's countenance. She did not mind the broken leg, for he was safe from her terror. She put on her bonnet, tied the strings with trembling hands, and went with Stephen.

"You see God wants to keep him out of prison too," he said, as they walked along the street.

But to Sara this hardly conveyed an idea. She walked by his side in silence.

"Charley! Charley!" she cried, when she saw him white on the bed, rolling his head from side to side. Charley ordered her away with words awful to hear, but which from him meant no more than words of ordinary temper in the mouth of the well-nurtured man or woman. She had spoiled and indulged him all his life, and now for the first time she was nothing to him, while the master who had lectured and restrained him was everything. When the surgeon wanted to change his dressings, he would not let him touch them till his master came. Before he was able to leave his bed, he had developed for Stephen a terrier-like attachment. But, after the first feverishness was over, his sister waited upon him.

Stephen got a lodging, and abandoned his back room to the brother and sister. But he had to attend to his shop, and therefore saw much of both of them. Finding then to his astonishment that Sara could not read, he gave all his odd moments to her instruction, and her mind being at rest about Charley so long as she had him in bed, her spirit had leisure to think of other things.

She learned rapidly. The lesson-book was of course the New Testament; and Stephen soon discovered that Sara's questions, moving his pity at first because of the ignorance they displayed, always left him thinking about some point that had never occurred to him before; so that at length he regarded Sara as a being of superior intelligence waylaid and obstructed by unfriendly powers upon her path towards the threshold of the kingdom, while she looked up to him as to one supreme in knowledge as in goodness. But she never could understand the pastor. This would have been a great trouble to Stephen, had not his vanity been flattered by her understanding of himself. He did not consider that growing love had enlightened his eyes to see into her heart, and enabled him thus to use an ordinary human language for the embodiment of common-sense ideas; whereas the speech of the pastor contained such an admixture of technicalities as to be unintelligible to the neophyte.

Stephen was now distressed to find that

whereas formerly he had received everything
without question that his minister spoke, he
now in general went home in a doubting,
questioning mood, begotten of asking himself
what Sara would say. He feared at first
that the old Adam was beginning to get the
upper hand of him, and that Satan was laying
snares for his soul. But when he found at
the same time that his conscience was growing more scrupulous concerning his business
affairs, his hope sprouted afresh.

One day, after Charley had been out for
the first time, Sara, with a little tremor of
voice and manner, addressed Stephen thus :—

" I shall take Charley home to-morrow, if
you please, Mr. Archer."

" You don't mean to say, Sara, you've been
paying for those lodgings all this time ? "
half-asked, half-exclaimed Stephen.

" Yes, Mr. Archer. We must have somewhere to go to. It ain't easy to get a room
at any moment, now them railways is every-
wheres."

" But I hope as how you're comfortable
where you are, Sara ? "

" Yes, Mr. Archer. But what am I to do
for all your kindness ? "

" You can pay me all in a lump, if you
like, Sara. Only you don't owe me nothing."

Her colour came and went. She was not
used to men. She could not tell what he
would have her understand, and could not
help trembling.

" What do you mean, Mr. Archer ? " she faltered out.

" I mean you can give me yourself, Sara, and that'll clear all scores."

" But, Mr. Archer—you've been a-teaching of me good things—— You *don't* mean to marry me ! " exclaimed Sara, bursting into tears.

" Of course I do, Sara. Don't cry about it. I won't if you don't like."

This is how Stephen came to change his mind about his stock in trade.

THE GIFTS OF THE CHILD CHRIST.

CHAPTER I.

" My hearers, we grow old," said the preacher.
" Be it summer or be it spring with us now,
autumn will soon settle down into winter,
that winter whose snow melts only in the
grave. The wind of the world sets for the
tomb. Some of us rejoice to be swept along
on its swift wings, and hear it bellowing in
the hollows of earth and sky; but it will
grow a terror to the man of trembling limb
and withered brain, until at length he will
long for the shelter of the tomb to escape its
roaring and buffeting. Happy the man who
shall then be able to believe that old age
itself, with its pitiable decays and sad dreams
of youth, is the chastening of the Lord, a
sure sign of his love and his fatherhood."

It was the first Sunday in Advent; but
" the chastening of the Lord " came into
almost every sermon that man preached.

" Eloquent! But after all, *can* this kind
of thing be true?" said to himself a man of

about thirty, who sat decorously listening. For many years he had thought he believed this kind of thing—but of late he was not so sure.

Beside him sat his wife, in her new winter bonnet, her pretty face turned up toward the preacher; but her eyes—nothing else—revealed that she was not listening. She was much younger than her husband — hardly twenty, indeed.

In the upper corner of the pew sat a pale-faced child about five, sucking her thumb, and staring at the preacher.

The sermon over, they walked home in proximity. The husband looked gloomy, and his eyes sought the ground. The wife looked more smiling than cheerful, and her pretty eyes went hither and thither. Behind them walked the child — steadily, " with level-fronting eyelids."

It was a late-built region of large, common-place houses, and at one of them they stopped and entered. The door of the dining-room was open, showing the table laid for their Sunday dinner. The gentleman passed on to the library behind it, the lady went up to her bedroom, and the child a stage higher to the nursery.

It wanted half an hour to dinner. Mr. Greatorex sat down, drummed with his fingers on the arm of his easy-chair, took up a book of arctic exploration, threw it again on the table, got up, and went to

the smoking-room. He had built it for his
wife's sake, but was often glad of it for his
own. Again he seated himself, took a cigar,
and smoked gloomily.

Having reached her bedroom, Mrs. Greatorex took off her bonnet, and stood for ten
minutes turning it round and round. Earn-
estly she regarded it—now gave a twist to
the wire-stem of a flower, then spread wider
the loop of a bow. She was meditating what
it lacked of perfection rather than brooding
over its merits : she was keen in bonnets.

Little Sophy—or, as she called herself by
a transposition of consonant sounds common
with children, Phosy—found her nurse Alice
in the nursery. But she was lost in the
pages of a certain London weekly, which had
found her in a mood open to its influences,
and did not even look up when the child
entered. With some effort Phosy drew off
her gloves, and with more difficulty untied
her hat. Then she took off her jacket,
smoothed her hair, and retreated to a corner.
There a large shabby doll lay upon her little
chair : she took it up, disposed it gently upon
the bed, seated herself in its place, got a little
book from where she had left it under the
chair, smoothed down her skirts, and began
simultaneously to read and suck her thumb.
The book was an unhealthy one, a cup filled
to the brim with a poverty-stricken and
selfish religion : such are always breaking
out like an eruption here and there over the

body of the Church, doing their part, doubtless, in carrying off the evil humours gener-
ated by poverty of blood, or the congestion of
self-preservation. It is wonderful out of what
spoiled fruit some children will suck sweetness.

But she did not read far : her thoughts
went back to a phrase which had haunted
her ever since first she went to church :
" Whom the Lord loveth, he chasteneth."

" I wish he would chasten me," she thought
for the hundredth time.

The small Christian had no suspicion that
her whole life had been a period of chastening—that few children indeed had to live
in such a sunless atmosphere as hers.

Alice threw down the newspaper, gazed
from the window into the back-yard of the
next house, saw nothing but an elderly man-
servant brushing a garment, and turned upon
Sophy.

" Why don't you hang up your jacket,
miss ? " she said, sharply.

The little one rose, opened the wardrobe-
door wide, carried a chair to it, fetched her
jacket from the bed, clambered up on the
chair, and, leaning far forward to reach a
peg, tumbled right into the bottom of the
wardrobe.

" You clumsy ! " exclaimed the nurse
angrily, and pulling her out by the arm,
shook her.

Alice was not generally rough to her, but
there were reasons to-day.

Phosy crept back to her seat, pale, frightened, and a little hurt. Alice hung up the
jacket, closed the wardrobe, and, turning, con-
templated her own pretty face and neat figure
in the glass opposite. The dinner-bell rang.

"There, I declare!" she cried, and wheeled
round on Phosy. "And your hair not
brushed yet, miss! Will you ever learn to
do a thing without being told it? Thank
goodness, I shan't be plagued with you long!
But I pity her as comes after me: I do!"

"If the Lord would but chasten me!" said
the child to herself, as she rose and laid
down her book with a sigh.

The maid seized her roughly by the
arm, and brushed her hair with an angry
haste that made the child's eyes water, and
herself feel a little ashamed at the sight of
them.

"How could anybody love such a troublesome chit?" she said, seeking the comfort of
justification from the child herself.

Another sigh was the poor little damsel's
only answer. She looked very white and
solemn as she entered the dining-room.

Mr. Greatorex was a merchant in the City.
But he was more of a man than a merchant,
which all merchants are not. Also, he was
more scrupulous in his dealings than some
merchants in the same line of business, who
yet stood as well with the world as he; but,
on the other hand, he had the meanness to
pride himself upon it as if it had been some-

thing he might have done without and yet held up his head.

Some six years before, he had married to please his parents ; and a year before, he had married to please himself. His first wife had intellect, education, and heart, but little individuality—not enough to reflect the individuality of her husband. The consequence was, he found her uninteresting. He was kind and indulgent however, and not even her best friend blamed him much for manifesting nothing beyond the average devotion of husbands. But in truth his wife had great capabilities, only they had never ripened, and when she died, a fortnight after giving birth to Sophy, her husband had not a suspicion of the large amount of undeveloped power that had passed away with her.

Her child was so like her both in countenance and manner that he was too constantly reminded of her unlamented mother ; and he loved neither enough to discover that, in a sense as true as marvellous, the child was the very flower-bud of her mother's nature, in which her retarded blossom had yet a chance of being slowly carried to perfection. Love alone gives insight, and the father took her merely for a miniature edition of the volume which he seemed to have laid aside for ever in the dust of the earth's lumber-room. Instead, therefore, of watering the roots of his little human slip from the well of his affections, he had scarcely as yet perceived more in relation to her than that he was legally accountable for her existence, and bound to give her shelter and food. If he had questioned himself on the matter, he would have replied that love was not wanting, only waiting upon her growth, and the development of something to interest him.

Little right as he had had to expect anything from his first marriage, he had yet cherished some hopes therein — tolerably vague, it is true, yet hardly faint enough, it would seem, for he was disappointed in them. When its bonds fell from him, however, he flattered himself that he had not worn them in vain, but had through them arrived at a knowledge of women as rare as profound. But whatever the reach of this knowledge, it was not sufficient to prevent him from harbouring the presumptuous hope of so choosing and so fashioning the heart and mind of a woman that they should be as concave mirrors to his own. I do not mean that he would have admitted the figure, but such was really the end he blindly sought. I wonder how many of those who have been disappointed in such an attempt have been thereby aroused to the perception of what a frightful failure their success would have been on both sides. It was bad enough that Augustus Greatorex's theories had cramped his own development ; it would have been ten-fold worse had they been operative to the stunting of another soul.

Letty Merewether was the daughter of a bishop *in partibus*. She had been born tolerably innocent, had grown up more than tolerably pretty, and was, when she came to England at the age of sixteen, as nearly a genuine example of Locke's sheet of white paper as could well have fallen to the hand of such an experimenter as Greatorex would fain become.

In his suit he had prospered—perhaps too easily. He loved the girl, or at least loved the modified reflection of her in his own mind; while she, thoroughly admiring the dignity, good looks, and accomplishments of the man whose attentions flattered her self-opinion, accorded him deference enough to encourage his vainest hopes. Although she knew little, fluttering over the merest surfaces of existence, she had sense enough to know that he talked sense to her, and foolishness enough to put it down to her own credit, while for the sense itself she cared little or nothing. And Greatorex, without even knowing what she was rough-hewn for, would take upon him to shape her ends!—an ambition the Divinity never permits to succeed: he who fancies himself the carver finds himself but the chisel, or indeed perhaps only the mallet, in the hand of the true workman.

During the days of his courtship, then, Letty listened and smiled, or answered with what he took for a spiritual response, when

D

it was merely a brain-echo. Looking down
into the pond of her being, whose surface
was not yet ruffled by any bubbling of
springs from below, he saw the reflection
of himself and was satisfied. An able man
on his hobby looks a centaur of wisdom
and folly; but if he be at all a wise man,
the beast will one day or other show him
the jade's favour of unseating him. Meantime Augustus Greatorex was fooled, not by
poor little Letty, who was not capable of
fooling him, but by himself. Letty had
made no pretences; had been interested, and
had shown her interest; had understood, or
seemed to understand, what he said to her,
and forgotten it the next moment—had no
pocket to put it in, did not know what to
do with it, and let it drop into the Limbo
of Vanity. They had not been married
many days before the scouts of advancing
disappointment were upon them. Augustus
resisted manfully for a time. But the truth
was each of the two had to become a great
deal more than either was, before any approach
to unity was possible. He tried to interest
her in one subject after another—tried her
first, I am ashamed to say, with political
economy. In that instance, when he came
home to dinner he found that she had not got
beyond the first page of the book he had left
with her. But she had the best of excuses,
namely, that of that page she had not understood a sentence. He saw his mistake, and

tried her with poetry. But Milton, with whom unfortunately he commenced his approaches, was to her, if not equally unintelligible, equally uninteresting. He tried her next with the elements of science, but with no better success. He returned to poetry, and read some of the Faerie Queene with her : she was, or seemed to be, interested in all his talk about it, and inclined to go on with it in his absence, but found the first stanza she tried more than enough without him to give life to it. She could give it none, and therefore it gave her none. I believe she read a chapter of the Bible every day, but the only books she read with any real interest were novels of a sort that Augustus despised. It never occurred to him that he ought at once to have made friends of this Momus of unrighteousness, for by them he might have found entrance to the sealed chamber. He ought to have read with her the books she did like, for by them only could he make her think, and from them alone could he lead her to better. It is but from the very step upon which one stands that one can move to the next. Besides these books, there was nothing in her scheme of the universe but fashion, dress, calls, the park, other-peopledom, concerts, plays, church-going—whatever could show itself on the frosted glass of her *camera obscura*—make an interest of motion and colour in her darkened chamber. Without these, her bosom's mis-

tress would have found life unendurable, for
not yet had she ascended her throne, but lay
on the floor of her nursery, surrounded with
toys that imitated life.

It was no wonder, therefore, that Augustus
was at length compelled to allow himself disappointed. That it was the fault of his self-
confidence made the thing no whit better.
He was too much of a man not to cherish
a certain tenderness for her, but he soon
found to his dismay that it had begun to be
mingled with a shadow of contempt. Against
this he struggled, but with fluctuating success. He stopped later and later at business,
and when he came home spent more and
more of his time in the smoking-room, where
by and by he had bookshelves put up.
Occasionally he would accept an invitation
to dinner and accompany his wife, but he
detested evening parties, and when Letty,
who never refused an invitation if she could
help it, went to one, he remained at home
with his books. But his power of reading
began to diminish. He became restless and
irritable. Something kept gnawing at his
heart. There was a sore spot in it. The
spot grew larger and larger, and by degrees
the centre of his consciousness came to be a
soreness : his cherished idea had been fooled ;
he had taken a silly girl for a woman of
undeveloped wealth ;—a bubble, a surface
whereon fair colours chased each other, for a
hearted crystal.

On her part, Letty too had her grief, which, unlike Augustus, she did not keep to herself, receiving in return from more than one of her friends the soothing assurance that Augustus was only like all other men ; that women were but their toys, which they cast away when weary of them. Letty did not see that she was herself making a toy of her life, or that Augustus was right in refusing to play with such a costly and delicate thing. Neither did Augustus see that, having, by his own blunder, married a mere child, he was bound to deal with her as one, and not let the child suffer for his fault more than what could not be helped. It is not by pressing our insights upon them, but by bathing the sealed eyelids of the human kittens, that we can help them.

And all the time poor little Phosy was left to the care of Alice, a clever, careless, good-hearted, self-satisfied damsel, who, although seldom so rough in her behaviour as we have just seen her, abandoned the child almost entirely to her own resources. It was often she sat alone in the nursery, wishing the Lord would chasten her—because then he would love her.

The first course was nearly over ere Augustus had brought himself to ask—

"What did you think of the sermon to-day, Letty ? "

"Not much," answered Letty. "I am not fond of finery. I prefer simplicity."

Augustus held his peace bitterly. For it was just finery in a sermon, without knowing it, that Letty was fond of: what seemed to him a flimsy syllabub of sacred things, beaten up with the whisk of composition, was charming to Letty; while, on the contrary, if a man such as they had been listening to was carried away by the thoughts that struggled in him for utterance, the result, to her judgment, was finery, and the object display. In excuse it must be remembered that she had been used to her father's style, which no one could have aspersed with lack of sobriety.

Presently she spoke again.

"Gus, dear, couldn't you make up your mind for once to go with me to Lady Ashdaile's to-morrow? I am getting quite ashamed of appearing so often without you."

"There is another way of avoiding that unpleasantness," remarked her husband drily.

"You cruel creature!" returned Letty playfully. "But I must go this once, for I promised Mrs. Holden."

"You know, Letty," said her husband, after a little pause, "it gets of more and more consequence that you should not fatigue yourself. By keeping such late hours in such stifling rooms you are endangering two lives—remember that, Letty. If you stay at home to-morrow, I will come home early, and read to you all the evening."

"Gussy, that _would_ be charming. You _know_ there is nothing in the world I should enjoy so much. But this time I really mustn't."

She launched into a list of all the great nobodies and small somebodies who were to be there, and whom she positively must see : it might be her only chance.

Those last words quenched a sarcasm on Augustus' lips. He was kinder than usual the rest of the evening, and read her to sleep with the Pilgrim's Progress.

Phosy sat in a corner, listened, and understood. Or where she misunderstood, it was an honest misunderstanding, which never does much hurt. Neither father nor mother spoke to her till they bade her good night. Neither saw the hungry heart under the mask of the still face. The father never imagined her already fit for the modelling she was better without, and the stepmother had to become a mother before she could value her.

Phosy went to bed to dream of the Valley of Humiliation.

CHAPTER II.

THE next morning Alice gave her mistress warning. It was quite unexpected, and she looked at her aghast.

" Alice," she said at length, " you're never going to leave me at such a time ! "

"I'm sorry it don't suit you, ma'am, but I must."

"Why, Alice? What is the matter? Has Sophy been troublesome?"

"No, ma'am; there's no harm in that child."

"Then what can it be, Alice? Perhaps you are going to be married sooner than you expected?"

Alice gave her chin a little toss, pressed her lips together, and was silent.

"I have always been kind to you," resumed her mistress.

"I'm sure, ma'am, I never made no complaints!" returned Alice, but as she spoke she drew herself up straighter than before.

"Then what is it?" said her mistress.

"The fact is, ma'am," answered the girl, almost fiercely, "I can*not* any longer endure a state of domestic slavery."

"I don't understand you a bit better," said Mrs. Greatorex, trying, but in vain, to smile, and therefore looking angrier than she was.

"I mean, ma'am—an' I see no reason as I shouldn't say it, for it's the truth—there's a worm at the root of society where one yuman bein' 's got to do the dirty work of another. I don't mind sweepin' up my own dust, but I won't sweep up nobody else's. I ain't a goin' to demean myself no longer! There!"

"Leave the room, Alice," said Mrs. Greatorex; and when, with a toss and a flounce,

the young woman had vanished, she burst
into tears of anger and annoyance.

The day passed. The evening came. She
dressed without Alice's usual help, and went
to Lady Ashdaile's with her friend. There
a reaction took place, and her spirits rose
unnaturally. She even danced—to the disgust of one or two quick-eyed matrons who
sat by the wall.

When she came home she found her husband sitting up for her. He said next to
nothing, and sat up an hour longer with his
book.

In the night she was taken ill. Her husband called Alice, and ran himself to fetch
the doctor. For some hours she seemed in
danger, but by noon was much better. Only
the greatest care was necessary.

As soon as she could speak, she told
Augustus of Alice's warning, and he sent
for her to the library.

She stood before him with flushed cheeks
and flashing eyes.

"I understand, Alice, you have given your
mistress warning," he said gently.

"Yes, sir."

"Your mistress is very ill, Alice."

"Yes, sir."

"Don't you think it would be ungrateful
of you to leave her in her present condition?
She's not likely to be strong for some time to
come."

The use of the word "ungrateful" was

an unfortunate one. Alice begged to know what she had to be grateful for. Was her work worth nothing? And her master, as every one must who claims that which can only be freely given, found himself in the wrong.

"Well, Alice," he said, "we won't dispute that point; and if you are really determined on going, you must do the best you can for your mistress for the rest of the month."

Alice's sense of injury was soothed by her master's forbearance. She had always rather approved of Mr. Greatorex, and she left the room more softly than she had entered it.

Letty had a fortnight in bed, during which she reflected a little.

The very day on which she left her room, Alice sought an interview with her master, and declared she could not stay out her month; she must go home at once.

She had been very attentive to her mistress during the fortnight: there must be something to account for her strange behaviour.

"Come now, Alice," said her master, "what's at the back of all this? You have been a good, well-behaved, obliging girl till now, and I am certain you would never be like this if there weren't something wrong somewhere."

"Something wrong, sir! No, indeed, sir! Except you call it wrong to have an old uncle as dies and leaves ever so much money as thousands on thousands, the lawyers say."

" And does it come to you then, Alice ? "

" I get my share, sir. He left it to be parted even between his nephews and nieces."

" Why, Alice, you are quite an heiress, then !" returned her master, scarcely however believing the thing so grand as Alice would have it. " But don't you think now it would be rather hard that your fortune should be Mrs. Greatorex's misfortune ? "

" Well, I don't see as how it shouldn't," replied Alice. " It's mis'ess's fortun' as 'as been my misfortun'—ain't it now, sir ? An' why shouldn't it be the other way next ? "

" I don't quite see how your mistress's fortune can be said to be your misfortune, Alice."

" Anybody would see that, sir, as wasn't blinded by class-prejudices."

" Class-prejudices !" exclaimed Mr. Greatorex, in surprise at the word.

" It's a term they use, I believe, sir ! But it's plain enough that if mis'ess hadn't 'a' been better off than me, she wouldn't ha' been able to secure my services— as you calls it."

" That is certainly plain enough," returned Mr. Greatorex. " But suppose nobody had been able to secure your services, what would have become of you ? "

" By that time the people'd have rose to assert their rights."

" To what ?—To fortunes like yours ? "

" To bread and cheese at least, sir," returned Alice, pertly.

" Well, but you've had something better than bread and cheese."

" I don't make no complaints as to the style of livin' in the house, sir, but that's all one, so long as it's on the vile condition of domestic slavery—which it's nothing can justify."

" Then of course, although you are now a woman of property, you will never dream of having any one to wait on you," said her master, amused with the volume of human nature thus opened to him.

" All I say, sir, is—it's my turn now ; and I ain't goin' to be sit upon by no one. I know my dooty to myself."

" I didn't know there was such a duty, Alice," said her master.

Something in his tone displeased her.

" Then you know now, sir," she said, and bounced out of the room.

The next moment, however, ashamed of her rudeness, she re-entered, saying,

"I don't want to be unkind, sir, but I must go home. I've got a brother that's ill, too, and wants to see me. If you don't object to me goin' home for a month, I promise you to come back and see mis'ess through her trouble —as a friend, you know, sir."

" But just listen to me first, Alice," said Mr. Greatorex. " I've had something to do with wills in my time, and I can assure you it is not likely to be less than a year before you can touch the money. You had much

better stay where you are till your uncle's
affairs are settled.   You don't know what
may happen.   There's many a slip between
cup and lip, you know."

"Oh! it's all right, sir.   Everybody knows
the money's left to his nephews and nieces,
and me and my brother's as good as any."

"I don't doubt it: still, if you'll take my
advice, you'll keep a sound roof over your
head till another's ready for you."

Alice only threw her chin in the air, and
said almost threateningly,

"Am I to go for the month, sir?"

"I'll talk to your mistress about it,"
answered Mr. Greatorex, not at all sure that
such an arrangement would be for his wife's
comfort.

But the next day Mrs. Greatorex had a
long talk with Alice, and the result was that
on the following Monday she was to go home
for a month, and then return for two months
more at least.   What Mr. Greatorex had said
about the legacy, had had its effect, and,
besides, her mistress had spoken to her with
pleasure in her good fortune.   About Sophy
no one felt any anxiety: she was no trouble
to any one, and the housemaid would see to
her.

CHAPTER III.

ON the Sunday evening, Alice's lover, having heard, not from herself, but by a side wind, that she was going home the next day, made his appearance in Wimborne Square, somewhat perplexed—both at the move, and at her leaving him in ignorance of the same. He was a cabinet-maker in an honest shop in the neighbourhood, and in education, faculty, and general worth, considerably Alice's superior—a fact which had hitherto rather pleased her, but now gave zest to the change which she imagined had subverted their former relation. Full of the sense of her new superiority, she met him draped in an indescribable strangeness. John Jephson felt, at the very first word, as if her voice came from the other side of the English Channel. He wondered what he had done, or rather what Alice could imagine he had done or said, to put her in such tantrums.

"Alice, my dear," he said—for John was a man to go straight at the enemy, "what's amiss? What's come over you? You ain't altogether like your own self to-night! And here I find you're goin' away, and ne'er a word to me about it! What have I done?"

Alice's chin alone made reply. She waited the fitting moment, with splendour to astonish, and with grandeur to subdue her

lover. To tell the sad truth, she was no
longer sure that it would be well to encourage
him on the old footing; was she not standing
on tiptoe, her skirts in her hand, on the
brink of the brook that parted serfdom from
gentility, on the point of stepping daintily
across, and leaving domestic slavery, red
hands, caps, and obedience behind her? How
then was she to marry a man that had black
nails, and smelt of glue? It was incumbent
on her at least, for propriety's sake, to render
him at once aware that it was in condescension ineffable she took any notice of him.

"Alice, my girl!" began John again, in
expostulatory tone.

"Miss Cox, if you please, John Jephson,"
interposed Alice.

"What on 'arth's come over you?" exclaimed John, with the first throb of rousing
indignation.   "But if you ain't your own
self no more, why, Miss Cox be it.   'T seems
to me 's if I warn't my own self no more—'s
if I'd got into some un else, or 't least hedn't
got my own ears on m' own head.— Never
saw or heerd Alice like this afore!" he added,
turning in gloomy bewilderment to the housemaid for a word of human sympathy.

The movement did not altogether please
Alice, and she felt she must justify her behaviour.

"You see, John," she said, with dignity,
keeping her back towards him, and pretending to dust the globe of a lamp, "there's

things as no woman can help, and therefore
as no man has no right to complain of them.
It's not as if I'd gone an' done it, or changed
myself, no more 'n if it 'ad took place in my
cradle.   What can I help it, if the world
goes and changes itself?   Am *I* to blame?—
tell me that.   It's not that I make no complaint, but I tell you it ain't me, it's circumstances as is gone and changed theirselves,
and bein' as circumstances is changed, things
ain't the same as they was, and Miss is the
properer term from you to me, John Jephson."

   "Dang it if I know what you're a drivin'
at, Alice!—Miss Cox!—and I beg yer pardon,
miss, I'm sure.—Dang me if I do!"

   "Don't swear, John Jephson—leastways
before a lady.   It's not proper."

   "It seems to me, Miss Cox, as if the wind
was a settin' from Bedlam, or may be Colney
Hatch," said John, who was considered a
humourist among his comrades.   "I wouldn't
take no liberties with a lady, Miss Cox; but
if I might be so bold as to arst the joke of
the thing——"

   "Joke, indeed!" cried Alice.   "Do you call
a dead uncle and ten thousand pounds a joke?"

   "God bless me!" said John.   "You don't
mean it, Alice?"

   "I do mean it, and that you'll find, John
Jephson.   I'm goin' to bid you good-bye to-
morrer."

   "Whoy, Alice!" exclaimed honest John,
aghast.

" It's truth I tell ye," said Alice.

" And for how long?" gasped John, fore-feeling illimitable misfortune.

" That depends," returned Alice, who did not care to lessen the effect of her communication by mentioning her promised return for a season. "—It ain't likely," she added, " as a heiress is a goin' to act the nuss-maid much longer."

" But Alice," said John, " you don't mean to say—it's not in your mind now—it can't be, Alice—you're only jokin' with me——"

" Indeed, and I'm not!" interjected Alice, with a sniff.

"I don't mean that way, you know.   What I mean is, you don't mean as how this 'ere money—dang it all!—as how it's to be all over between you and me?—You *can't* mean that, Alice!" ended the poor fellow, with a choking in his throat.

It was very hard upon him!   He must either look as if he wanted to share her money, or else as if he were ready to give her up.

" Arst yourself, John Jephson," answered Alice, " whether it's likely a young lady of fortun' would be keepin' company with a young man as didn't know how to take off his hat to her in the park?"

Alice did not above half mean what she said: she wished mainly to enhance her own importance.   At the same time she did mean it half, and that would have been enough for Jephson.   He rose, grievously wounded.

E

"Good-bye, Alice," he said, taking the hand she did not refuse. "Ye're throwin' from ye what all yer money won't buy."

She gave a scornful little laugh, and John walked out of the kitchen.

At the door he turned with one lingering look; but in Alice there was no sign of softening. She turned scornfully away, and no doubt enjoyed her triumph to the full.

The next morning she went away.

CHAPTER IV.

MR. GREATOREX had ceased to regard the advent of Christmas with much interest. Naturally gifted with a strong religious tendency, he had, since his first marriage, taken, not to denial, but to the side of objection, spending much energy in contempt for the foolish opinions of others, a self-indulgence which does less than little to further the growth of one's own spirit in truth and righteousness. The only person who stands excused—I do not say justified—in so doing, is the man who, having been taught the same opinions, has found them a legion of adversaries barring his way to the truth. But having got rid of them for himself, it is, I suspect, worse than useless to attack them again, save as the ally of those who are fighting their way through the same ranks to the truth. Greatorex had been indulging his intellect at the expense of his heart. A man may have light in the brain and darkness in the heart. It were better to be an owl than a strong-eyed apteryx. He was on the path which naturally ends in blindness and unbelief. I fancy, if he had not been neglectful of his child, she would ere this time have relighted his Christmas-candles for him; but now his second disappointment in marriage had so dulled his heart that he had begun to regard life as a stupid affair, in which the most enviable fool was the man who could still expect to realize an ideal. He had set out on a false track altogether, but had not yet discovered that there had been an immoral element at work in his mistake.

For what right had he to desire the fashioning of any woman after his ideas? did not the angel of her eternal Ideal for ever behold the face of her Father in heaven? The best that can be said for him is, that, notwithstanding his disappointment and her faults, yea, notwithstanding his own faults, which were, with all his cultivation and strength of character, yet more serious than hers, he was still kind to her; yes, I may say for him, that, notwithstanding even her silliness, which is a sickening fault, and one which no supremacy of beauty can over-shadow, he still loved her a little. Hence the care he showed for her in respect of the coming sorrow was genuine; it did not all belong to his desire for a son to whom he might be a father indeed—after his own fancies, however. Letty, on her part, was as full of expectation as the girl who has been promised a doll that can shut and open its eyes, and cry when it is pinched; her carelessness of its safe arrival came of ignorance and not indifference.

It cannot but seem strange that such a man should have been so careless of the child he had. But from the first she had painfully reminded him of her mother, with whom in truth he had never quarrelled, but with whom he had not found life the less irksome on that account. Add to this that he had been growing fonder of business,—a fact which indicated, in a man of his endowment and development, an inclination downwards of the plane of his life. It was some time since he had given up reading poetry. History had almost followed : he now read little except politics, travels, and popular expositions of scientific progress.

That year Christmas Eve fell upon a Monday. The day before, Letty not feeling very well, her husband thought it better not to leave her, and gave up going to church. Phosy was utterly forgotten, but she dressed herself, and at the usual hour appeared with her prayer-book in her hand ready for church. When her father told her that he was not going, she looked so blank that he took pity

upon her, and accompanied her to the church-
door, promising to meet her as she came out.
Phosy sighed from relief as she entered, for
she had a vague idea that by going to church
to pray for it she might move the Lord to
chasten her.   At least he would see her
there, and might think of it.   She had never
had such an attention from her father before,
never such dignity conferred upon her as to
be allowed to appear in church alone, sitting
in the pew by herself like a grown damsel.
But I doubt if there was any pride in her
stately step, or any vanity in the smile—no,
not smile, but illuminated mist, the vapour of
smiles, which haunted her sweet little solemn
church-window of a face, as she walked up
the aisle.

The preacher was one of whom she had
never heard her father speak slighting word,
in whom her unbounded trust had never been
shaken.   Also he was one who believed with
his whole soul in the things that make
Christmas precious.   To him the birth of
the wonderful baby hinted at hundreds of
strange things in the economy of the planet.
That a man could so thoroughly persuade
himself that he believed the old fable, was
matter of marvel to some of his friends who
held blind Nature the eternal mother, and
Night the everlasting grandmother of all
things.   But the child Phosy, in her dreams
or out of them, in church or nursery, with
her book or her doll, was never out of the

region of wonders, and would have believed,
or tried to believe, anything that did not
involve a moral impossibility.

What the preacher said I need not even
partially repeat; it is enough to mention
a certain metamorphosed deposit from the
stream of his eloquence carried home in her
mind by Phosy: from some of his sayings
about the birth of Jesus into the world, into
the family, into the individual human bosom,
she had got it into her head that Christmas
Day was not a birthday like that she had
herself last year, but that, in some wonderful
way, to her requiring no explanation, the
baby Jesus was born every Christmas Day
afresh. What became of him afterwards she
did not know, and indeed she had never yet
thought to ask how it was that he could
come to every house in London as well as
No. 1, Wimborne Square. Little of a home
as another might think it, that house was
yet to her the centre of all houses, and the
wonder had not yet widened rippling beyond
it: into that spot of the pool the eternal gift
would fall.

Her father forgot the time over his book,
but so entranced was her heart with the
expectation of the promised visit, now so
near—the day after to-morrow—that, if she
did not altogether forget to look for him as
she stepped down the stair from the church
door to the street, his absence caused her
no uneasiness; and when, just as she reached

it, he opened the house-door in tardy haste
to redeem his promise, she looked up at him
with a solemn, smileless repose, born of
spiritual tension and speechless anticipation,
upon her face, and walking past him without change in the rhythm of her motion,
marched stately up the stairs to the nursery.
I believe the centre of her hope was that
when the baby came she would beg him on
her knees to ask the Lord to chasten her.

When dessert was over, her mother on
the sofa in the drawing-room, and her father
in an easy-chair, with a bottle of his favourite
wine by his side, she crept out of the room
and away again to the nursery. There she
reached up to her little bookshelf, and, full
of the sermon as spongy mists are full of
the sunlight, took thence a volume of stories
from the German, the re-reading of one of
which, narrating the visit of the Christ-child,
laden with gifts, to a certain household, and
what he gave to each and all therein, she
had, although sorely tempted, saved up until
now, and sat down with it by the fire, the
only light she had. When the housemaid,
suddenly remembering she must put her to
bed, and at the same time discovering it was
a whole hour past her usual time, hurried
to the nursery, she found her fast asleep in
her little armchair, her book on her lap,
and the fire self-consumed into a dark cave
with a sombre glow in its deepest hollows.
Dreams had doubtless come to deepen the

impressions of sermon and *mährchen*, for as she slowly yielded to the hands of Polly putting her to bed, her lips, unconsciously moved of the slumbering but not sleeping spirit, more than once murmured the words *Lord loveth* and *chasteneth.* Right blessedly would I enter the dreams of such a child— revel in them, as a bee in the heavenly gulf of a cactus-flower.

CHAPTER V.

On Christmas Eve the church bells were ringing through the murky air of London, whose streets lay flaring and steaming below. The brightest of their constellations were the butchers' shops, with their shows of prize beef; around them, the eddies of the human tides were most confused and knotted. But the toy-shops were brilliant also. To Phosy they would have been the treasure-caves of the Christ-child—all mysteries, all with insides to them—boxes, and desks, and windmills, and dove-cots, and hens with chickens, and who could tell what all? In every one of those shops her eyes would have searched for the Christ-child, the giver of all their wealth. For to her he was everywhere that night—ubiquitous as the luminous mist that brooded all over London —of which, however, she saw nothing but

the glow above the mews. John Jephson
was out in the middle of all the show,
drifting about in it : he saw nothing that
had pleasure in it, his heart was so heavy.
He never thought once of the Christ-child,
or even of the Christ-man, as the giver
of anything. Birth is the one standing
promise-hope for the race, but for poor John
this Christmas held no promise. With all
his humour, he was one of those people,
generally dull and slow—God grant me and
mine such dulness and such sloth—who
having once loved, cannot cease. During
the fortnight he had scarce had a moment's
ease from the sting of his Alice's treatment.
The honest fellow's feelings were no study
to himself; he knew nothing but the pleasure
and the pain of them; but I believe it was
not mainly for himself that he was sorry.
Like Othello, " the pity of it " haunted him :
he had taken Alice for a downright girl,
about whom there was and could be no
mistake; and the first hot blast of pros-
perity had swept her away like a hectic leaf.
What were all the shops dressed out in holly
and mistletoe, what were all the rushing
flaming gas-jets, what the fattest of prize-
pigs to John, who could never more imagine
a spare-rib on the table between Alice and
him of a Sunday ? His imagination ran on
seeing her pass in her carriage, and drop
him a nod of condescension as she swept
noisily by him—trudging home weary from

his work to his loveless fireside. *He* didn't
want her money! Honestly, he would rather
have her without than with money, for he
now regarded it as an enemy, seeing what
evil changes it could work. " There be some
devil in it, sure! " he said to himself. True,
he had never found any in his week's wages,
but he did remember once finding the devil
in a month's wages received in the lump.

As he was thus thinking with himself, a
carriage came suddenly from a side street
into the crowd, and while he stared at it,
thinking Alice might be sitting inside it
while he was tramping the pavement alone,
she passed him on the other side on foot—was
actually pushed against him: he looked round,
and saw a young woman, carrying a small
bag, disappearing in the crowd. " There's
an air of Alice about *her*," said John to himself, seeing her back only. But of course it
couldn't be Alice; for her he must look in
the carriages now! And what a fool he was:
every young woman reminded him of the
one he had lost! Perhaps if he was to call
the next day — Polly was a good-natured
creature—he might hear some news of her.

It had been a troubled fortnight with Mrs.
Greatorex. She wished much that she could
have talked to her husband more freely, but
she had not learned to feel at home with him.
Yet he had been kinder and more attentive
than usual all the time, so much so that
Letty thought with herself—if she gave him

a boy, he would certainly return to his first devotion. She said *boy*, because any one might see he cared little for Phosy. She had never discovered that he was disappointed in herself, but, since her disregard of his wishes had brought evil upon her, she had begun to suspect that he had some ground for being dissatisfied with her. She never dreamed of his kindness as the effort of a conscientious nature to make the best of what could not now be otherwise helped. Her own poverty of spirit and lack of worth achieved, she knew as little of as she did of the riches of Michael the archangel. One must have begun to gather wisdom before he can see his own folly.

That evening she was seated alone in the drawing-room, her husband having left her to smoke his cigar, when the butler entered and informed her that Alice had returned, but was behaving so oddly that they did not know what to do with her. Asking wherein her oddness consisted, and learning that it was mostly in silence and tears, she was not sorry to gather that some disappointment had befallen her, and felt considerable curiosity to know what it was. She therefore told him to send her upstairs.

Meantime Polly, the housemaid, seeing plainly enough from her return in the middle of her holiday, and from her utter dejection, that Alice's expectations had been frustrated, and cherishing no little resentment against

her because of her *uppishness* on the first
news of her good fortune, had been un-
generous enough to take her revenge in a
way as stinging in effect as bitter in intention; for she loudly protested that no
amount of such luck as she pretended to
suppose in Alice's possession, would have
induced *her* to behave herself so that a hand-
some honest fellow like John Jephson should
be driven to despise her, and take up with
her betters.   When her mistress's message
came, Alice was only too glad to find refuge
from the kitchen in the drawing-room.

The moment she entered, she fell on her
knees at the foot of the couch on which her
mistress lay, covered her face with her hands,
and sobbed grievously.

Nor was the change more remarkable in
her bearing than in her person.   She was
pale and worn, and had a hunted look—was
in fact a mere shadow of what she had been.
For a time her mistress found it impossible
to quiet her so as to draw from her her
story: tears and sobs combined with repug-
nance to hold her silent.

" Oh, ma'am ! " she burst out at length,
wringing her hands, " how ever *can* I tell
you ? You will never speak to me again.
Little did I think such a disgrace was
waiting me ! "

" It was no fault of yours if you were mis-
informed," said her mistress, " or that your
uncle was not the rich man you fancied."

"Oh, ma'am, there was no mistake there! He was more than twice as rich as I fancied. If he had only died a beggar, and left things as they was!"

"Then he didn't leave it to his nephews and nieces as they told you?—Well, there's no disgrace in that."

"Oh! but he did, ma'am: that was all right; no mistake there either, ma'am.—And to think o' me behavin' as I did—to you and master as was so good to me! Who'll ever take any more notice of me now, after what has come out—as I'm sure I no more dreamed on than the child unborn!"

An agonized burst of fresh weeping followed, and it was with prolonged difficulty, and by incessant questioning, that Mrs. Greatorex at length drew from her the following facts.

Before Alice and her brother could receive the legacy to which they laid claim, it was necessary to produce certain documents, the absence of which, as of any proof to take their place, led to the unavoidable publication of a fact previously known only to a living few—namely, that the father and mother of Alice Hopwood had never been married, which fact deprived them of the smallest claim on the legacy, and fell like a millstone upon Alice and her pride. From the height of her miserable arrogance she fell prone— not merely hurled back into the lowly condition from which she had raised her head

only to despise it with base unrighteousness,
and to adopt and reassert the principles she
had abhorred when they affected herself— not
merely this, but, in her own judgment at
least, no longer the respectable member of
society she had hitherto been justified in
supposing herself. The relation of her
father and mother she felt overshadow her
with a disgrace unfathomable — the more
overwhelming that it cast her from the gates
of the Paradise she had seemed on the point
of entering : her fall she measured by the
height of the social ambition she had
cherished, and had seemed on the point of
attaining. But it is not an evil that the
devil's money, which this legacy had from
the first proved to Alice, should turn to a
hot cinder in the hand. Rarely had a more
haughty spirit than hers gone before a fall,
and rarely has the fall been more sudden
or more abject. And the consciousness of
the behaviour into which her false riches
had seduced her, changed the whip of her
chastisement into scorpions. Worst of all,
she had insulted her lover as beneath her
notice, and the next moment had found herself too vile for his. Judging by herself,
in the injustice of bitter humiliation she
imagined him scoffing with his mates at
the base-born menial who would set up for
a fine lady. But had she been more worthy
of honest John, she would have understood
him better. As it was, no really good for-

tune could have befallen her but such as
now seemed to her the depth of evil fortune.
Without humiliation to prepare the way for
humility, she must have become capable of
more and more baseness, until she lost all
that makes life worth having.

When Mrs. Greatorex had given her what
consolation she found handy, and at length
dismissed her, the girl, unable to endure her
own company, sought the nursery, where
she caught Sophy in her arms and embraced
her with fervour.   Never in her life having
been the object of any such display of feeling, Phosy was much astonished : when
Alice had set her down and she had resumed
her seat by the fireside, she went on staring
for a while—and then a strange sort of
miming ensued.

It was Phosy's habit—one less rare with
children than may by most be imagined—
to do what she could to enter into any
state of mind whose shows were sufficiently
marked for her observation.   She sought
to lay hold of the feeling that produced the
expression : less than the reproduction of a
similar condition in her own imaginative
sensorium, subject to her leisurely examina-
tion, would in no case satisfy the little meta-
physician.   But what was indeed very odd
was the means she took for arriving at the
sympathetic knowledge she desired.   As if
she had been the most earnest student of dra-
matic expression through the facial muscles,

she would sit watching the countenance of the object of her solicitude, all the time, with full consciousness, fashioning her own as nearly as she could into the lines and forms of the other : in proportion as she succeeded, the small psychologist imagined she felt in herself the condition that produced the phenomenon she observed — as if the shape of her face cast inward its shadow upon her mind, and so revealed to it, through the two faces, what was moving and shaping in the mind of the other.

In the present instance, having at length, after modelling and remodelling her face like that of a gutta-percha doll for some time, composed it finally into the best correspondence she could effect, she sat brooding for a while, with Alice's expression as it were frozen upon it. Gradually the forms assumed melted away, and allowed her still, solemn face to look out from behind them. The moment this evanishment was complete, she rose and went to Alice, where she sat staring into the fire, unconscious of the scrutiny she had been undergoing, and, looking up in her face, took her thumb out of her mouth, and said,

" Is the Lord chastening Alice ? I wish he would chasten Phosy."

Her face was calm as that of the Sphinx ; there was no mist in the depth of her gray eyes, not a cloud on the wide heaven of her forehead.

Was the child crazed ? What could the atom mean, with her big eyes looking right into her ? Alice never had understood her : it were indeed strange if the less should comprehend the greater ! She was not yet capable of recognising the word of the Lord in the mouth of babes and sucklings. But there was a something in Phosy's face besides its calmness and unintelligibility. What it was Alice could never have told—yet it did her good. She lifted the child on her lap. There she soon fell asleep. Alice undressed her, laid her in her crib, and went to bed herself.

But, weary as she was, she had to rise again before she got to sleep. Her mistress was again taken ill. Doctor and nurse were sent for in hot haste ; hansom cabs came and went throughout the night, like noisy moths to the one lighted house in the street; there were soft steps within, and doors were gently opened and shut. The waters of Mara had risen and filled the house.

Towards morning they were ebbing slowly away. Letty did not know that her husband was watching by her bedside. The street was quiet now. So was the house. Most of its people had been up throughout the night, but now they had all gone to bed except the strange nurse and Mr. Greatorex.

It was the morning of Christmas Day, and little Phosy knew it in every cranny of her soul. She was not of those who had been

F

up all night, and now she was awake, early
and wide, and the moment she awoke she
was speculating : He was coming to-day—
how would he come ?   Where should she find
the baby Jesus ?   And when would he come ?
In the morning, or the afternoon, or in the
evening ?   Could such a grief be in store for
her as that he would not appear until night,
when she would be again in bed ?   But she
would not sleep till all hope was gone.
Would everybody be gathered to meet him,
or would he show himself to one after
another, each alone ?   Then her turn would
be last, and oh, if he would come to the
nursery !   But perhaps he would not appear
to her at all !—for was she not one whom the
Lord did not care to chasten ?

Expectation grew and wrought in her
until she could lie in bed no longer.
Alice was fast asleep.   It must be early, but
whether it was yet light or not she could
not tell for the curtains.   Anyhow she would
get up and dress, and then she would be
ready for Jesus whenever he should come.
True, she was not able to dress herself very
well, but he would know, and would not
mind.   She made all the haste she could,
consistently with taking pains, and was soon
attired after a fashion.

She crept out of the room and down the
stair.   The house was very still.   What if
Jesus should come and find nobody awake ?
Would he go again and give them no

presents ?   She couldn't expect any herself
—but might he not let her take theirs for
the rest ?   Perhaps she ought to wake them
all, but she dared not without being sure.

On the last landing above the first floor,
she saw, by the low gaslight at the end of
the corridor, an unknown figure pass the foot
of the stair : could she have anything to do
with the marvel of the day ?   The woman
looked up, and Phosy dropped the question.
Yet she might be a charwoman, whose assist-
ance the expected advent rendered necessary.
When she reached the bottom of the stair
she saw her disappearing in her step-mother's
room.   That she did not like.   It was the
one room into which she could not go.   But,
as the house was so still, she would search
everywhere else, and if she did not find him,
would then sit down in the hall and wait
for him.

The room next the foot of the stair, and
opposite her step-mother's, was the spare
room, with which she associated ideas of
state and grandeur : where better could she
begin than at the guest-chamber ?—There !
—Could it be ? Yes !—Through the chink of
the scarce-closed door she saw light.   Either
he was already there or there they were expecting him.   From that moment she felt
as if lifted out of the body.   Far exalted
above all dread, she peeped modestly in, and
then entered.   Beyond the foot of the bed,
a candle stood on a little low table, but

nobody was to be seen. There was a stool
near the table : she would sit on it by the
candle, and wait for him. But ere she
reached it, she caught sight of something
upon the bed that drew her thither. She
stood entranced.—*Could* it be ?—It *might* be.
Perhaps he had left it there while he went
into her mamma's room with something for
her.—The loveliest of dolls ever imagined!
She drew nearer. The light was low, and
the shadows were many : she could not be
sure what it was. But when she had gone
close up to it, she concluded with certainty
that it was in very truth a doll—perhaps
intended for her—but beyond doubt the most
exquisite of dolls. She dragged a chair to
the bed, got up, pushed her little arms softly
under it, and drawing it gently to her, slid
down with it. When she felt her feet firm
on the floor, filled with the solemn composure
of holy awe she carried the gift of the child
Jesus to the candle, that she might the better
admire its beauty and know its preciousness.
But the light had no sooner fallen upon it
than a strange undefinable doubt awoke
within her. Whatever it was, it was the
very essence of loveliness—the tiny darling
with its alabaster face, and its delicately
modelled hands and fingers ! A long night-
gown covered all the rest.—Was it possible ?
—Could it be ?—Yes, indeed ! it must be—it
could be nothing else than a *real* baby !
What a goose she had been ! Of course it

was baby Jesus himself!—for was not this
his very own Christmas Day on which he was
always born ?—If she had felt awe of his
gift before, what a grandeur of adoring love,
what a divine dignity possessed her, holding
in her arms the very child himself!   One
shudder of bliss passed through her, and in
an agony of possession she clasped the baby
to her great heart—then at once became still
with the satisfaction of eternity, with the
peace of God.   She sat down on the stool,
near the little table, with her back to the
candle, that its rays should not fall on the
eyes of the sleeping Jesus and wake him :
there she sat, lost in the very majesty of
bliss, at once the mother and the slave of
the Lord Jesus.

   She sat for a time still as marble waiting
for marble to awake, heedful as tenderest
woman not to rouse him before his time,
though her heart was swelling with the eager
petition that he would ask his Father to be
as good as chasten her.   And as she sat, she
began, after her wont, to model her face to
the likeness of his, that she might understand
his stillness—the absolute peace that dwelt
on his countenance.   But as she did so, again
a sudden doubt invaded her : Jesus lay so
very still—never moved, never opened his
pale eye-lids !   And now set thinking, she
noted that he did not breathe.   She had seen
babies asleep, and their breath came and
went—their little bosoms heaved up and

down, and sometimes they would smile, and sometimes they would moan and sigh. But Jesus did none of all these things : was it not strange ? And then he was cold—oh, so cold!

A blue silk coverlid lay on the bed : she half rose and dragged it off, and contrived to wind it around herself and the baby. Sad at heart, very sad, but undismayed, she sat and watched him on her lap.

CHAPTER VI.

MEANTIME the morning of Christmas Day grew. The light came and filled the house. The sleepers slept late, but at length they stirred. Alice awoke last—from a troubled sleep, in which the events of the night mingled with her own lost condition and destiny. After all Polly had been kind, she thought, and got Sophy up without disturbing her.

She had been but a few minutes down, when a strange and appalling rumour made itself—I cannot say audible, but—somehow known through the house, and every one hurried up in horrible dismay.

The nurse had gone into the spare room, and missed the little dead thing she had laid there. The bed was between her and Phosy, and she never saw her. The doctor had been sharp with her about something the night

before : she now took her revenge in suspicion of him, and after a hasty and fruitless
visit of inquiry to the kitchen, hurried to
Mr. Greatorex.

The servants crowded to the spare room,
and when their master, incredulous indeed,
yet shocked at the tidings brought him,
hastened to the spot, he found them all in
the room, gathered at the foot of the bed. A
little sunlight filtered through the red win-
dow-curtains, and gave a strange pallid expression to the flame of the candle, which had
now burned very low.   At first he saw
nothing but the group of servants, silent,
motionless, with heads leaning forward, in-
tently gazing : he had come just in time :
another moment and they would have ruined
the lovely sight.   He stepped forward, and
saw Phosy, half shrouded in blue, the candle
behind illuminating the hair she had found
too rebellious to the brush, and making of
it a faint aureole about her head and white
face, whence cold and sorrow had driven all
the flush, rendering it colourless as that upon
her arm which had never seen the light.
She had pored on the little face until she
knew death, and now she sat a speechless
mother of sorrow, bending in the dim light
of the tomb over the body of her holy infant.

How it was I cannot tell, but the moment
her father saw her she looked up, and the
spell of her dumbness broke.

" Jesus is dead," she said, slowly and sadly,

but with perfect calmness. " He is dead,"
she repeated. " He came too early, and there
was no one up to take care of him, and he's
dead—dead—dead ! "

But as she spoke the last words, the frozen
lump of agony gave way ; the well of her
heart suddenly filled, swelled, overflowed ;
the last word was half sob, half shriek of
utter despair and loss.

Alice darted forward and took the dead
baby tenderly from her. The same moment
her father raised the little mother and clasped
her to his bosom. Her arms went round his
neck, her head sank on his shoulder, and sobbing in grievous misery, yet already a little
comforted, he bore her from the room.

" No, no, Phosy ! " they heard him say.
" Jesus is not dead, thank God. It is only
your little brother that hadn't life enough,
and is gone back to God for more."

Weeping the women went down the stairs.
Alice's tears were still flowing, when John
Jephson entered. Her own troubles forgotten
in the emotion of the scene she had just
witnessed, she ran to his arms and wept on
his bosom.

John stood as one astonied.

" O Lord! this *is* a Christmas ! " he sighed
at last.

" Oh John ! " cried Alice, and tore herself
from his embrace, " I forgot ! You'll never
speak to me again, John ! Don't do it,
John."

And with the words she gave a stifled cry, and fell a weeping again, behind her two shielding hands.

"Why, Alice!—you ain't married, are you?" gasped John, to whom that was the only possible evil.

"No, John, and never shall be : a respectable man like you would never think of looking twice at a poor girl like me!"

"Let's have one more look anyhow," said John, drawing her hands from her face. "Tell me what's the matter, and if there's anything can be done to right you, I'll work day and night to do it, Alice."

"There's nothing *can* be done, John," replied Alice, and would again have floated out on the ocean of her misery, but in spite of wind and tide, that is sobs and tears, she held on by the shore at his entreaty, and told her tale, not even omitting the fact that when she went to the eldest of the cousins, inheriting through the misfortune of her and her brother so much more than their expected share, and "demeaned herself" to beg a little help for her brother, who was dying of consumption, he had all but ordered her out of the house, swearing he had nothing to do with her or her brother, and saying she ought to be ashamed to show her face.

"And that when we used to make mud pies together!" concluded Alice with indignation. "There, John! you have it all," she added.   "——And now?"

With the word she gave a deep, humbly questioning look into his honest eyes.

"Is that all, Alice?" he asked.

"Yes, John; ain't it enough?" she returned.

"More'n enough," answered John. "I swear to you, Alice, you're worth to me ten times what you would ha' been, even if you'd ha' had me, with ten thousand pounds in your ridicule. Why, my woman, I never saw you look one 'alf so 'an'some as you do now!"

"But the disgrace of it, John!" said Alice, hanging her head, and so hiding the pleasure that would dawn through all the mist of her misery.

"Let your father and mother settle that betwixt 'em, Alice. 'Tain't none o' my business. Please God, we'll do different.—When shall it be, my girl?"

"When you like, John," answered Alice, without raising her head, thoughtfully.

When she had withdrawn herself from the too rigorous embrace with which he received her consent, she remarked—

"I do believe, John, money ain't a good thing! Sure as I live, with the very wind o' that money, the devil entered into me. Didn't you hate me, John? Speak the truth now."

"No, Alice. I did cry a bit over you, though. You *was* possessed like."

"I *was* possessed. I do believe if that

money hadn't been took from me, I'd never ha' had you, John. Ain't it awful to think on?"

"Well, no. O' coorse! How could ye?" said Jephson—with reluctance.

"Now, John, don't ye talk like that, for I won't stand it. Don't you go for to set me up again with excusin' of me. I'm a nasty conceited cat, I am—and all for nothing but mean pride."

"Mind ye, ye're mine now, Alice; an' what's mine's mine, an' I won't have it abused. I knows you twice the woman you was afore, and all the world couldn't gi' me such another Christmas-box—no, not if it was all gold watches and roast beef."

When Mr. Greatorex returned to his wife's room, and thought to find her asleep as he had left her, he was dismayed to hear sounds of soft weeping from the bed. Some tone or stray word, never intended to reach her ear, had been enough to reveal the truth concerning her baby.

"Hush! hush!" he said, with more love in his heart than had moved there for many months, and therefore more in his tone than she had heard for as many ;—"if you cry you will be ill. Hush, my dear!"

In a moment, ere he could prevent her, she had flung her arms around his neck as he stooped over her.

"Husband! husband!" she cried, "is it my fault?"

"You behaved perfectly," he returned. "No woman could have been braver."

"Ah, but I wouldn't stay at home when you wanted me."

"Never mind that now, my child," he said.

At the word she pulled his face down to hers.

"I have *you*, and I don't care," he added.

"*Do* you care to have me?" she said, with a sob that ended in a loud cry. "Oh! I don't deserve it. But I *will* be good after this. I promise you I will."

"Then you must begin now, my darling. You must lie perfectly still, and not cry a bit, or you will go after the baby, and I shall be left alone."

She looked up at him with such a light in her face as he had never dreamed of there before. He had never seen her so lovely. Then she withdrew her arms, repressed her tears, smiled, and turned her face away. He put her hands under the clothes, and in a minute or two she was again fast asleep.

CHAPTER VII.

THAT day, when Phosy and her father had sat down to their Christmas dinner, he rose again, and taking her up as she sat, chair and all, set her down close to him, on the

other side of the corner of the table.   It was
the first of a new covenant between them.
The father's eyes having been suddenly
opened to her character and preciousness, as
well as to his own neglected duty in regard
to her, it was as if a well of life had burst
forth at his feet.   And every day, as he
looked in her face and talked to her, it was
with more and more respect for what he
found in her, with growing tenderness for
her predilections, and reverence for the
divine idea enclosed in her ignorance, for her
childish wisdom, and her calm seeking—until
at length he would have been horrified at the
thought of training her up in *his* way : had
she not a way of her own to go—following—
not the dead Jesus, but Him who liveth for
evermore ?   In the endeavour to help her, he
had to find his own position towards the
truth ; and the results were weighty.—Nor
did the child's influence work forward merely.
In his intercourse with her he was so often
reminded of his first wife, and that with the
gloss or comment of a childish reproduction,
that his memories of her at length grew a
little tender, and through the child he began
to understand the nature and worth of the
mother.   In her child she had given him
what she could not be herself.   Unable to
keep up with him, she had handed him her
baby, and dropped on the path.

Nor was little Sophy his only comfort.
Through their common loss and her hus-

band's tenderness, Letty began to grow a
woman.   And her growth was the more
rapid that, himself taught through Phosy,
her husband no longer desired to make her
adopt his tastes, and judge with his experiences, but, as became the elder and the tried,
entered into her tastes and experiences—became, as it were, a child again with her,
that, through the thing she was, he might
help the thing she had to be.

As soon as she was able to bear it, he told
her the story of the dead Jesus, and with the
tale came to her heart love for Phosy.   She
had lost a son for a season, but she had
gained a daughter for ever.

Such were the gifts the Christ-child
brought to one household that Christmas.
And the days of the mourning of that household were ended.

THE HISTORY OF PHOTOGEN AND NYCTERIS.

A DAY AND NIGHT MÄHRCHEN.

———◦◦◦———

CHAPTER I.

WATHO.

THERE was once a witch who desired to know everything. But the wiser a witch is, the harder she knocks her head against the wall when she comes to it. Her name was Watho, and she had a wolf in her mind. She cared for nothing in itself—only for knowing it. She was not naturally cruel, but the wolf had made her cruel.

She was tall and graceful, with a white skin, red hair, and black eyes, which had a red fire in them. She was straight and strong, but now and then would fall bent together, shudder, and sit for a moment with her head turned over her shoulder, as if the wolf had got out of her mind on to her back.

CHAPTER II.

AURORA.

THIS witch got two ladies to visit her. One of them belonged to the court, and her husband had been sent on a far and difficult embassy. The other was a young widow whose husband had lately died, and who had since lost her sight. Watho lodged them in different parts of her castle, and they did not know of each other's existence.

The castle stood on the side of a hill sloping gently down into a narrow valley, in which was a river, with a pebbly channel and a continual song. The garden went down to the bank of the river, enclosed by high walls, which crossed the river and there stopped. Each wall had a double row of battlements, and between the rows was a narrow walk.

In the topmost story of the castle the Lady Aurora occupied a spacious apartment of several large rooms looking southward. The windows projected oriel-wise over the garden below, and there was a splendid view from them both up and down and across the river. The opposite side of the valley was steep, but not very high. Far away snow-peaks were visible. These rooms Aurora seldom left, but their airy spaces, the bril-

liant landscape and sky, the plentiful sunlight, the musical instruments, books, pictures,
curiosities, with the company of Watho who
made herself charming, precluded all dulness.
She had venison and feathered game to eat,
milk and pale sunny sparkling wine to drink.

She had hair of the yellow gold, waved
and rippled; her skin was fair, not white
like Watho's, and her eyes were of the blue
of the heavens when bluest; her features
were delicate but strong, her mouth large
and finely curved, and haunted with smiles.

CHAPTER III.

VESPER.

BEHIND the castle the hill rose abruptly; the
north-eastern tower, indeed, was in contact
with the rock, and communicated with the
interior of it. For in the rock was a series
of chambers, known only to Watho and the
one servant whom she trusted, called Falca.
Some former owner had constructed these
chambers after the tomb of an Egyptian
king, and probably with the same design,
for in the centre of one of them stood what
could only be a sarcophagus, but that and
others were walled off. The sides and roofs
of them were carved in low relief, and curiously painted. Here the witch lodged the

G

blind lady, whose name was Vesper. Her
eyes were black, with long black lashes;
her skin had a look of darkened silver, but
was of purest tint and grain; her hair was
black and fine and straight-flowing; her
features were exquisitely formed, and if less
beautiful yet more lovely from sadness; she
always looked as if she wanted to lie down
and not rise again. She did not know she
was lodged in a tomb, though now and then
she wondered she never touched a window.
There were many couches, covered with
richest silk, and soft as her own cheek, for
her to lie upon; and the carpets were so
thick, she might have cast herself down anywhere—as befitted a tomb. The place was
dry and warm, and cunningly pierced for
air, so that it was always fresh, and lacked
only sunlight. There the witch fed her
upon milk, and wine dark as a carbuncle,
and pomegranates, and purple grapes, and
birds that dwell in marshy places; and she
played to her mournful tunes, and caused
wailful violins to attend her, and told her
sad tales, thus holding her ever in an atmosphere of sweet sorrow.

CHAPTER IV.

WATHO at length had her desire, for witches often get what they want : a splendid boy was born to the fair Aurora. Just as the sun rose, he opened his eyes. Watho carried him immediately to a distant part of the castle, and persuaded the mother that he never cried but once, dying the moment he was born. Overcome with grief, Aurora left the castle as soon as she was able, and Watho never invited her again.

And now the witch's care was, that the child should not know darkness. Persistently she trained him until at last he never slept during the day, and never woke during the night. She never let him see anything black, and even kept all dull colours out of his way. Never, if she could help it, would she let a shadow fall upon him, watching against shadows as if they had been live things that would hurt him. All day he basked in the full splendour of the sun, in the same large rooms his mother had occupied. Watho used him to the sun, until he could bear more of it than any dark-blooded African. In the hottest of every day, she stript him and laid him in it, that he might ripen like a peach ; and the boy rejoiced in it, and would resist being dressed again. She brought all her knowledge to bear on making his muscles strong and elastic and swiftly responsive—that his soul, she said laughing, might sit in every fibre, be all in every part, and awake the moment of call. His hair was of the red gold, but his eyes grew darker as he grew, until they were as black as Vesper's. He was the merriest of creatures, always laughing, always loving, for a moment raging, then laughing afresh. Watho called him Photogen.

CHAPTER V.

NYCTERIS.

FIVE or six months after the birth of Photogen, the dark lady also gave birth to a baby: in the windowless tomb of a blind mother, in the dead of night, under the feeble rays of a lamp in an alabaster globe, a girl came into the darkness with a wail. And just as she was born for the first time, Vesper was born for the second, and passed into a world as unknown to her as this was to her child—who would have to be born yet again before she could see her mother.

Watho called her Nycteris, and she grew as like Vesper as possible—in all but one particular. She had the same dark skin, dark eyelashes and brows, dark hair, and gentle sad look; but she had just the eyes of Aurora, the mother of Photogen, and if they grew darker as she grew older, it was only a darker blue. Watho, with the help of Falca, took the greatest possible care of her—in every way consistent with her plans, that is,—the main point in which was that she should never see any light but what came from the lamp. Hence her optic nerves, and indeed her whole apparatus for seeing, grew both larger and more sensitive; her eyes, indeed, stopped short only of being too large. Under her dark hair and forehead and eyebrows, they looked like two breaks in a cloudy night-sky, through which peeped the heaven where the stars and no clouds live. She was a sadly dainty little creature. No one in the world except those two was aware of the being of the little bat. Watho trained her to sleep during the day, and wake during the night. She taught her music, in which she was herself a proficient, and taught her scarcely anything else.

CHAPTER VI.

HOW PHOTOGEN GREW.

THE hollow in which the castle of Watho lay, was a cleft in a plain rather than a valley among hills, for at the top of its steep sides, both north and south, was a table-land, large and wide. It was covered with rich grass and flowers, with here and there a wood, the outlying colony of a great forest. These grassy plains were the finest hunting grounds in the world. Great herds of small, but fierce cattle, with humps and shaggy manes, roved about them, also antelopes and gnus, and the tiny roedeer, while the woods were swarming with wild creatures. The tables of the castle were mainly supplied from them. The chief of Watho's huntsmen was a fine fellow, and when Photogen began to outgrow the training she could give him, she handed him over to Fargu. He with a will set about teaching him all he knew. He got him pony after pony, larger and larger as he grew, every one less manageable than that which had preceded it, and advanced him from pony to horse, and from horse to horse, until he was equal to anything in that kind which the country produced. In similar fashion he trained him to the use of bow and arrow, substituting every

three months a stronger bow and longer
arrows; and soon he became, even on horse-
back, a wonderful archer. He was but four-
teen when he killed his first bull, causing
jubilation among the huntsmen, and, indeed,
through all the castle, for there too he was the
favourite. Every day, almost as soon as the
sun was up, he went out hunting, and would
in general be out nearly the whole of the day.
But Watho had laid upon Fargu just one
commandment, namely, that Photogen should
on no account, whatever the plea, be out until
sundown, or so near it as to wake in him the
desire of seeing what was going to happen;
and this commandment Fargu was anxiously
careful not to break; for, although he would
not have trembled had a whole herd of bulls
come down upon him, charging at full speed
across the level, and not an arrow left in his
quiver, he was more than afraid of his mistress. When she looked at him in a certain
way, he felt, he said, as if his heart turned
to ashes in his breast, and what ran in his
veins was no longer blood, but milk and
water. So that, ere long, as Photogen grew
older, Fargu began to tremble, for he found
it steadily growing harder to restrain him.
So full of life was he, as Fargu said to his
mistress, much to her content, that he was
more like a live thunderbolt than a human
being. He did not know what fear was, and
that not because he did not know danger;
for he had had a severe laceration from the

razor-like tusk of a boar—whose spine, however, he had severed with one blow of his hunting-knife, before Fargu could reach him with defence. When he would spur his horse into the midst of a herd of bulls, carrying only his bow and his short sword, or shoot an arrow into a herd, and go after it as if to reclaim it for a runaway shaft, arriving in time to follow it with a spear-thrust before the wounded animal knew which way to charge, Fargu thought with terror how it would be when he came to know the temptation of the huddle-spot leopards, and the knife-clawed lynxes, with which the forest was haunted. For the boy had been so steeped in the sun, from childhood so saturated with his influence, that he looked upon every danger from a sovereign height of courage. When, therefore, he was approaching his sixteenth year, Fargu ventured to beg of Watho that she would lay her commands upon the youth himself, and release him from responsibility for him. One might as soon hold a tawny-maned lion as Photogen, he said. Watho called the youth, and in the presence of Fargu laid her command upon him never to be out when the rim of the sun should touch the horizon, accompanying the prohibition with hints of consequences, none the less awful that they were obscure. Photogen listened respectfully, but, knowing neither the taste of fear nor the temptation of the night, her words were but sounds to him.

CHAPTER VII.

HOW NYCTERIS GREW.

THE little education she intended Nycteris to
have, Watho gave her by word of mouth.
Not meaning she should have light enough
to read by, to leave other reasons unmen-
tioned, she never put a book in her hands.
Nycteris, however, saw so much better than
Watho imagined, that the light she gave her
was quite sufficient, and she managed to
coax Falca into teaching her the letters, after
which she taught herself to read, and Falca
now and then brought her a child's book.
But her chief pleasure was in her instru-
ment. Her very fingers loved it, and would
wander about over its keys like feeding sheep.
She was not unhappy. She knew nothing
of the world except the tomb in which she
dwelt, and had some pleasure in everything
she did. But she desired, nevertheless, something more or different. She did not know
what it was, and the nearest she could come
to expressing it to herself was—that she
wanted more room. Watho and Falca would
go from her beyond the shine of the lamp,
and come again ; therefore surely there must
be more room somewhere. As often as she
was left alone, she would fall to poring over
the coloured bas-reliefs on the walls. These

were intended to represent various of the
powers of Nature under allegorical simili-
tudes, and as nothing can be made that does
not belong to the general scheme, she could
not fail at least to imagine a flicker of re-
lationship between some of them, and thus a
shadow of the reality of things found its way
to her.

There was one thing, however, which
moved and taught her more than all the
rest—the lamp, namely, that hung from the
ceiling, which she always saw alight,
though she never saw the flame, only the
slight condensation towards the centre of the
alabaster globe. And besides the operation
of the light itself after its kind, the indefinite-
ness of the globe, and the softness of the
light, giving her the feeling as if her eyes
could go in and into its whiteness, were somehow also associated with the idea of space
and room. She would sit for an hour together gazing up at the lamp, and her
heart would swell as she gazed. She would
wonder what had hurt her, when she found
her face wet with tears, and then would
wonder how she could have been hurt without knowing it. She never looked thus at
the lamp except when she was alone.

CHAPTER VIII.

WATHO having given orders, took it for granted they were obeyed, and that Falca was all night long with Nycteris, whose day it was. But Falca could not get into the habit of sleeping through the day, and would often leave her alone half the night. Then it seemed to Nycteris that the white lamp was watching over her. As it was never permitted to go out—while she was awake at least—Nycteris, except by shutting her eyes, knew less about darkness than she did about light. Also, the lamp being fixed high overhead, and in the centre of everything, she did not know much about shadows either. The few there were fell almost entirely on the floor, or kept like mice about the foot of the walls.

Once, when she was thus alone, there came the noise of a far-off rumbling: she had never before heard a sound of which she did not know the origin, and here therefore was a new sign of something beyond these chambers. Then came a trembling, then a shaking; the lamp dropped from the ceiling to the floor with a great crash, and she felt as if both her eyes were hard shut and both her hands over them. She concluded that it was the darkness that had made the rumbling and the shaking, and rushing into the room, had thrown down the lamp. She sat trembling. The noise and the shaking ceased, but the light did not return. The darkness had eaten it up!

Her lamp gone, the desire at once awoke to get out of her prison. She scarcely knew what *out* meant; out of one room into another, where there was not even a dividing door, only an open arch, was all she knew of the world. But suddenly she remembered that she had heard Falca speak of the lamp *going out*: this must be what she had meant? And if the lamp had gone out, where had it gone? Surely where Falca went, and like her it would come again. But she could not wait. The desire to go out grew irresistible. She must follow her beautiful lamp! She must find it! She must see what it was about!

Now there was a curtain covering a recess in the wall, where some of her toys and gymnastic things were kept; and from behind that curtain Watho and Falca always appeared, and behind it they vanished. How they came out of solid wall, she had not an idea, all up to the wall was open space, and all beyond it seemed wall; but clearly the first and only thing she could do, was to feel her way behind the curtain. It was so dark that a cat could not have caught the largest of mice. Nycteris could see better than any cat, but now her great eyes were not of the smallest use to her. As she went she trod upon a piece of the broken lamp. She had never worn shoes or stockings, and the fragment, though, being of soft alabaster, it did not cut, yet hurt her foot. She did not know what it was, but as it had not been there before the darkness came, she suspected that it had to do with the lamp. She kneeled therefore, and searched with her hands, and bringing two large pieces together, recognized the shape of the lamp. Therewith it flashed upon her that the lamp was dead, that this brokenness was the death of which she had read without understanding, that the darkness had killed the lamp. What then could Falca have meant when she spoke of the lamp *going out?* There was the lamp—dead, indeed, and so changed that she would never have taken it for a lamp but for the shape! No, it was not the lamp any more now it was dead, for all that made it a lamp was gone, namely, the bright shining of it. Then it must be the shine, the light, that had gone out! That must be what Falca meant—and it must be somewhere in the other place in the wall. She started afresh after it, and groped her way to the curtain.

Now she had never in her life tried to get out, and did not know how; but instinctively she began to move her hands about over one of the walls behind the curtain, half expecting them to go into it, as she supposed

Watho and Falca did. But the wall repelled her with inexorable hardness, and she turned to the one opposite. In so doing, she set her foot upon an ivory die, and as it met sharply the same spot the broken alabaster had already hurt, she fell forward with her outstretched hands against the wall. Something gave way, and she tumbled out of the cavern.

CHAPTER IX.

OUT.

BUT alas! *out* was very much like *in*, for the same enemy, the darkness, was here also. The next moment, however, came a great gladness—a firefly, which had wandered in from the garden. She saw the tiny spark in the distance. With slow pulsing ebb and throb of light, it came pushing itself through the air, drawing nearer and nearer, with that motion which more resembles swimming than flying, and the light seemed the source of its own motion.

"My lamp! my lamp!" cried Nycteris. "It is the shiningness of my lamp, which the cruel darkness drove out. My good lamp has been waiting for me here all the time! It knew I would come after it, and waited to take me with it."

She followed the firefly, which, like herself, was seeking the way out. If it did not know the way, it was yet light; and, because all light is one, any light may serve to guide to more light. If she was mistaken in thinking it the spirit of her lamp, it was of the same spirit as her lamp—and had wings. The gold-green jet-boat, driven by light, went throbbing before her through a long narrow passage. Suddenly it rose higher, and the same moment Nycteris fell upon an ascending stair. She had never seen a stair before, and found going-up a curious sensation. Just as she reached what seemed the top, the firefly ceased to shine, and so disappeared. She was in utter darkness once more. But when we are following the light, even its extinction is a guide. If the firefly had gone on shining, Nycteris would have seen the stair turn, and would have gone up to Watho's bedroom; whereas now, feeling straight before her, she came to a latched door, which after a good deal of trying she managed to open—and stood in a maze of wondering perplexity, awe, and delight. What was it? Was it outside of her, or something taking place in her head? Before her was a very long and very narrow passage, broken up she could not tell how, and spreading out above and on all sides to an infinite height and breadth and distance—as if space itself were growing out of a trough. It was brighter than her rooms had ever been—brighter than if six alabaster lamps had been burning in them. There was a quantity of strange streaking and mottling about it, very different from the shapes on her walls. She was in a dream of pleasant perplexity, of delightful bewilderment. She could not tell whether she was upon her feet or drifting about like the firefly, driven by the pulses of an inward bliss. But she knew little as yet of her inheritance. Unconsciously she took one step forward from the threshold, and the girl who had been from her very birth a troglodyte, stood in the ravishing glory of a southern night, lit by a perfect moon—not the moon of our northern clime, but a moon like silver glowing in a furnace—a moon one could see to be a globe—not far off, a mere flat disc on the face of the blue, but hanging down halfway, and looking as if one could see all round it by a mere bending of the neck.

"It is my lamp!" she said, and stood dumb with parted lips. She looked and felt as if she had been standing there in silent ecstasy from the beginning.

"No, it is not my lamp," she said after a while; "it is the mother of all the lamps."

And with that she fell on her knees, and spread out her hands to the moon. She could not in the least have told what was in her mind, but the action was in reality just a begging of the moon to be what she was— that precise incredible splendour hung in the far-off roof, that very glory essential to the being of poor girls born and bred in caverns.

It was a resurrection—nay, a birth itself, to
Nycteris. What the vast blue sky, studded
with tiny sparks like the heads of diamond
nails, could be ; what the moon, looking so
absolutely content with light,—why, she
knew less about them than you and I ! but
the greatest of astronomers might envy the
rapture of such a first impression at the age
of sixteen. Immeasurably imperfect it was,
but false the impression could not be, for she
saw with the eyes made for seeing, and saw
indeed what many men are too wise to see.

As she knelt, something softly flapped her,
embraced her, stroked her, fondled her. She
rose to her feet, but saw nothing, did not
know what it was. It was likest a woman's
breath. For she knew nothing of the air
even, had never breathed the still newborn
freshness of the world. Her breath had
come to her only through long passages and
spirals in the rock. Still less did she know
of the air alive with motion—of that thrice
blessed thing, the wind of a summer night.
It was like a spiritual wine, filling her whole
being with an intoxication of purest joy. To
breathe was a perfect existence. It seemed
to her the light itself she drew into her
lungs. Possessed by the power of the
gorgeous night, she seemed at one and the
same moment annihilated and glorified.

She was in the open passage or gallery
that ran round the top of the garden walls,
between the cleft battlements, but she did not

H

once look down to see what lay beneath.
Her soul was drawn to the vault above her,
with its lamp and its endless room.   At last
she burst into tears, and her heart was relieved, as the night itself is relieved by its
lightning and rain.

And now she grew thoughtful. She must
hoard this splendour! What a little ignorance her gaolers had made of her! Life
was a mighty bliss, and they had scraped
hers to the bare bone! They must not know
that she knew. She must hide her knowledge—hide it even from her own eyes,
keeping it close in her bosom, content to
know that she had it, even when she could
not brood on its presence, feasting her eyes
with its glory. She turned from the vision,
therefore, with a sigh of utter bliss, and with
soft quiet steps and groping hands, stole back
into the darkness of the rock. What was
darkness or the laziness of Time's feet to one
who had seen what she had that night seen?
She was lifted above all weariness—above all
wrong.

When Falca entered, she uttered a cry of
terror. But Nycteris called to her not to be
afraid, and told her how there had come a
rumbling and a shaking, and the lamp had
fallen. Then Falca went and told her mistress, and within an hour a new globe hung
in the place of the old one. Nycteris
thought it did not look so bright and clear
as the former, but she made no lamentation

over the change; she was far too rich to heed it. For now, prisoner as she knew herself, her heart was full of glory and gladness; at times she had to hold herself from jumping up, and going dancing and singing about the room. When she slept, instead of dull dreams, she had splendid visions. There were times, it is true, when she became restless, and impatient to look upon her riches, but then she would reason with herself, saying, "What does it matter if I sit here for ages with my poor pale lamp, when out there a lamp is burning at which ten thousand little lamps are glowing with wonder?"

She never doubted she had looked upon the day and the sun, of which she had read; and always when she read of the day and the sun, she had the night and the moon in her mind; and when she read of the night and the moon, she thought only of the cave and the lamp that hung there.

CHAPTER X.

THE GREAT LAMP.

IT was some time before she had a second opportunity of going out, for Falca, since the fall of the lamp, had been a little more careful, and seldom left her for long. But one night, having a little headache, Nycteris

lay down upon her bed, and was lying with
her eyes closed, when she heard Falca come
to her, and felt she was bending over her.
Disinclined to talk, she did not open her
eyes, and lay quite still. Satisfied that she
was asleep, Falca left her, moving so softly
that her very caution made Nycteris open
her eyes and look after her—just in time to
see her vanish—through a picture, as it
seemed, that hung on the wall a long way
from the usual place of issue. She jumped
up, her headache forgotten, and ran in the
opposite direction; got out, groped her way
to the stair, climbed, and reached the top of
the wall.—Alas! the great room was not so
light as the little one she had left. Why?—
Sorrow of sorrows! the great lamp was gone!
Had its globe fallen? and its lovely light
gone out upon great wings, a resplendent
firefly, oaring itself through a yet grander
and lovelier room? She looked down to see
if it lay anywhere broken to pieces on the
carpet below; but she could not even see
the carpet. But surely nothing very dreadful could have happened—no rumbling or
shaking, for there were all the little lamps
shining brighter than before, not one of
them looking as if any unusual matter had
befallen. What if each of those little lamps
was growing into a big lamp, and after
being a big lamp for a while, had to go
out and grow a bigger lamp still—out
there, beyond this *out?*—Ah! here was the

living thing that would not be seen, come
to her again—bigger to-night! with such
loving kisses, and such liquid strokings
of her cheeks and forehead, gently tossing
her hair, and delicately toying with it! But
it ceased, and all was still. Had it gone
out? What would happen next? Perhaps
the little lamps had not to grow great lamps,
but to fall one by one and go out first?—
With that, came from below a sweet scent,
then another, and another. Ah, how de-
licious! Perhaps they were all coming to
her only on their way out after the great
lamp!—Then came the music of the river,
which she had been too absorbed in the sky
to note the first time. What was it? Alas!
alas! another sweet living thing on its way
out. They were all marching slowly out in
long lovely file, one after the other, each
taking its leave of her as it passed! It must
be so: here were more and more sweet
sounds, following and fading! The whole
of the *Out* was going out again; it was all
going after the great lovely lamp! She
would be left the only creature in the soli-
tary day! Was there nobody to hang up
a new lamp for the old one, and keep the
creatures from going?—She crept back to
her rock very sad. She tried to comfort
herself by saying that anyhow there would
be room out there; but as she said it she
shuddered at the thought of *empty* room.

When next she succeeded in getting out,

a half-moon hung in the east: a new lamp had come, she thought, and all would be well.

It would be endless to describe the phases of feeling through which Nycteris passed, more numerous and delicate than those of a thousand changing moons. A fresh bliss bloomed in her soul with every varying aspect of infinite nature. Ere long she began to suspect that the new moon was the old moon, gone out and come in again like herself; also that, unlike herself, it wasted and grew again; that it was indeed a live thing, subject like herself to caverns, and keepers, and solitudes, escaping and shining when it could. Was it a prison like hers it was shut in? and did it grow dark when the lamp left it? Where could be the way into it?—With that first she began to look below, as well as above and around her; and then first noted the tops of the trees between her and the floor. There were palms with their red-fingered hands full of fruit; eucalyptus trees crowded with little boxes of powder-puffs; oleanders with their half-caste roses; and orange trees with their clouds of young silver stars, and their aged balls of gold. Her eyes could see colours invisible to ours in the moonlight, and all these she could distinguish well, though at first she took them for the shapes and colours of the carpet of the great room. She longed to get down among them, now she saw they were real creatures, but she did

not know how. She went along the whole
length of the wall to the end that crossed the
river, but found no way of going down.
Above the river she stopped to gaze with
awe upon the rushing water. She knew
nothing of water but from what she drank
and what she bathed in ; and, as the moon
shone on the dark, swift stream, singing
lustily as it flowed, she did not doubt the
river was alive, a swift rushing serpent of
life, going—out?—whither? And then she
wondered if what was brought into her rooms
had been killed that she might drink it, and
have her bath in it.

Once when she stepped out upon the wall,
it was into the midst of a fierce wind. The
trees were all roaring. Great clouds were
rushing along the skies, and tumbling over
the little lamps : the great lamp had not
come yet. All was in tumult. The wind
seized her garments and hair, and shook
them as if it would tear them from her.
What could she have done to make the gentle
creature so angry? Or was this another
creature altogether—of the same kind, but
hugely bigger, and of a very different temper
and behaviour? But the whole place was
angry! Or was it that the creatures dwelling
in it, the wind, and the trees, and the clouds,
and the river, had all quarrelled, each with
all the rest? Would the whole come to confusion and disorder? But, as she gazed
wondering and disquieted, the moon, larger

than ever she had seen her, came lifting
herself above the horizon to look, broad and
red, as if she, too, were swollen with anger
that she had been roused from her rest by
their noise, and compelled to hurry up to see
what her children were about, thus rioting in
her absence, lest they should rack the whole
frame of things. And as she rose, the loud
wind grew quieter and scolded less fiercely,
the trees grew stiller and moaned with a
lower complaint, and the clouds hunted and
hurled themselves less wildly across the sky.
And as if she were pleased that her children
obeyed her very presence, the moon grew
smaller as she ascended the heavenly stair ;
her puffed cheeks sank, her complexion grew
clearer, and a sweet smile spread over her
countenance, as peacefully she rose and rose.
But there was treason and rebellion in her
court; for, ere she reached the top of her
great stairs, the clouds had assembled, forgetting their late wars, and very still they
were as they laid their heads together and
conspired. Then combining, and lying
silently in wait until she came near, they
threw themselves upon her, and swallowed
her up. Down from the roof came spots of
wet, faster and faster, and they wetted the
cheeks of Nycteris; and what could they be
but the tears of the moon, crying because her
children were smothering her ? Nycteris
wept too, and not knowing what to think,
stole back in dismay to her room.

The next time, she came out in fear and trembling. There was the moon still! away in the west—poor, indeed, and old, and looking dreadfully worn, as if all the wild beasts in the sky had been gnawing at her—but there she was, alive still, and able to shine!

CHAPTER XI.

THE SUNSET.

KNOWING nothing of darkness, or stars, or moon, Photogen spent his days in hunting. On a great white horse he swept over the grassy plains, glorying in the sun, fighting the wind, and killing the buffaloes.

One morning, when he happened to be on the ground a little earlier than usual, and before his attendants, he caught sight of an animal unknown to him, stealing from a hollow into which the sunrays had not yet reached. Like a swift shadow it sped over the grass, slinking southward to the forest. He gave chase, noted the body of a buffalo it had half eaten, and pursued it the harder. But with great leaps and bounds the creature shot farther and farther ahead of him, and vanished. Turning therefore defeated, he met Fargu, who had been following him as fast as his horse could carry him.

"What animal was that, Fargu?" he asked. "How he did run!"

Fargu answered he might be a leopard, but he rather thought from his pace and look that he was a young lion.

"What a coward he must be!" said Photogen.

"Don't be too sure of that," rejoined Fargu. "He is one of the creatures the sun makes uncomfortable. As soon as the sun is down, he will be brave enough."

He had scarcely said it, when he repented nor did he regret it the less when he found that Photogen made no reply. But alas! said was said.

"Then," said Photogen to himself, "that contemptible beast is one of the terrors of sundown, of which Madam Watho spoke!"

He hunted all day, but not with his usual spirit. He did not ride so hard, and did not kill one buffalo. Fargu to his dismay observed also that he took every pretext for moving farther south, nearer to the forest. But all at once, the sun now sinking in the west, he seemed to change his mind, for he turned his horse's head, and rode home so fast that the rest could not keep him in sight. When they arrived, they found his horse in the stable, and concluded that he had gone into the castle. But he had in truth set out again by the back of it. Crossing the river a good way up the valley, he re-ascended to the ground they had left, and just before sunset reached the skirts of the forest.

The level orb shone straight in between the bare stems, and saying to himself he could not fail to find the beast, he rushed into the wood. But even as he entered, he turned, and looked to the west. The rim of the red was touching the horizon, all jagged with broken hills. " Now," said Photogen, we shall see ; " but he said it in the face of a darkness he had not proved. The moment the sun began to sink among the spikes and saw-edges, with a kind of sudden flap at his heart a fear inexplicable laid hold of the youth ; and as he had never felt anything of the kind before, the very fear itself terrified him. As the sun sank, it rose like the shadow of the world, and grew deeper and darker. He could not even think what it might be, so utterly did it enfeeble him. When the last flaming scimitar-edge of the sun went out like a lamp, his horror seemed to blossom into very madness. Like the closing lids of an eye—for there was no twilight, and this night no moon—the terror and the darkness rushed together, and he knew them for one. He was no longer the man he had known, or rather thought himself. The courage he had had was in no sense his own—he had only had courage, not been courageous ; it had left him, and he could scarcely stand—certainly not stand straight, for not one of his joints could he make stiff or keep from trembling. He was but a spark of the sun, in himself nothing.

The beast was behind him—stealing upon him! He turned. All was dark in the wood, but to his fancy the darkness here and there broke into pairs of green eyes, and he had not the power even to raise his bow-hand from his side. In the strength of despair he strove to rouse courage enough —not to fight—that he did not even desire —but to run. Courage to flee home was all he could ever imagine, and it would not come. But what he had not, was ignominiously given him. A cry in the wood, half a screech, half a growl, sent him running like a boar-wounded cur. It was not even himself that ran, it was the fear that had come alive in his legs: he did not know that they moved. But as he ran he grew able to run—gained courage at least to be a coward. The stars gave a little light. Over the grass he sped, and nothing followed him. "How fallen, how changed," from the youth who had climbed the hill as the sun went down! A mere contempt to himself, the self that contemned was a coward with the self it contemned! There lay the shapeless black of a buffalo, humped upon the grass : he made a wide circuit, and swept on like a shadow driven in the wind. For the wind had arisen, and added to his terror : it blew from behind him. He reached the brow of the valley, and shot down the steep descent like a falling star. Instantly the whole upper country behind him arose and pursued him! The wind came howling after him, filled with screams, shrieks, yells, roars, laughter, and chattering, as if all the animals of the forest were careering with it. In his ears was a trampling rush, the thunder of the hoofs of the cattle, in career from every quarter of the wide plains to the brow of the hill above him! He fled straight for the castle, scarcely with breath enough to pant.

As he reached the bottom of the valley, the moon peered up over its edge. He had never seen the moon before—except in the daytime, when he had taken her for a thin bright cloud. She was a fresh terror to him —so ghostly! so ghastly! so gruesome!— so knowing as she looked over the top of her garden-wall upon the world outside! That was the night itself! the darkness alive —and after him! the horror of horrors coming down the sky to curdle his blood, and turn his brain to a cinder! He gave a sob, and made straight for the river, where it ran between the two walls, at the bottom of the garden. He plunged in, struggled through, clambered up the bank, and fell senseless on the grass.

CHAPTER XII.

THE GARDEN.

ALTHOUGH Nycteris took care not to stay out long at a time, and used every precaution, she could hardly have escaped discovery so long, had it not been that the strange attacks to which Watho was subject had been more frequent of late, and had at last settled into an illness which kept her to her bed. But whether from an access of caution or from suspicion, Falca, having now to be much with her mistress both day and night, took it at length into her head to fasten the door as often as she went by her usual place of exit; so that one night, when Nycteris pushed, she found, to her surprise and dismay, that the wall pushed her again, and would not let her through; nor with all her searching could she discover wherein lay the cause of the change. Then first she felt the pressure of her prison-walls, and turning, half in despair, groped her way to the picture where she had once seen Falca disappear. There she soon found the spot by pressing upon which the wall yielded. It let her through into a sort of cellar, where was a glimmer of light from a sky whose blue was paled by the moon. From the cellar she got into a long passage, into which the moon was shining, and came to a door. She managed to open it, and, to her great joy, found herself in *the other place*, not on the top of the wall, however, but in the garden she had longed to enter. Noiseless as a fluffy moth she flitted away into the covert of the trees and shrubs, her bare feet welcomed by the softest of carpets, which, by the very touch, her feet knew to be alive, whence it came that it was so sweet and friendly to them. A soft little wind was out among the trees, running now here, now there, like a child that had got its will. She went dancing over the grass, looking behind her at her shadow, as she went. At first she had taken it for a little black creature that made game of her, but when she perceived that it was only where she kept the moon away, and that every tree, however great and grand a creature, had also one of these strange attendants, she soon learned not to mind it, and by and by it became the source of as much amusement to her, as to any kitten its tail. It was long before she was quite at home with the trees, however. At one time they seemed to disapprove of her; at another not even to know she was there, and to be altogether taken up with their own business. Suddenly, as she went from one to another of them, looking up with awe at the murmuring mystery of their branches and leaves, she spied one a little way off, which was very different from all

the rest. It was white, and dark, and
sparkling, and spread like a palm—a small
slender palm, without much head ; and it
grew very fast, and sang as it grew. But
it never grew any bigger, for just as fast
as she could see it growing, it kept falling
to pieces. When she got close to it, she
discovered that it was a water-tree—made
of just such water as she washed with—only
it was alive of course, like the river—a different sort of water from that, doubtless,
seeing the one crept swiftly along the floor,
and the other shot straight up, and fell, and
swallowed itself, and rose again. She put
her feet into the marble basin, which was
the flower-pot in which it grew. It was
full of real water, living and cool—so nice,
for the night was hot !

But the flowers ! ah, the flowers ! she
was friends with them from the very first.
What wonderful creatures they were !—and
so kind and beautiful—always sending out
such colours and such scents—red scent, and
white scent, and yellow scent—for the other
creatures ! The one that was invisible and
everywhere, took such a quantity of their
scents, and carried it away ! yet they did
not seem to mind. It was their talk, to
show they were alive, and not painted like
those on the walls of her rooms, and on the
carpets.

She wandered along down the garden
until she reached the river. Unable then

to get any further — for she was a little
afraid, and justly, of the swift watery serpent—she dropped on the grassy bank,
dipped her feet in the water, and felt it
running and pushing against them. For a
long time she sat thus, and her bliss seemed
complete, as she gazed at the river, and
watched the broken picture of the great lamp
overhead, moving up one side of the roof,
to go down the other.

CHAPTER XIII.

SOMETHING QUITE NEW.

A BEAUTIFUL moth brushed across the great
blue eyes of Nycteris. She sprang to her
feet to follow it—not in the spirit of the
hunter, but of the lover. Her heart—like
every heart, if only its fallen sides were
cleared away—was an inexhaustible fountain
of love : she loved everything she saw. But
as she followed the moth, she caught sight of
something lying on the bank of the river,
and not yet having learned to be afraid of
anything, ran straight to see what it was.
Reaching it, she stood amazed. Another
girl like herself ! But what a strange-
looking girl !—so curiously dressed too !—
and not able to move ! Was she dead ?
Filled suddenly with pity, she sat down, lifted

I

Photogen's head, laid it on her lap, and began stroking his face. Her warm hands brought him to himself. He opened his black eyes, out of which had gone all the fire, and looked up with a strange sound of fear, half moan, half gasp. But when he saw her face, he drew a deep breath, and lay motionless— gazing at her : those blue marvels above him, like a better sky, seemed to side with courage and assuage his terror. At length, in a trembling, awed voice, and a half whisper, he said, " Who are you ? "

" I am Nycteris," she answered.

" You are a creature of the darkness, and love the night," he said, his fear beginning to move again.

" I may be a creature of the darkness," she replied. " I hardly know what you mean. But I do not love the night. I love the day —with all my heart ; and I sleep all the night long."

" How can that be ? " said Photogen, rising on his elbow, but dropping his head on her lap again the moment he saw the moon ; "—how can it be," he repeated, " when I see your eyes there—wide awake ? "

She only smiled and stroked him, for she did not understand him, and thought he did not know what he was saying.

" Was it a dream then ? " resumed Photogen, rubbing his eyes. But with that his memory came clear, and he shuddered, and cried, " Oh horrible ! horrible ! to be turned

all at once into a coward! a shameful, contemptible, disgraceful coward! I am ashamed
—ashamed—and *so* frightened! It is all so
frightful!"

"What is so frightful?" asked Nycteris,
with a smile like that of a mother to her child
waked from a bad dream.

"All, all," he answered; "all this darkness
and the roaring."

"My dear," said Nycteris, "there is no
roaring. How sensitive you must be! What
you hear is only the walking of the water,
and the running about of the sweetest of all
the creatures. She is invisible, and I call
her Everywhere, for she goes through all
the other creatures and comforts them. Now
she is amusing herself, and them too, with
shaking them and kissing them, and blowing
in their faces. Listen : do you call that roaring? You should hear her when she is
rather angry though! I don't know why,
but she is sometimes, and then she does roar
a little."

"It is so horribly dark!" said Photogen,
who, listening while she spoke, had satisfied
himself that there was no roaring.

"Dark!" she echoed. "You should be in
my room when an earthquake has killed my
lamp. I do not understand. How *can* you
call this dark? Let me see : yes, you have
eyes, and big ones, bigger than Madam
Watho's or Falca's—not so big as mine, I
fancy—only I never saw mine. But then—

oh yes!—I know now what is the matter! You can't see with them because they are so black. Darkness can't see, of course. Never mind: I will be your eyes, and teach you to see. Look here—at these lovely white things in the grass, with red sharp points all folded together into one. Oh, I love them so! I could sit looking at them all day, the darlings!"

Photogen looked close at the flowers, and thought he had seen something like them before, but could not make them out. As Nycteris had never seen an open daisy, so had he never seen a closed one.

Thus instinctively Nycteris tried to turn him away from his fear; and the beautiful creature's strange lovely talk helped not a little to make him forget it.

" You call it dark!" she said again, as if she could not get rid of the absurdity of the idea; " why, I could count every blade of the green hair—I suppose it is what the books call grass—within two yards of me! And just look at the great lamp! It is brighter than usual to-day, and I can't think why you should be frightened, or call it dark!"

As she spoke, she went on stroking his cheeks and hair, and trying to comfort him. But oh how miserable he was! and how plainly he looked it! He was on the point of saying that her great lamp was dreadful to him, looking like a witch, walking in the sleep of death; but he was not so ignorant

as Nycteris, and knew even in the moonlight
that she was a woman, though he had never
seen one so young or so lovely before; and
while she comforted his fear, her presence
made him the more ashamed of it. Besides,
not knowing her nature, he might annoy her,
and make her leave him to his misery. He
lay still therefore, hardly daring to move:
all the little life he had seemed to come from
her, and if he were to move, she might move;
and if she were to leave him, he must weep
like a child.

"How did you come here?" asked Nycteris, taking his face between her hands.

"Down the hill," he answered.

"Where do you sleep?" she asked.

He signed in the direction of the house.
She gave a little laugh of delight.

"When you have learned not to be frightened, you will always be wanting to come
out with me," she said.

She thought with herself she would ask
her presently, when she had come to herself
a little, how she had made her escape, for
she must, of course, like herself have got out
of a cave, in which Watho and Falca had
been keeping her.

"Look at the lovely colours," she went on,
pointing to a rose-bush, on which Photogen
could not see a single flower. "They are far
more beautiful—are they not?—than any of
the colours upon your walls. And then they
are alive, and smell so sweet!"

He wished she would not make him keep opening his eyes to look at things he could not see; and every other moment would start and grasp tight hold of her, as some fresh pang of terror shot into him.

"Come, come, dear!" said Nycteris; "you must not go on this way. You must be a brave girl, and—— "

"A girl!" shouted Photogen, and started to his feet in wrath. "If you were a man, I should kill you."

"A man?" repeated Nycteris: "what is that? How could I be that? We are both girls—are we not?"

"No, I am not a girl," he answered; "—although," he added, changing his tone, and casting himself on the ground at her feet, "I have given you too good reason to call me one."

"Oh, I see!" returned Nycteris. "No, of course! you can't be a girl: girls are not afraid—without reason. I understand now: it is because you are not a girl that you are so frightened."

Photogen twisted and writhed upon the grass.

"No, it is not," he said sulkily; "it is this horrible darkness that creeps into me, goes all through me, into the very marrow of my bones—that is what makes me behave like a girl. If only the sun would rise!"

"The sun! what is it?" cried Nycteris, now in her turn conceiving a vague fear.

Then Photogen broke into a rhapsody, in which he vainly sought to forget his.

"It is the soul, the life, the heart, the glory of the universe," he said. "The worlds dance like motes in his beams. The heart of man is strong and brave in his light, and when it departs his courage grows from him —goes with the sun, and he becomes such as you see me now."

"Then that is not the sun?" said Nycteris, thoughtfully, pointing up to the moon.

"That!" cried Photogen, with utter scorn; "I know nothing about *that*, except that it is ugly and horrible. At best it can be only the ghost of a dead sun. Yes, that is it! That is what makes it look so frightful."

"No," said Nycteris, after a long, thoughtful pause; "you must be wrong there. I think the sun is the ghost of a dead moon, and that is how he is so much more splendid as you say.—Is there, then, another big room, where the sun lives in the roof?"

"I do not know what you mean," replied Photogen. "But you mean to be kind, I know, though you should not call a poor fellow in the dark a girl. If you will let me lie here, with my head in your lap, I should like to sleep. Will you watch me, and take care of me?"

"Yes, that I will," answered Nycteris, forgetting all her own danger.

So Photogen fell asleep.

CHAPTER XIV.

THE SUN.

THERE Nycteris sat, and there the youth lay, all night long, in the heart of the great cone-shadow of the earth, like two Pharaohs in one pyramid. Photogen slept, and slept; and Nycteris sat motionless lest she should wake him, and so betray him to his fear.

The moon rode high in the blue eternity; it was a very triumph of glorious night; the river ran babble-murmuring in deep soft syllables; the fountain kept rushing moon-ward, and blossoming momently to a great silvery flower, whose petals were for ever falling like snow, but with a continuous musical clash, into the bed of its exhaustion beneath; the wind woke, took a run among the trees, went to sleep, and woke again; the daisies slept on their feet at hers, but she did not know they slept; the roses might well seem awake, for their scent filled the air, but in truth they slept also, and the odour was that of their dreams; the oranges hung like gold lamps in the trees, and their silvery flowers were the souls of their yet unem-bodied children; the scent of the acacia blooms filled the air like the very odour of the moon herself.

At last, unused to the living air, and weary

with sitting so still and so long, Nycteris grew drowsy. The air began to grow cool. It was getting near the time when she too was accustomed to sleep. She closed her eyes just a moment, and nodded—opened them suddenly wide, for she had promised to watch.

In that moment a change had come. The moon had got round, and was fronting her from the west, and she saw that her face was altered, that she had grown pale, as if she too were wan with fear, and from her lofty place espied a coming terror. The light seemed to be dissolving out of her; she was dying—she was going out! And yet everything around looked strangely clear—clearer than ever she had seen anything before: how could the lamp be shedding more light when she herself had less? Ah, that was just it! See how faint she looked! It was because the light was forsaking her, and spreading itself over the room, that she grew so thin and pale! She was giving up everything! She was melting away from the roof like a bit of sugar in water.

Nycteris was fast growing afraid, and sought refuge with the face upon her lap. How beautiful the creature was!—what to call it she could not think, for it had been angry when she called it what Watho called her. And, wonder upon wonder! now, even in the cold change that was passing upon the great room, the colour as of a red rose

was rising in the wan cheek. What beautiful
yellow hair it was that spread over her lap!
What great huge breaths the creature took!
And what were those curious things it
carried? She had seen them on her walls,
she was sure.

Thus she talked to herself while the lamp
grew paler and paler, and everything kept
growing yet clearer. What could it mean?
The lamp was dying—going out into the
other place of which the creature in her lap
had spoken, to be a sun! But why were
the things growing clearer before it was
yet a sun? That was the point. Was it her
growing into a sun that did it? Yes! yes!
it was coming death! She knew it, for it
was coming upon her also! She felt it
coming! What was she about to grow into?
Something beautiful, like the creature in her
lap? It might be! Anyhow, it must be
death; for all her strength was going out
of her, while all around her was growing
so light she could not bear it! She must
be blind soon! Would she be blind or dead
first?

For the sun was rushing up behind her.
Photogen woke, lifted his head from her lap,
and sprang to his feet. His face was one
radiant smile. His heart was full of daring
—that of the hunter who will creep into the
tiger's den. Nycteris gave a cry, covered
her face with her hands, and pressed her
eyelids close. Then blindly she stretched

out her arms to Photogen, crying, "Oh, I am *so* frightened! What is this? It must be death! I don't wish to die yet. I love this room and the old lamp. I do not want the other place! This is terrible. I want to hide. I want to get into the sweet, soft, dark hands of all the other creatures. Ah me! ah me!"

"What is the matter with you, girl?" said Photogen, with the arrogance of all male creatures until they have been taught by the other kind. He stood looking down upon her over his bow, of which he was examining the string. "There is no fear of anything now, child. It is day. The sun is all but up. Look! he will be above the brow of yon hill in one moment more! Good-bye. Thank you for my night's lodging. I'm off. Don't be a goose. If ever I can do anything for you—and all that, you know!"

"Don't leave me; oh, don't leave me!" cried Nycteris. "I am dying! I am dying! I cannot move. The light sucks all the strength out of me. And oh, I am *so* frightened!"

But already Photogen had splashed through the river, holding high his bow that it might not get wet. He rushed across the level, and strained up the opposing hill. Hearing no answer, Nycteris removed her hands. Photogen had reached the top, and the same moment the sunrays alighted upon him: the glory of the king of day crowded blazing upon the golden-haired youth. Radiant as Apollo, he stood in mighty strength, a flashing shape in the midst of flame. He fitted a glowing arrow to a gleaming bow. The arrow parted with a keen musical twang of the bowstring, and Photogen darting after it, vanished with a shout. Up shot Apollo himself, and from his quiver scattered astonishment and exultation. But the brain of poor Nycteris was pierced through and through. She fell down in utter darkness. All around her was a flaming furnace. In despair and feebleness and agony, she crept back, feeling her way with doubt and difficulty and enforced persistence to her cell. When at last the friendly darkness of her chamber folded her about with its cooling and consoling arms, she threw herself on her bed and fell fast asleep. And there she slept on, one alive in a tomb, while Photogen, above in the sun-glory, pursued the buffaloes on the lofty plain, thinking not once of her where she lay dark and forsaken, whose presence had been his refuge, her eyes and her hands his guardians through the night. He was in his glory and his pride; and the darkness and its disgrace had vanished for a time.

CHAPTER XV.

THE COWARD HERO.

BUT no sooner had the sun reached the noonstead, than Photogen began to remember the past night in the shadow of that which was at hand, and to remember it with shame. He had proved himself—and not to himself only, but to a girl as well—a coward!—one bold in the daylight, while there was nothing to fear, but trembling like any slave when the night arrived. There was, there must be, something unfair in it! A spell had been cast upon him! He had eaten, he had drunk something that did not agree with courage! In any case he had been taken unprepared! How was he to know what the going down of the sun would be like? It was no wonder he should have been surprised into terror, seeing it was what it was—in its very nature so terrible! Also, one could not see where danger might be coming from! You might be torn in pieces, carried off, or swallowed up, without even seeing where to strike a blow! Every possible excuse he caught at, eager as a self-lover to lighten his self-contempt. That day he astonished the huntsmen—terrified them with his reckless daring—all to prove to himself he was no coward. But nothing eased his shame. One thing only had hope in it—the resolve to encounter the dark in solemn earnest, now that he knew something of what it was. It was nobler to meet a recognized danger than to rush contemptuously into what seemed nothing—nobler still to encounter a nameless horror. He could conquer fear and wipe out disgrace together. For a marksman and swordsman like him, he said, one with his strength and courage, there was but danger. Defeat there was not. He knew the darkness now, and when it came he would meet it as fearless and cool as now he felt himself. And again he said, " We shall see ! "

He stood under the boughs of a great beech as the sun was going down, far away over the jagged hills : before it was half down, he was trembling like one of the leaves behind him in the first sigh of the night-wind. The moment the last of the glowing disc vanished, he bounded away in terror to gain the valley, and his fear grew as he ran. Down the side of the hill, an abject creature, he went bounding and rolling and running ; fell rather than plunged into the river, and came to himself, as before, lying on the grassy bank in the garden.

But when he opened his eyes, there were no girl-eyes looking down into his ; there were only the stars in the waste of the sunless Night—the awful all-enemy he had

again dared, but could not encounter. Perhaps the girl was not yet come out of the
water! He would try to sleep, for he dared
not move, and perhaps when he woke he
would find his head on her lap, and the
beautiful dark face, with its deep blue eyes,
bending over him. But when he woke he
found his head on the grass, and although
he sprang up with all his courage, such as it
was, restored, he did not set out for the
chase with such ʼn *elan* as the day before;
and, despite the sun-glory in his heart and
veins, his hunting was this day less eager;
he ate little, and from the first was thoughtful
even to sadness. A second time he was
defeated and disgraced! Was his courage
nothing more than the play of the sunlight
on his brain? Was he a mere ball tossed
between the light and the dark? Then
what a poor contemptible creature he was!
But a third chance lay before him. If he
failed the third time, he dared not foreshadow
what he must then think of himself! It was
bad enough now—but then!

Alas! it went no better. The moment the
sun was down, he fled as if from a legion
of devils.

Seven times in all, he tried to face the
coming night in the strength of the past
day, and seven times he failed—failed with
such increase of failure, with such a growing
sense of ignominy, overwhelming at length
all the sunny hours and joining night to

right, that, what with misery, self-accusa-
tion, and loss of confidence, his daylight
courage too began to fade, and at length,
from exhaustion, from getting wet, and then
lying out of doors all night, and night after
night,—worst of all, from the consuming of
the deathly fear, and the shame of shame,
his sleep forsook him, and on the seventh
morning, instead of going to the hunt, he
crawled into the castle, and went to bed.
The grand health, over which the witch had
taken such pains, had yielded, and in an
hour or two he was moaning and crying out
in delirium.

CHAPTER XVI.

AN EVIL NURSE.

Watho was herself ill, as I have said, and
was the worse tempered; and, besides, it is
a peculiarity of witches, that what works in
others to sympathy, works in them to re-
pulsion. Also, Watho had a poor, helpless,
rudimentary spleen of a conscience left, just
enough to make her uncomfortable, and
therefore more wicked. So, when she heard
that Photogen was ill, she was angry. Ill,
indeed! after all she had done to saturate
him with the life of the system, with the
solar might itself! He was a wretched
failure, the boy! And because he was *her*

failure, she was annoyed with him, began
to dislike him, grew to hate him. She
looked on him as a painter might upon a
picture, or a poet upon a poem, which he
had only succeeded in getting into an irre-
coverable mess. In the hearts of witches,
love and hate lie close together, and often
tumble over each other. And whether it
was that her failure with Photogen foiled
also her plans in regard to Nycteris, or that
her illness made her yet more of a devil's
wife, certainly Watho now got sick of the
girl too, and hated to know her about the
castle.

She was not too ill, however, to go to
poor Photogen's room and torment him.
She told him she hated him like a serpent,
and hissed like one as she said it, looking
very sharp in the nose and chin, and flat in
the forehead. Photogen thought she meant
to kill him, and hardly ventured to take
anything brought him. She ordered every
ray of light to be shut out of his room;
but by means of this he got a little used to
the darkness. She would take one of his
arrows, and now tickle him with the feather
end of it, now prick him with the point till
the blood ran down. What she meant finally
I cannot tell, but she brought Photogen
speedily to the determination of making his
escape from the castle: what he should do
then he would think afterwards. Who could
tell but he might find his mother somewhere

K

beyond the forest! If it were not for the broad patches of darkness that divided day from day, he would fear nothing!

But now, as he lay helpless in the dark, ever and anon would come dawning through it the face of the lovely creature who on that first awful night nursed him so sweetly: was he never to see her again? If she was, as he had concluded, the nymph of the river, why had she not re-appeared? She might have taught him not to fear the night, for plainly she had no fear of it herself! But then, when the day came, she did seem frightened :—why was that, seeing there was nothing to be afraid of then? Perhaps one so much at home in the darkness, was correspondingly afraid of the light! Then his selfish joy at the rising of the sun, blinding him to her condition, had made him behave to her, in ill return for her kindness, as cruelly as Watho behaved to him! How sweet and dear and lovely she was! If there were wild beasts that came out only at night, and were afraid of the light, why should there not be girls too, made the same way— who could not endure the light, as he could not bear the darkness? If only he could find her again! Ah, how differently he would behave to her! But alas! perhaps the sun had killed her—melted her—burned her up!—dried her up—that was it, if she was the nymph of the river!

CHAPTER XVII

WATHO'S WOLF

FROM that dreadful morning Nycteris had never got to be herself again. The sudden light had been almost death to her; and now she lay in the dark with the memory of a terrific sharpness—a something she dared scarcely recall, lest the very thought of it should sting her beyond endurance. But this was as nothing to the pain which the recollection of the rudeness of the shining creature whom she had nursed through his fear caused her; for, the moment his suffering passed over to her, and he was free, the first use he made of his returning strength had been to scorn her! She wondered and wondered; it was all beyond her comprehension.

Before long, Watho was plotting evil against her. The witch was like a sick child weary of his toy: she would pull her to pieces, and see how she liked it. She would set her in the sun, and see her die, like a jelly from the salt ocean cast out on a hot rock. It would be a sight to soothe her wolf-pain. One day, therefore, a little before noon, while Nycteris was in her deepest sleep, she had a darkened litter brought to the door, and in that she made two of her men carry her to the plain above. There they took her out, laid her on the grass, and left her.

Watho watched it all from the top of her high tower, through her telescope; and scarcely was Nycteris left, when she saw her sit up, and the same moment cast herself down again with her face to the ground.

"She'll have a sunstroke," said Watho, "and that'll be the end of her."

Presently, tormented by a fly, a huge-humped buffalo, with great shaggy mane, came galloping along, straight for where she lay. At sight of the thing on the grass, he started, swerved yards aside, stopped dead, and then came slowly up, looking malicious. Nycteris lay quite still, and never even saw the animal.

"Now she'll be trodden to death!" said Watho. "That's the way those creatures do."

When the buffalo reached her, he sniffed at her all over, and went away; then came back, and sniffed again; then all at once went off as if a demon had him by the tail.

Next came a gnu, a more dangerous animal still, and did much the same; then a gaunt wild boar. But no creature hurt her, and Watho was angry with the whole creation.

At length, in the shade of her hair, the blue eyes of Nycteris began to come to themselves a little, and the first thing they saw was a comfort. I have told already how she

knew the night-daisies, each a sharp-pointed
little cone with a red tip ; and once she had
parted the rays of one of them, with trembling fingers, for she was afraid she was
dreadfully rude, and perhaps was hurting it ;
but she did want, she said to herself, to see
what secret it carried so carefully hidden ;
and she found its golden heart. But now,
right under her eyes, inside the veil of her
hair, in the sweet twilight of whose blackness
she could see it perfectly, stood a daisy with
its red tip opened wide into a carmine ring,
displaying its heart of gold on a platter of
silver. She did not at first recognize it as
one of those cones come awake, but a
moment's notice revealed what it was. Who
then could have been so cruel to the lovely
little creature, as to force it open like that,
and spread it heart-bare to the terrible death-
lamp? Whoever it was, it must be the same
that had thrown her out there to be burned
to death in its fire! But she had her hair,
and could hang her head, and make a small
sweet night of her own about her! She tried
to bend the daisy down and away from the
sun, and to make its petals hang about it like
her hair, but she could not. Alas ! it was
burned and dead already! She did not know
that it could not yield to her gentle force
because it was drinking life, with all the
eagerness of life, from what she called the
death-lamp. Oh, how the lamp burned her !

But she went on thinking—she did not

know how; and by and by began to reflect that, as there was no roof to the room except that in which the great fire went rolling about, the little Red-tip must have seen the lamp a thousand times, and must know it quite well! and it had not killed it! Nay, thinking about farther, she began to ask the question whether this, in which she now saw it, might not be its more perfect condition. For not only now did the whole seem perfect, as indeed it did before, but every part showed its own individual perfection as well, which perfection made it capable of combining with the rest into the higher perfection of a whole. The flower was a lamp itself! The golden heart was the light, and the silver border was the alabaster globe, skilfully broken, and spread wide to let out the glory. Yes; the radiant shape was plainly its perfection! If, then, it was the lamp which had opened it into that shape, the lamp could not be unfriendly to it, but must be of its own kind, seeing it made it perfect! And again, when she thought of it, there was clearly no little resemblance between them. What if the flower then was the little great-grandchild of the lamp, and he was loving it all the time? And what if the lamp did not mean to hurt her, only could not help it? The red tips looked as if the flower had some time or other been hurt: what if the lamp was making the best it could of her—opening her out somehow like the flower? She would bear it patiently, and see. But how coarse the colour of the grass was! Perhaps, however, her eyes not being made for the bright lamp, she did not see them as they were! Then she remembered how different were the eyes of the creature that was not a girl and was afraid of the darkness! Ah, if the darkness would only come again, all arms, friendly and soft everywhere about her! She would wait and wait, and bear, and be patient.

She lay so still that Watho did not doubt she had fainted. She was pretty sure she would be dead before the night came to revive her.

CHAPTER XVIII.

REFUGE.

FIXING her telescope on the motionless form, that she might see it at once when the morning came, Watho went down from the tower to Photogen's room. He was much better by this time, and before she left him, he had resolved to leave the castle that very night. The darkness was terrible indeed, but Watho was worse than even the darkness, and he could not escape in the day. As soon, therefore, as the house seemed still, he tightened his belt, hung to it his hunting-knife, put a flask of wine and some bread in his pocket, and took his bow and arrows. He got from the house, and made his way at once up to the plain. But what with his illness, the terrors of the night, and his dread of the wild beasts, when he got to the level he could not walk a step further, and sat down, thinking it better to die than to live. In spite of his fears, however, sleep contrived to overcome him, and he fell at full length on the soft grass.

He had not slept long when he woke with such a strange sense of comfort and security, that he thought the dawn at least must have arrived. But it was dark night about him. And the sky—no, it was not the sky, but the blue eyes of his naiad looking down upon him! Once more he lay with his head in her lap, and all was well, for plainly the girl feared the darkness as little as he the day.

"Thank you," he said. "You are like live armour to my heart; you keep the fear off me. I have been very ill since then. Did you come up out of the river when you saw me cross?"

"I don't live in the water," she answered. "I live under the pale lamp, and I die under the bright one."

"Ah, yes! I understand now," he returned. "I would not have behaved as I did last time if I had understood; but I thought you were mocking me; and I am so made that I cannot help being frightened at the darkness. I beg your pardon for leaving you as I did, for, as I say, I did not understand. Now I believe you were really frightened. Were you not?"

"I was, indeed," answered Nycteris, "and shall be again. But why you should be, I cannot in the least understand. You must know how gentle and sweet the darkness is, how kind and friendly, how soft and velvety! It holds you to its bosom and loves you. A little while ago, I lay faint and dying under your hot lamp.—What is it you call it?"

"The sun," murmured Photogen: "how I wish he would make haste!"

"Ah! do not wish that. Do not, for my sake, hurry him. I can take care of you from the darkness, but I have no one to take care of me from the light.—As I was telling you, I lay dying in the sun. All at once I drew a deep breath. A cool wind came and ran over my face. I looked up. The torture was gone, for the death-lamp itself was gone. I hope he does not die and grow brighter yet. My terrible headache was all gone, and my sight was come back. I felt as if I were new made. But I did not get up at once, for I was tired still. The grass grew cool about me, and turned soft in colour. Something wet came upon it, and it was now so pleasant to my feet, that I rose and ran about. And when I had been running about a long time, all at once I found you lying, just as I had been lying a little while before. So I sat down beside you to take care of you, till your life—and my death—should come again."

"How good you are, you beautiful creature! —Why, you forgave me before ever I asked you!" cried Photogen.

Thus they fell a talking, and he told her what he knew of his history, and she told him what she knew of hers, and they agreed they must get away from Watho as far as ever they could.

"And we must set out at once," said Nycteris.

"The moment the morning comes," returned Photogen.

"We must not wait for the morning," said Nycteris, "for then I shall not be able to move, and what would you do the next night? Besides, Watho sees best in the daytime. Indeed, you must come now, Photogen.—You must."

"I can not; I dare not," said Photogen. "I cannot move. If I but lift my head from your lap, the very sickness of terror seizes me."

"I shall be with you," said Nycteris soothingly. "I will take care of you till your dreadful sun comes, and then you may leave me, and go away as fast as you can. Only please put me in a dark place first, if there is one to be found."

"I will never leave you again, Nycteris," cried Photogen. "Only wait till the sun comes, and brings me back my strength, and we will go away together, and never, never part any more."

"No, no," persisted Nycteris; "we must go now. And you must learn to be strong in the dark as well as in the day, else you will always be only half brave. I have begun already—not to fight your sun, but to try to get at peace with him, and understand what he really is, and what he means with me— whether to hurt me or to make the best of me. You must do the same with my darkness."

"But you don't know what mad animals there are away there towards the south," said Photogen. "They have huge green eyes, and they would eat you up like a bit of celery, you beautiful creature!"

"Come, come! you must," said Nycteris, "or I shall have to pretend to leave you, to make you come. I have seen the green eyes you speak of, and I will take care of you from them."

"You! How can you do that? If it were day now, I could take care of you from the worst of them. But as it is, I can't even see them for this abominable darkness. I could not see your lovely eyes but for the light that is in them; that lets me see straight into heaven through them. They are windows into the very heaven beyond the sky. I believe they are the very place where the stars are made."

"You come then, or I shall shut them," said Nycteris, "and you shan't see them any more till you are good. Come. If you can't see the wild beasts, I can."

"You can! and you ask me to come!" cried Photogen.

"Yes," answered Nycteris. "And more than that, I see them long before they can see me, so that I am able to take care of you."

"But how?" persisted Photogen. "You can't shoot with bow and arrow, or stab with a hunting-knife."

"No, but I can keep out of the way of them all. Why, just when I found you, I was having a game with two or three of them at once. I see, and scent them too, long before they are near me—long before they can see or scent me."

"You don't see or scent any now, do you?" said Photogen, uneasily, rising on his elbow."

"No—none at present. I will look," replied Nycteris, and sprang to her feet.

"Oh, oh! do not leave me—not for a moment," cried Photogen, straining his eyes to keep her face in sight through the darkness.

"Be quiet, or they will hear you," she returned. "The wind is from the south, and they cannot scent us. I have found out all about that. Ever since the dear dark came, I have been amusing myself with them, getting every now and then just into the edge of the wind, and letting one have a sniff of me."

"Oh, horrible!" cried Photogen. "I

hope you will not insist on doing so any more. What was the consequence?"

"Always, the very instant, he turned with flashing eyes, and bounded towards me— only he could not see me, you must remember. But my eyes being so much better than his, I could see him perfectly well, and would run away round him until I scented him, and then I knew he could not find me anyhow. If the wind were to turn, and run the other way now, there might be a whole army of them down upon us, leaving no room to keep out of their way. You had better come."

She took him by the hand. He yielded and rose, and she led him away. But his steps were feeble, and as the night went on, he seemed more and more ready to sink.

"Oh dear! I am so tired! and so frightened!" he would say.

"Lean on me," Nycteris would return, putting her arm round him, or patting his cheek. "Take a few steps more. Every step away from the castle is clear gain. Lean harder on me. I am quite strong and well now."

So they went on. The piercing night-eyes of Nycteris descried not a few pairs of green ones gleaming like holes in the darkness, and many a round she made to keep far out of their way; but she never said to Photogen she saw them. Carefully she kept him off the uneven places, and on the softest and smoothest of the grass, talking to him gently all the way as they went— of the lovely flowers and the stars — how comfortable the flowers looked, down in their green beds, and how happy the stars up in their blue beds!

When the morning began to come, he began to grow better, but was dreadfully tired with walking instead of sleeping, especially after being so long ill. Nycteris too, what with supporting him, what with growing fear of the light which was beginning to ooze out of the east, was very tired. At length, both equally exhausted, neither was able to help the other. As if by consent they stopped. Embracing each the other, they stood in the midst of the wide grassy land, neither of them able to move a step, each supported only by the leaning weakness of the other, each ready to fall if the other should move. But while the one grew weaker still, the other had begun to grow stronger. When the tide of the night began to ebb, the tide of the day began to flow; and now the sun was rushing to the horizon, borne upon its foaming billows. And ever as he came, Photogen revived. At last the sun shot up into the air, like a bird from the hand of the Father of Lights. Nycteris gave a cry of pain, and hid her face in her hands.

"Oh me!" she sighed; "I am *so* frightened! The terrible light stings so!"

But the same instant, through her blindness, she heard Photogen give a low exultant laugh, and the next felt herself caught up : she who all night long had tended and protected him like a child, was now in his arms, borne along like a baby, with her head lying on his shoulder. But she was the greater, for, suffering more, she feared nothing.

CHAPTER XIX.

THE WEREWOLF.

AT the very moment when Photogen caught up Nycteris, the telescope of Watho was angrily sweeping the table-land. She swung it from her in rage, and running to her room, shut herself up. There she anointed herself from top to toe with a certain ointment; shook down her long red hair, and tied it round her waist; then began to dance, whirling round and round faster and faster, growing angrier and angrier, until she was foaming at the mouth with fury. When Falca went looking for her, she could not find her anywhere.

As the sun rose, the wind slowly changed and went round, until it blew straight from the north. Photogen and Nycteris were drawing near the edge of the forest, Photogen still carrying Nycteris, when she moved a little on his shoulder uneasily, and murmured in his ear,

"I smell a wild beast—that way, the way the wind is coming."

Photogen turned, looked back towards the castle, and saw a dark speck on the plain. As he looked, it grew larger: it was coming across the grass with the spee l of the wind. It came nearer and nearer. It looked long and low, but that might be because it was running at a great stretch. He set Nycteris down under a tree, in the black shadow of its bole, strung his bow, and picked out his heaviest, longest, sharpest arrow. Just as he set the notch on the string, he saw that the creature was a tremendous wolf, rushing straight at him. He loosened his knife in its sheath, drew another arrow half-way from the quiver, lest the first should fail, and took his aim—at a good distance, to leave time for a second chance. He shot. The arrow rose, flew straight, descended, struck the beast, and started again into the air, doubled like a letter V. Quickly Photogen snatched the other, shot, cast his bow from him, and drew his knife. But the arrow was in the brute's chest, up to the feather; it tumbled heels over head with a great thud of its back on the earth, gave a groan, made a struggle or two, and lay stretched out motionless.

"I've killed it, Nycteris," cried Photogen. "It is a great red wolf."

"Oh, thank you!" answered Nycteris feebly from behind the tree. "I was sure you would. I was not a bit afraid."

Photogen went up to the wolf. It *was* a monster! But he was vexed that his first arrow had behaved so badly, and was the less willing to lose the one that had done him such good service: with a long and a strong pull, he drew it from the brute's chest. Could he believe his eyes? There lay—no wolf, but Watho, with her hair tied round her waist! The foolish witch had made herself invulnerable, as she supposed, but had forgotten that, to torment Photogen therewith, she had handled one of his arrows. He ran back to Nycteris and told her.

She shuddered and wept, and would not look.

CHAPTER XX.

ALL IS WELL.

THERE was now no occasion to fly a step farther. Neither of them feared any one but Watho. They left her there, and went back. A great cloud came over the sun, and rain began to fall heavily, and Nycteris was much refreshed, grew able to see a little, and with Photogen's help walked gently over the cool wet grass.

They had not gone far before they met Fargu and the other huntsmen. Photogen told them he had killed a great red wolf, and

L

it was Madam Watho. The huntsmen looked grave, but gladness shone through.

" Then," said Fargu, " I will go and bury my mistress."

But when they reached the place, they found she was already buried—in the maws of sundry birds and beasts which had made their breakfast of her.

Then Fargu, overtaking them, would, very wisely, have Photogen go to the king, and tell him the whole story. But Photogen, yet wiser than Fargu, would not set out until he had married Nycteris ; " for then," he said, " the king himself can't part us ; and if ever two people couldn't do the one without the other, those two are Nycteris and I. She has got to teach me to be a brave man in the dark, and I have got to look after her until she can bear the heat of the sun, and he helps her to see, instead of blinding her."

They were married that very day. And the next day they went together to the king, and told him the whole story. But whom should they find at the court but the father and mother of Photogen, both in high favour with the king and queen. Aurora nearly died for joy, and told them all how Watho had lied, and made her believe her child was dead.

No one knew anything of the father or mother of Nycteris ; but when Aurora saw in the lovely girl her own azure eyes shining through night and its clouds, it made her think strange things, and wonder how even the wicked themselves may be a link to join together the good. Through Watho, the mothers, who had never seen each other, had changed eyes in their children.

The king gave them the castle and lands of Watho, and there they lived and taught each other for many years that were not long. But hardly had one of them passed, before Nycteris had come to love the day best, because it was the clothing and crown of Photogen, and she saw that the day was greater than the night, and the sun more lordly than the moon; and Photogen had come to love the night best, because it was the mother and home of Nycteris.

"But who knows," Nycteris would say to Photogen, "that, when we go out, we shall not go into a day as much greater than your day as your day is greater than my night?"

THE BUTCHER'S BILLS.

CHAPTER I.

HUSBAND AND WIFE.

I AM going to tell a story of married life. My title will prepare the reader for something hardly heroic; but I trust it will not be found lacking in the one genuine and worthy interest a tale ought to have— namely, that it presents a door through which we may walk into one region or another of the human heart, and there find ourselves not altogether unacquainted or from home.

There was a law among the Jews which forbade the yoking together of certain animals, either because, being unequal in size or strength, one of them must be oppressed, or for the sake of some lesson thus embodied to the Eastern mind—possibly for both reasons. Half the tragedy would be taken out of social life if this law could be applied to human beings in their various relations. I do not say that this would be

well, or that we could afford to lose the result
of the tragedy thus occasioned. Neither do
I believe that there are so many instances of
unequal yoking as the misprising judgments
of men by men and women by women might
lead us to imagine. Not every one declared
by the wisdom of acquaintance to have
thrown himself or herself away must therefore be set down as unequally yoked. Or it
may even be that the inequality is there, but
the loss on the other side. How some people
could ever have come together must always
be a puzzle until one knows the history of
the affair; but not a few whom most of us
would judge quite unsuited to each other do
yet get on pretty well from the first, and
better and better the longer they are together, and that with mutual advantage,
improvement, and development. Essential
humanity is deeper than the accidents of
individuality; the common is more powerful
than the peculiar; and the honest heart will
always be learning to act more and more in
accordance with the laws of its being. It
must be of much more consequence to any
lady that her husband should be a man on
whose word she can depend than that he
should be of a gracious presence. But if
instead of coming nearer to a true understanding of each other, the two should from
the first keep falling asunder, then something
tragic may almost be looked for.

Duncan and Lucy Dempster were a couple

the very mention of whose Christian names
together would have seemed amusing to the
friends who had long ceased to talk of their
unfitness. Indeed, I doubt if in their innermost privacy they ever addressed each other
except as Mr. and Mrs. Dempster. For the
first time to see them together, no one could
help wondering how the conjunction could
have been effected. Dempster was of Scotch
descent, but the hereditary high cheek-bone
seemed to have got into his nose, which was
too heavy a pendant for the low forehead
from which it hung. About an inch from
the end it took a swift and unexpected curve
downwards, and was a curious and abnormal
nose, which could not properly be assorted
with any known class of noses. A long
upper lip, a large, firm, and not quite ugly
mouth, with a chin both long and square,
completed a face which, with its low forehead, being yet longer than usual, had a
particularly equine look. He was rather
under the middle height, slender, and well
enough made—altogether an ordinary mortal,
known on 'Change as an able, keen, and
laborious man of business. What his special
business was I do not know. He went to
the city by the eight o'clock omnibus every
morning, dived into a court, entered a little
square, rushed up two flights of stairs to a
couple of rooms, and sat down in the back
one before an office table on a hair-seated
chair. It was a dingy place—not so dirty as

it looked, I daresay. Even the windows,
being of bad glass, did, I believe, look dirtier
than they were. It was a place where, so
far as the eye of an outsider could tell, much
or nothing might be doing. Its occupant
always wore his hat in it, and his hat always
looked shabby. Some people said he was
rich, others that he would be one day. Some
said he was a responsible man, whatever the
epithet may have been intended to mean. I
believe he was quite as honest as the recognized laws of his trade demanded—and for
how many could I say more? Nobody said
he was avaricious—but then he moved
amongst men whose very notion was first
to make money, after that to be religious, or
to enjoy themselves, as the case might be.
And no one either ever said of him that he
was a good man, or a generous. He was
about forty years of age, looking somehow
as if he had never been younger. He had
had a fair education—better than is generally
considered necessary for mercantile purposes
—but it would have been hard to discover
any signs of it in the spending of his leisure.
On Sunday mornings he went with his wife
to church, and when he came home had a
good dinner, of which now and then a friend
took his share. If no stranger was present
he took his wine by himself, and went to
sleep in his easy chair of marone-coloured
leather, while his wife sat on the other side
of the fire if it was winter, or a little way

off by the open window if it was summer,
gently yawned now and then, and looked at
him with eyes a little troubled.   Then he
went off again by the eight o'clock omnibus
on Monday morning, and not an idea more or
less had he in his head, not a hair's-breadth of
difference was there in his conduct or pur-
suits, that he had been to church and had
spent the day out of business. That may,
however, for anything I know, have been as
much the clergyman's fault as his. He was
the sort of man you might call machine-made,
one in whom humanity, if in no wise cari-
catured, was yet in no wise ennobled.

His wife was ten years younger than he—
hardly less than beautiful—only that over her
countenance seemed to have gathered a kind
of haze of commonness. At first sight, notwithstanding, one could not help perceiving
that she was china and he was delft. She
was graceful as she sat, long-necked, slope-
shouldered, and quite as tall as her husband,
with a marked daintiness about her in the
absence of the extremes of the fashion, in the
quality of the lace she wore on her black silk
dress, and in the wide white sleeves of fine
cambric that covered her arms from the
shoulder to the wrist. She had a morally
delicate air, a look of scrupulous nicety and
lavender-stored linen. She had long dark
lashes ; and when they rose, the eyelids revealed eyes of uncommon beauty. She had
good features, good teeth, and a good com-

plexion. The main feeling she produced and left was of ladyhood—little more.

Sunday afternoon came fifty-two times in the year. I mention this because then always, and nearly then only, could one calculate on seeing them together. It came to them in a surburb of London, and the look of it was dull. Doubtless Mr. Dempster's dinner and his repose after it were interesting to him, but I cannot help thinking his wife found it dreary. She had, however, got used to it. The house was a good old one, of red brick, much larger than they required, but not expensive, and had a general look of the refinement of its mistress. In the summer the windows of the dining-room would generally be open, for they looked into a really lovely garden behind the house, and the scent of the jasmine that crept all around them would come in plentifully. I wonder what the scent of jasmine did in Duncan Dempster's world. Perhaps it never got farther than the general ante-chamber of the sensorium. It often made his wife sad—she could not tell why. To him I daresay it smelt agreeable, but I can hardly believe it ever woke in him that dreamy sensation it gave her— of something she had not had enough of, she could not say what. When the heat was gone off a little he would walk out on the lawn, which was well kept and well watered, with many flowering shrubs about it. Why he did so, I cannot tell. He looked at nothing in particular, only walked about for a few minutes, no doubt derived some pleasure of a mild nature from something, and walked in again to tea. One might have expected he would have cultivated the acquaintance of his garden a little, if it were only for the pleasure the contrast would give him when he got back to his loved office, for a greater contrast could not well have been found than between his dingy dreary haunt on week-days—a place which nothing but duty could have made other than repugnant to any free soul—and this nest of greenery and light and odour. Sweet scents floated in clouds invisible about the place; flower eyes and stars and bells and bunches shone and glowed and lurked all around; his very feet might have learned a lesson of that which is beyond the sense from the turf he trod; but all the time, if he were not exactly seeing in his mind's eye the walls and tables of his office in the City square, his thoughts were not the less brooding over such business as he there transacted. For Mr. Dempster's was not a free soul. How could it be when all his energies were given to making money? This he counted his *calling*—and I believe actually contrived to associate some feeling of duty with the notion of leaving behind him a plump round sum of money, as if money in accumulation and following flood, instead of money in peaceful current, were the good thing for the world! Hence the

whole realm of real life, the universe of
thought and growth, was a high-hedged park
to him, within which he never even tried to
look—not even knowing that he was shut
out from it, for the hedge was of his own
growing.   What shall ever wake such a man
to a sense of indwelling poverty, or make
him begin to hunger after any lowliest ex-
pansion?   Does a reader retort, "The man
was comfortable, and why should he be
troubled?"   If the end of being, I answer,
is only comfort in self, I yield.   But what if
there should be at the heart of the universe
a Thought to which the being of such men
is distasteful?   What if to that Thought
they look blots in light, ugly things?   May
there not lie in that direction some possible
reason why they should bethink themselves?
Dempster, however, was not yet a clinker
out of which all the life was burned, however
much he looked like one.   There was in him
that which might yet burn—and give light
and heat.

On the Sunday evenings Mrs. Dempster
would have gladly gone to church again, if
only—though to herself she never allowed
this for one of her reasons—to slip from
under the weight of her husband's presence.
He seldom spoke to her more than a sentence
at a time, but he did like to have **her** near
him, and I suppose held, through the bare
presence, some kind of dull one-sided communication with her; what did a woman

know about business ? and what did he know
about except business ? It is true he had a
rudimentary pleasure in music—and would
sometimes ask her to play to him, when he
would listen, and after his fashion enjoy.
But although here was a gift that might be
developed until his soul could echo the music
of the spheres, the embodied souls of Handel
or Mendelssohn were to him but clouds of
sound wrapped about kernels—let me say of
stock or bonds.

For a year or so after their marriage it had
been the custom that, the first thing after
breakfast on Monday morning, she should
bring him her account-book, that they might
together go over her week's expenses. She
must cultivate the business habits in which,
he said, he found her more than deficient.
How could he endure in a wife what would
have been preposterous in a clerk, and would
have led to his immediate dismissal ? It was
in his eyes necessary that the same strict
record of receipt and expenditure should be
kept in the household as in the office; how
else was one to know in what direction
things were going ? he said. He required of
his wife, therefore, that every individual
thing that cost money, even to what she
spent upon her own person, should be entered in her book. She had no money of her
own, neither did he allow her any special
sum for her private needs ; but he made her
a tolerably liberal weekly allowance, from

which she had to pay everything except house-rent and taxes, an arrangement which I cannot believe a good one, as it will inevitably lead some conscientious wives to self-denial severer than necessary, and on the other hand will tempt the vulgar nature to make a purse for herself by mean savings off everybody else. It was especially distasteful to Mrs. Dempster to have to set down every little article of personal requirement that she bought. It would probably have seemed to her but a trifle had they both been young when they married, and had there been that tenderness of love between them which so soon sets everything more than right; but as it was, she could never get over the feeling that the man was strange to her. As it was she would have got over this. But there was in her a certain constitutional lack of precision, combined with a want of energy and a weakness of will, that rendered her more than careless where her liking was not interested. Hence, while she would have been horrified at playing a wrong note or singing out of tune, she not only had no anxiety, for the thing's own sake, to have her accounts correct, but shrunk from every effort in that direction. Now I can perfectly understand her recoil from the whole affair, with her added dislike to the smallness of the thing required of her; but seeing she did begin with doing it after a fashion, it is not so easy to understand why, doing it, she should

not make a consolation of doing it with absolute exactness. Not even her dread of her
husband's dissatisfaction—which was by no
means small—could prevail to make her, instead of still trusting a memory that constantly played her false, put down a thing
at once, nor postpone it to a far less convenient season. Hence it came that her
accounts, though never much out, never
balanced; and the weekly audit, while it
grew more and more irksome to the one,
grew more and more unsatisfactory to the
other. For to Mr. Dempster's dusty eyes
exactitude wore the robe of rectitude, and
before long, precisely and merely from the
continued unsatisfactory condition of her accounts, he began, in a hidden corner of his
righteous soul, to reflect on the moral condition of his wife herself as unsatisfactory.
Now such it certainly was, but he was not
the man to judge it correctly, or to perceive
the true significance of her failing. In business, while scrupulous as to the requirements
of custom and recognized right, he nevertheless did things from which her soul would
have recoiled like "the tender horns of
cockled snails;" yet it was to him not merely
a strange and inexplicable fact that she
should *never* be able to show to a penny, nay,
often not to a shilling or eighteenpence, how
the week's allowance went, but a painful one
as indicating something beyond perversity.
And truly it was no very hard task he re-

quired of her, for, seeing they had no children, only three servants, and saw little
company, her housekeeping could not be a
very heavy or involved affair. Perhaps if it
had been more difficult she would have done
it better, but anyhow she hated the whole
thing, procrastinated, and setting down
several things together, was *sure* to forget
some article or mistake some price ; yet not
one atom more would she distrust her memory
the next time she was tempted. But it was
a small fault at worst, and if her husband had
loved her enough to understand the bearings
of it in relation to her mental and moral condition he would have tried to content himself
that at least she did not exceed her allowance ; and would of all things have avoided
making such a matter a burden upon the
consciousness of one so differently educated,
if not constituted, from himself. It is but
fair to add on the other side that, if she had
loved him after anything like a wifely ideal,
which I confess was not yet possible to her,
it would not have been many weeks before
she had a first correct account to show him.
Convinced, at length, that accuracy was not
to be had from her, and satisfying himself
with dissatisfaction, he one morning threw
from him the little ruled book, and declared,
in a wrath which he sought to smother into
dignified but hopeless rebuke, that he would
trouble himself with her no further. She
burst into tears, took up the book, left the

room, cried a little, resolved to astonish him
the next Monday, and never set down another
item.   When it came, and breakfast was
over, he gave her the usual cheque, and left
at once for town.   Nor had the accounts ever
again been alluded to between them.

Now this might have been very well, or
at least not very ill, if both had done tolerably well thereafter—that is, if the one had
continued to attend to her expenditure as
well as before, and the other, when he threw
away the account-book, had dismissed from
his mind the whole matter.   But Dempster
was one of those dangerous men—more
dangerous, however, to themselves than to
others—who never forget, that is, get over,
an offence or disappointment.   They respect
themselves so much, and, out of their respect
for themselves, build so much upon success,
set so much by never being defeated but
always gaining their point, that when they
are driven to confess themselves foiled, the
confession is made from the " poor dumb
mouth " of a wound that cannot be healed.
It is there for ever—will be there at least
until they find another God to worship than
their own paltry selves.   Hence it came that
the bourn between the two spiritual estates
yawned a little wider at one point, and a
mist of dissatisfaction would not unfrequently
rise from a certain stagnant pool in its
hollow.   The cause was paltry in one sense,
but nothing to which belongs the name of

Cause can fail to mingle the element of awfulness even with its paltriness. Its worst effect was that it hindered approximation in other parts of their marching natures.

And as to Mrs. Dempster, I am sorry for the apparent justification which what I have to confess concerning her must give to the severe whims of such husbands as hers : from that very Monday morning she began to grow a little careless about her expenditure —which she had never been before. By degrees bill after bill was allowed to filch from the provision of the following week, and when that was devoured, then from that of the week after. It was not that she was in the least more expensive upon herself, or that she consciously wasted anything ; but, altogether averse to housekeeping, she ceased to exercise the same outlook upon the expenditure of the house, did not keep her horses together, left the management more and more to her cook ; while the consciousness that she was not doing her duty made her more and more uncomfortable, and the knowledge that things were going farther and farther wrong, made her hate the idea of accounts worse and worse, until she came at length to regard them with such a loathing as might have fitted some extreme of moral evil. The bills which were supposed by her husband to be regularly settled every week were at last months behind, and the week's money spent in meeting the most pressing of its demands,

M

while what it could no longer cover was cast upon the growing heap of evil for the time to come.

I must say this for her, however, that there was a small sum of money she expected on the death of a crazy aunt, which, if she could but lay hold of it without her husband's knowledge, she meant to devote to the clearing off of everything, when she vowed to herself to do better in the time to come.

The worst thing in it all was that her fear of her husband kept increasing, and that she felt more and more uncomfortable in his presence. Hence that troubled look in her eye, always more marked when her husband sat dozing in his chair of a Sunday afternoon.

It was natural, too, that, although they never quarrelled, their intercourse should not grow of a more tender character. Seldom was there a salient point in their few scattered sentences of conversation, except, indeed, it were some piece of news either had to communicate. Occasionally the wife read something from the newspaper, but never except at her husband's request. In general he enjoyed his newspaper over a chop at his office. Two or three times since their marriage—now eight years—he had made a transient resolve pointing at the improvement of her mind, and to that end had taken from his great glass-armoured bookcase some *standard* work—invariably, I believe, upon party-politics—from which he had made

her read him a chapter. But, unhappily,
she had always got to the end of it without gaining the slightest glimmer of a true
notion of what the author was driving at.

It almost moves me to pity to think of the
vagueness of that rudimentary humanity in
Mr. Dempster which made him dream of
doing something to improve his wife's mind.
What did he ever do to improve his own?
It is hard to understand how horses find
themselves so comfortable in their stables
that, be the day ever so fine, the country
ever so lovely, the air ever so exhilarating,
they are always rejoiced to get back into
their dull twilight : it is harder to me to
understand how Mr. Dempster could be so
comfortable in his own mind that he never
wanted to get out of it, even at the risk of
being beside himself; but no doubt the dim-
ness of its twilight had a good deal to do
with his content. And then there is that in
every human mind which no man's neighbour, nay, no man himself, can understand.
My neighbour may in his turn be regarding
my mind as a gloomy place to live in, while
I find it no undesirable residence—though
chiefly because of the number of windows it
affords me for looking out of it. Still, if
Dempster's dingy office in the City was not
altogether a sufficing type of the mind that
used it, I consider it a very fairly good one

But wherein was Mrs. Dempster so very
different from her husband as I rudely fancy

some of my readers imagining her? Whatever may have been her reasons for marrying
him — one would suppose they must have
been weighty—to do so she must have been
in a very undeveloped condition, and in that
condition she still remained. I do not mean
that she was less developed than ninty-nine
out of the hundred : most women affect me
only as valuable crude material out of which
precious things are making. How much they
might be, must be, shall be ! For now they
stand like so many Lot's-wives—so many
rough-hewn marble blocks, rather, of which
a Divinity is shaping the ends. Mrs. Dempster had all the making of a lovely woman,
but notwithstanding her grace, her beauty,
her sweetness, her lark-like ballading too,
she was a very ordinary woman in that
region of her which knew what she meant
when she said " I." Of this fact she had
hardly a suspicion, however; for until aspi-
ration brings humility, people are generally
pretty well satisfied with themselves, having
no idea what poor creatures they are. She
saw in her mirror a superior woman, regarded herself as one of the finer works of
creation. The worst was that from the first
she had counted herself superior to her husband, and in marrying him had felt not
merely that she was conferring a favour,
which every husband would allow, but that
she was lowering herself without elevating
him. Now it is true that she was pleasanter

to look at, that her manners were sweeter, and
her notions of the becoming far less easily
satisfied than his; also that she was a little
less deficient in vague reverence for certain
forms of the higher than he.   But I know
of nothing in her to determine her classifi-
cation as of greater value than he, except
indeed that she was on the whole rather
more honest.   She read novels and he did
not; she passed shallow judgment, where he
scorned to judge; she read all the middling
poetry that came in her way, and copied
books full of it; but she could no more have
appreciated one of Milton's or Shakspere's
smallest poems than she could have laughed
over a page of Chinese.   She liked to hear
this and that popular preacher, and when her
husband called his sermons humbug, she
heard it with a shocked countenance; but
was she better or worse than her husband
when, admiring them as she did, she permitted them to have no more influence upon
her conduct than if they had been the merest
humbug ever uttered by ambitious dema-
gogue?   In truth, I cannot see that in the
matter of worth there was much as yet to
choose between them.

It is hardly necessary, then, to say that
there was little appreciable approximation of
any kind going on between them.   If only
they would have read Dickens together!
Who knows what might have come of it!
But this dull close animal proximity, without

the smallest conscious nearness of heart or
mind or soul—and so little chance, from very
lack of wants, for showing each other kind-
nesses—surely it is a killing sort of thing!
And yet, and yet, there is always a something—call it habit, or any poorest name you
please—grows up between two who are much
together, at least when they neither quarrel
nor thwart each other's designs, which, tend-
ing with its roots towards the deeper human,
blossoms into—a wretched little flower indeed, yet afar off partaking of the nature of
love.   The Something seldom reveals its
existence until they are parted.   I suspect
that with not a few, Death is the love-
messenger at the stroke of whose dart the
stream of love first begins to flow in the
selfish bosom.

It is now necessary to mention a little
break in the monotony of Mrs. Dempster's
life, which, but for what came afterwards,
could claim no record.   One morning her
page announced Major Strong, and possibly
she received the gentleman who entered with
a brighter face than she had ever shown her
husband.   The major had just arrived from
India.   He had been much at her father's
house while she was yet a mere girl, being
then engaged to one of her sisters, who died
after he went abroad, and before he could
return to marry her.   He was now a widower,
a fine-looking, frank, manly fellow.   The expression of his countenance was little altered,

and the sight of him revived in the memory
of Mrs. Dempster many recollections of a
happy girlhood, when the prospect of such a
life as she now led with tolerable content
would have seemed simply unendurable.
When her husband came home she told him
as much as he cared to hear of the visitor
she had had, and he made no objection to
her asking him to dine the next Sunday.
When he arrived Mr. Dempster saw a man
of his own age, bronzed and big, with not
much waist left, but a good carriage and
pleasant face. He made himself agreeable
at dinner, appreciated his host's wine, and
told good stories that pleased the business
man as showing that he knew " what was
what." He accorded him his more particular approval, speaking to his wife, on
the ground that he was a man of the world,
with none of the army slang about him. Mr.
Dempster was not aware that he had himself
more business peculiarities than any officer
in her majesty's service had military ones.

After this Major Strong frequently called
upon Mrs. Dempster. They were good
friends, and did each other no harm whatever, and the husband neither showed nor
felt the least jealousy. They sang together,
occasionally went out shopping, and three
or four times went together to the play. Mr.
Dempster, so long as he had his usual comforts, did not pine in his wife's absence, but
did show a little more pleasure when she

came home to him than usually when he came home to her. This lasted for a few months. Then the major went back to India, and for a time the lady missed him a good deal, which, considering the dulness of her life, was not very surprising or reprehensible.

CHAPTER II.

AN ASTONISHMENT.

Now comes the strange part of my story.

One evening the housemaid opened the door to Mr. Dempster on his return from the city; and perhaps the fact that it was the maid, and not the page as usual, roused his observation, which, except in business matters, was not remarkably operative. He glanced at the young woman, when an eye far less keen than his could not have failed to remark a strangely excited expression on her countenance.

"Where is the boy?" he asked.

"Just run to the doctor's, sir," she answered.

Then first he remembered that when he left in the morning his wife had not been feeling altogether well, but he had never thought of her since.

"How is your mistress?" he said.

"She's rather poorly, sir, but—but—she's as well as could be expected."

" What does the fool mean ? " said Dempster to himself, and very nearly said it aloud, for he was not over polite to any in his service. But he did not say it aloud. He advanced into the hall with deliberation, and made for the stair.

" Oh, please sir," the maid cried in a tone of perturbation, when, turning from shutting the door, she saw his intention, " you can't go up to mis'ess's room just at this minute, sir. Please go in the dining-room, sir."

" What do you mean ? " he asked, turning angrily upon the girl, for of all things he hated mystery.

Like every one else in the house, and office both, she stood in awe of him, and his look frightened her.

" Please go in the dining-room," she gasped entreatingly

" What ! " he said and did turn towards the dining-room, " is your mistress so ill she can't see me ? "

" Oh, no, sir !—at least I don't know exactly. Cook's with her, sir. She's over the worst, anyhow."

" What on earth do you mean, girl ? Speak out, will you ? What is the matter with your mistress ? "

As he spoke he stepped into the room, the maid following him. The same moment he spied a whitish bundle of something on the rug in front of the fire.

" What do you mean by leaving things

like that in the dining-room ? " he went on more angrily still.

" Please, sir," answered the girl, going and lifting the bundle carefully, " it's the baby ! "

" The baby ! " shouted Mr. Dempster, and looked at her from head to foot. " What baby ? " Then bethinking himself that it must belong to some visitor in the drawing-room with his wife, he moderated his tone. " Make haste; take it away ! " he said. " I don't want babies here ! There's a time and a place for everything !—What *are* you about ? "

For, instead of obeying her master and taking it away, the maid was carefully looking in the blanket for the baby. Having found it and turned aside the covering from its face, she came nearer, and holding up the little vision, about the size and colour of a roll of red wax taper, said :—

" Look at it, sir ! It's your own, and worth looking at."

Never before had she dared speak to him so !

I will not venture to assert that Mr. Dempster turned white, but his countenance changed, and he dropped into the chair behind him, feeling less of a business man than had been his consciousness for the last twenty years. He was hit hard. The absolutely Incredible had hit him. Babies might be born in a day, but surely not without previous preparation on the part of nature at least, if not on that of the mother ; and in this case if the mother had prepared herself, certainly she had not prepared him for the event. It was as if the treasure of Nature's germens were tumbling all together. His head swam. He could not speak a word.

"Yes, sir," the maid went on, relieved of her trepidation in perceiving that her master too was mortal, and that her word had such power over him—proud also of knowing more of his concerns than he did himself, "she was took about an hour and a half ago. We've kep' sendin' an' sendin' after the doctor, but he ain't never been yet ; only cook, she knows a deal an' she says she's been very bad, sir. But the young gentleman come at last, bless him! and now she's doin' as well as could be expected, sir— cook says."

"God bless me!" said the astonished father, and relapsed into the silence of bewilderment.

Eight years married with never a glimmer of offspring—and now, all at once, and without a whisper of warning, the father of a "young gentleman!" How could it be other than perplexing—discomposing, indeed!—yet it was right pleasant too. Only it would have been more pleasant if experience could have justified the affair! Nature—no, not Nature —or, if Nature, then Nature sure in some unnatural mood, had stolen a march upon

him, had gone contrary to all that had ever
been revealed of her doings before! and
why had she pitched on him—just him,
Duncan Dempster, to exercise one of her
more grotesque and wayward moods upon?
—to play at hide-and-seek with after this
fashion? She had not treated him with
exactly proper respect, he thought, or, rather
vaguely felt.

"Business is business," he remarked, under
his breath, "and this cannot be called proper
business behaviour. What is there about
me to make game of? Really, my wife
ought—— "

What his wife ought or ought not to have
done, however, had not yet made itself clear
to him, and his endeavour to excogitate being
in that direction broken off, gave way to the
pleasure of knowing himself a father, or perhaps more truly of having an heir. In the
strength of it he rose, went to the cellaret,
and poured himself out a glass of his
favourite port, which he sat down to drink
in silence and meditation. He was rather
a picture just then and there, though not a
very lovely one, seated, with his hat still on
his head, in the middle of the room, upon a
chair half-way between the dining-table and
the sideboard, with his glass of wine in his
hand. He was pondering partly the pleasure,
but still mainly the peculiarity of his position.
A bishop once told me that, shortly after he
had been raised to the episcopal dignity, a

friend's horses, whose driver had tumbled off the box drunk, ran away with him, and upset the carriage. He crept out of the window over his head, and the first thought that came to him as he sat perched on the side of the carriage, while it was jumbled along by the maddened horses, was, "What do bishops do in such circumstances?" Equally perplexing was the question Dempster had to ask himself: how husbands who, after being married eight years, suddenly and unexpectedly received the gift of a first-born, were in the habit of comporting themselves! He poured himself out another glass, and with it came the reflection, both amusing and consoling, that his brother, who was confidently expecting his tidy five figures to crown the earthly bliss of one or more of his large family some day, would be equally but less agreeably surprised. "Serve him right!" he said to himself. "What business have they to be looking out for my death?" And for a moment the heavens appeared a little more just than he was ordinarily in the habit of regarding them. He said to himself he would work harder than ever now. There would now be some good in making money! He had never given his mind to it yet, he said: now the world should see what he could do when he did give his mind to it!

Hitherto gathering had been his main pleasure, but with the thought of his money would now not seldom be mingled the

thought of the little thing in the blanket!
He began to find himself strangely happy.
I use the wrong phrase—for the fact is, he
had never yet found himself at all; he knew
nothing of the person except a self-painted
and immensely flattered portrait that hung
in the innermost chamber of his heart—I
mean the innermost chamber he knew anything of: there were many chambers there of
which he did not even know the doors. Yet
a few minutes as he sat there, and he was
actually cherishing a little pride in the wife
who had done so much better for him than
he had at length come to expect. If not a
good accountant, she was at least a good
wife, and a very fair housekeeper: he had
no doubt she would prove a good mother.
He would gladly have gone to her at once, to
let her know how much he was pleased with
her behaviour. As for that little bit of red
clay—" terra cotta," he called it to himself,
as he looked round with a smile at the
blanket, which the housemaid had replaced on
the rug before the fire—who could imagine
him a potentate upon 'Change—perhaps in
time a director of European affairs! He was
not in the way of joking—of all things about
money; the very thought of business filled
him from top to toe with seriousness; but he
did make that small joke, and accompany it
with a grim smile.

He was startled from his musing by the
entrance of the doctor, who had in the mean-

time arrived and seen the lady, and now came to look at the baby. He congratulated Mr. Dempster on having at length a son and heir, but warned him that his wife was far from being beyond danger yet. The whole thing was entirely out of the common, he said, and she must be taken the greatest possible care of. The words woke a gentle pity in the heart of the man, for by nature all men have some tenderness for women in such circumstances, but they did not trouble him greatly—for such dangers belonged to their calling, their *business* in life, and, doubtless, if she had attended to that business earlier she would have found it easier.

"Did you ever know such a thing before, doctor?" he asked, with the importance of one honoured by a personal visit from the Marvellous.

"Never in my own practice," answered the doctor, whom the cook had instructed in the wonders of the case, "but I have read of such a thing." And Mr. Dempster swelled like a turkey-cock.

It was several days before he was allowed to see the mother. Perhaps had she expressed a strong desire to see him, it might have been risked sooner, but she had neither expressed nor manifested any. He kissed her, spoke a few stupid words in a kind tone, asking her how she did, but paying no heed to her answer, and turned aside to look at the baby.

Mrs. Dempster recovered but slowly, and not very satisfactorily. She did not seem to care much about the child. She tried to nurse him, but was not very successful. She took him when the nurse brought him, and yielded him again with the same indifference, showing neither pleasure to receive nor unwillingness to part with him. The nurse did not fail to observe it and remark upon it : *she* had never seen a mother care so little for her child! there was little of the mother in *her* any way! it was no wonder she was so long about it. It troubled the father a little that she should not care for his child : some slight fermentation had commenced in the seemingly dead mass of human affection that had lain so long neglected in his being, and it seemed strange to him that, while he was living for the child in the City, she should be so indifferent to him at home. For already he had begun to keep his vow, already his greater keenness in business was remarked in the City. But it boded little good for either that the gift of God should stir up in him the worship of Mammon. More sons are damned by their fathers' money than by anything else whatever outside of themselves.

There was the excuse to be made for Mrs. Dempster that she continued far from strong —and her husband made it : he would have made it more heartily if he had himself ever in his life known what it was to be ill. By degrees she grew stronger, however, until, to persons who had not known her before, she would have seemed in tolerable health. For a week or two after she was again going about the house, she continued to nurse the baby, but after that she became unable to do so, and therewith began to neglect him entirely. She never asked to see him, and when the nurse brought him would turn her head aside, and tell her to take it away. So far from his being a pleasure to her, the very sight of the child brought the hot dew upon her forehead. Her husband frowned and wondered, but, unaccustomed to open his mind either to her or to any one else, not unwisely sought to understand the thing before speaking of it, and in the meantime commenced a genuine attempt to make up to the baby for his mother's neglect. Almost without a notion how even to take him in his arms, he would now send for him the moment he had had his tea, and after a fashion, ludicrous in the eyes of the nurse, would dandle and caress him, and strut about with him before his wife, glancing up at her every now and then, to point the lesson that such was the manner in which a parent ought to behave to a child. In his presence she never made any active show of her dislike, but her look seemed all the time fixed on something far away, as if she had nothing to do with the affair.

N

CHAPTER III.

ANOTHER ASTONISHMENT.

BUT a second and very different astonishment awaited Mr. Dempster. Again one
evening, on his return from the City, he
saw a strange look on the face of the girl
who opened the door—but this time it was
a look of fear.

"Well?" he said, in a tone at once alarmed
and peremptory.

She made no answer, but turned whiter
than before.

"Where is your mistress?" he demanded.

"Nobody knows, sir," she answered.

"Nobody knows! What would you have
me understand by such an answer?"

"It's the bare truth, sir. Nobody knows
where she is."

"God bless me!" cried the husband.
"What does it all mean?"

And again he sunk down upon a chair—
this time in the hall, and stared at the girl
as if waiting further enlightenment.

But there was little enough to be had.
Only one point was clear: his wife was
nowhere to be found. He sent for every
one in the house, and cross-questioned each
to discover the last occasion on which she
had been seen. It was some time since she

had been missed ; how long before that she
had been seen there was no certainty to be
had. He ran to the doctor, then from one
to another of her acquaintance, then to her
mother, who lived on the opposite side of
London. She, like the rest, could tell him
nothing. In her anxiety she would have
gone back with him, but he was surly, and
would not allow her. It was getting towards
morning before he reached home, but no
relieving news awaited him. What to think
was as much a perplexity to him as what
to do. He was not in the agony in which a
man would have been who thoroughly loved
his wife, but he cared enough about her to
feel uncomfortable; and the cries of the child,
who was suffering from some ailment, made
him miserable : in his perplexity and dull
sense of helplessness he wondered whether
she might not have given the baby poison
before she went. Then the thing would
make such a talk ! and, of all things, Duncan
Dempster hated being talked about. How
busy people's brains would be with all his
affairs ! How many explanations of the mystery would be suggested on 'Change ! Some
would say, "What business had a man like
him with a fine lady for a wife ? one so much
younger than himself too !" He could remember making the same remark of another,
before he was married. "Served him right!"
they would say. And with that the first
movement of suspicion awoke in him—purely

and solely from his own mind's reflection of the imagined minds of others. While in his mind's ear he heard them talking, almost before he knew what they meant the words came to him: "There was that Major Strong, you know!"

"She's gone to him!" he cried aloud, and, springing from the bed on which he had thrown himself, he paced the chamber in a fury. He had no word for it but hers that he was now in India! They had only been waiting till—By heaven, that child was none of his! And therewith rushed into his mind the conviction that everything was thus explained. No man ever yet entertained an unhappy suspicion, but straightway an army of proofs positive came crowding to the service of the lie. It is astounding with what manifest probability everything will fall in to prove that a fact which has no foundation whatever! There is no end to the perfection with which a man may fool himself while taking absolute precautions against being fooled by others. Every fact, being a living fact, has endless sides and relations; but of all these, the man whose being hangs upon one thought, will see only those sides and relations which fall in with that thought. Dempster even recalled the words of the maid, "It's mis'ess's," as embodying the girl's belief that it was not master's. Where a man, whether by nature jealous or not, is in a jealous condition, there is no need of an Iago to parade before him the proofs of his wrong. It was because Shakespere would neither have Desdemona less than perfect, nor Othello other than the most trusting and least suspicious of men, that he had to invent an all but incredible villain to effect the needful catastrophe.

But why should a man, who has cared so little for his wife, become instantly, upon the bare suspicion, so utter a prey to consuming misery? There was a character in his suffering which could not be attributed to any degree of anger, shame, or dread of ridicule. The truth was, there lay in his being a possibility of love to his wife far beyond anything his miserably stunted consciousness had an idea of; and the conviction of her faithlessness now wrought upon him in the office of Death, to let him know what he had lost. It magnified her beauty in his eyes, her gentleness, her grace; and he thought with a pang how little he had made of her or it.

But the next moment wrath at the idea of another man's child being imposed upon him as his, with the consequent loss of his precious money, swept every other feeling before it. For by law the child was his, whoever might be the father of it. During a whole minute he felt on the point of tying a stone about its neck, carrying it out, and throwing it into the river Lea. Then, with the laugh of a hyena, he set about arranging in his mind the proofs of her guilt. First

came eight childless years with himself;
next the concealment of her condition, and
the absurd pretence that she had known
nothing of it; then the trouble of mind into
which she had fallen; then her strange unnatural aversion to her own child; and now,
last of all, conclusive of a guilty conscience,
her flight from his house. He would give
himself no trouble to find her; why should
he search after his own shame! He would
neither attempt to conceal nor to explain the
fact that she had left him—people might say
what they pleased—try him for murder if
they liked! As to the child she had so
kindly left to console him for her absence, he
would not drown him, neither would he bring
him up in his house; he would give him an
ordinary education, and apprentice him to a
trade. For his money, he would leave it to
a hospital—a rich one, able to defend his
will if disputed. For what was the child?
A monster—a creature that had no right to
existence!

Not one of those who knew him best
would have believed him capable of being
so moved, nor did one of them now know it,
for he hid his suffering with the success of a
man not unaccustomed to make a mask of his
face. There are not a few men who, except
something of the nature of a catastrophe
befall them, will pass through life without
having or affording a suspicion of what is
in them. Everything hitherto had tended

to suppress the live elements of Duncan Dempster; but now, like the fire of a volcano in a land of ice, the vitality in him had begun to show itself.

Sheer weariness drove him, as the morning began to break, to lie down again; but he neither undressed nor slept, and rose at his usual hour. When he entered the dining-room, where breakfast was laid as usual— only for one instead of two—he found by his plate, among letters addressed to his wife, a packet directed to himself. It had not been through the post, and the address was in his wife's hand. He opened it. A sheet of paper was wrapped around a roll of unpaid butcher's bills, amounting to something like eighty pounds, and a note from the butcher craving immediate settlement. On the sheet of paper was written, also in his wife's hand, these words : " I am quite unworthy of being your wife any longer;" that was all.

Now here, to a man who had loved her enough to understand her, was a clue to the whole — to Dempster it was the strongest possible confirmation of what he had already concluded. To him it appeared as certain as anything he called truth, that for years, while keeping a fair face to her husband— a man who had never refused her anything —he did not recall the fact that almost never had she asked or he offered anything—she had been deceiving him, spending money she would not account for, pretending to pay

everything when she had been ruining his
credit with the neighbourhood, making him,
a far richer man than any but himself knew,
appear to be living beyond his means, when
he was every month investing far more than
he spent. It was injury upon injury! Then,
as a last mark of her contempt, she had
taken pains that these beggarly butcher's
bills should reach him from her own hand!
He would trouble himself about such a
woman not a moment longer!

He went from breakfast to his omnibus as
usual, walked straight to his office, and spent
the day according to custom. I need hardly
say that the first thing he did was to
write a cheque for the butcher. He made
no further inquiry after her whatever, nor
was any made of him there, for scarcely one
of the people with whom he did business had
been to his house, or had even seen his wife.

In the suburb where he lived it was different; but he paid no heed to any inquiry,
beyond saying he knew nothing about her.
To her relatives he said that if they wanted
her they might find her for themselves. She
had gone to please herself, and he was not
going to ruin himself by running about the
world after her.

Night after night he came home to his
desolate house; took no comfort from his
child; made no confession that he stood in
need of comfort. But he had a dull sensation as if the sun had forsaken the world,

and an endless night had begun. The simile, of course, is mine—the sensation only was his; *he* could never have expressed anything that went on in the region wherein men suffer.

A few days made a marked difference in his appearance. He was a hard man; but not so hard as people had thought him; and besides, *no* man can rule his own spirit except he has the spirit of right on his side; neither is any man proof against the inroads of good. Even Lady Macbeth was defeated by the imagination she had braved. Add to this, that no man can, even by those who understand him best, be labelled as a box containing such and such elements, for the humanity in him is deeper than any individuality, and may manifest itself at some crisis in a way altogether beside expectation.

His feeling was not at first of an elevated kind. After the grinding wrath had abated, self-pity came largely to the surface—not by any means a grand emotion, though very dear to boys and girls in their first consciousness of self, and in them pardonable enough. On the same ground it must be pardoned in a man who, with all his experience of the world, was more ignorant of the region of emotion, and more undeveloped morally, than multitudes of children: in him it was an indication that the shell was beginning to break. He said to himself that he was old beside her, and that she had begun **to weary**

of him, and despise him. Gradually upon
this, however, supervened at intervals a faint
shadow of pity for her who could not have
been happy or she would not have left him.

Days and weeks passed, and there was no
sign of Mrs. Dempster. The child was not
sent out to nurse, and throve well enough.
His father never took the least notice of him.

CHAPTER IV.

WHAT IT MEANT.

SOME of my readers, perhaps all of them, will
have concluded that Mrs. Dempster was a
little out of her mind. Such, indeed, was the
fact, and one not greatly to be wondered at,
after such a peculiar experience as she had
had. Some small degree of congestion, and
the consequent pressure on some portion of
the brain, had sent certain faculties to sleep,
and, perhaps, roused others into morbid ac-
tivity. That it is impossible to tell where
sanity ends and insanity begins, is a trite
remark indeed ; but like many things which
it is useless to say, it has the more need to
be thought of. If I yield to an impulse of
which I know I shall be ashamed, is it not
the act of a madman ? And may not the
act lead to a habit, and at length to a despised, perhaps feared and hated, old age,

twisting at the ragged ends of a miserable life ?

However certain it is that mental disorder had to do with Mrs. Dempster's departure from her home, it is almost as certain she would never have gone had it not been for the unpaid bills haunting her consciousness, a combination of demon and ghost. The misery had all the time been growing upon her, and must have had no small share in the subversion of her microcosm. When that was effected, the evil thing that lay at the root of it all rose and pounced upon her. Wrong is its own avenger. She had been doing wrong, and knowingly for years, and now the plant of evil was blossoming towards its fruit. If one say the evil was but a trifle, I take her judgment, not his, upon that. She had been lazy towards duty, had persistently turned aside from what she knew to be her business, until she dared not even look at it. And now that the crisis was at hand, as omened by that letter from the butcher, with the sense of her wrong-doing was mingled the terror of her husband. What would he think, say, and do ? Not yet had she, after all these years, any deep insight into his character; else perhaps she might have read there that, much as he loved money, the pleasure of seeing signal failure follow the neglect of his instructions would quite compensate him for the loss. What the bills amounted to, she had not an idea. Not until she had made up her mind to leave her home could she muster the courage to get them together. Then she even counted up the total and set down the sum in her memory— which sum thereafter haunted her like the name of her devil.

As to the making up of her mind—she could remember very little of that process— or indeed of the turning of her resolve into action. She left the house in the plainest dress her wardrobe could afford her, and with just one half-crown in her pocket. Her design was to seek a situation, as a refuge from her husband and his wrath. It was a curious thing, that, while it gave her no trouble to leave her baby, whom indeed she had not that day seen, and to whom for some time she had ceased to be necessary, her only notion was to get a place as nurse.

At that time, I presume, there were few or no such offices for engaging servants as are now common; at all events, the plan Mrs. Dempster took, when she had reached a part of London she judged sufficiently distant for her purpose, was to go from shop to shop inquiring after a situation. But she met with no prospect of success, and at last, greatly in need of rest and refreshment, went into a small coffee shop. The woman who kept it was taken by her appearance, her manners, and her evident trouble, and, happening to have heard of a lady who wanted a nurse, gave her the address. She went at once, and applied for the place. The lady was much pleased with her, and agreed to take her, provided she received a satisfactory character of her. For such a demand Mrs Dempster was unprepared; she had never thought what reference she could give, and, her resources for deception easily exhausted, gave, driven to extremity, the name and address of her mother. So met the extremes of loss and salvation! She returned to the coffee shop, and the lady wrote at once to the address of the young woman's late mistress, as she supposed.

The kindness of her new friend was not exhausted; she gave her a share of her own bed that night. Mrs. Dempster had now but two shillings, which she offered her, promising to pay her the rest out of the first wages she received. But the good woman would take no more than one of them, and that in full payment of what she owed her, and Mrs. Dempster left the shop in tears, to linger about the neighbourhood until the hour should arrive at which the lady had told her to call again. Apparently she must have cherished the hope that her mother, divining her extremity, would give her the character she could honestly claim. But as she drew near the door which she hoped would prove a refuge, her mother was approaching it also, and at the turning of a corner they ran into each other's arms. The elderly lady had a hackney coach waiting for her in the next street, and Mrs. Dempster, too tired to resist, got into it at once at her mother's desire. Ere they reached the mother's house, which, as I have said, was a long way from Mr. Dempster's, the daughter told everything, and the mother had perceived more than the daughter could tell : her eyes had revealed that all was not right behind them. She soothed her as none but a mother can, easily persuading her she would make everything right, and undertaking herself to pay the money owing to the butcher. But it was soon evident that for the present there must be no suggestion of her going back to her husband ; for, imagining from something, that her mother was taking her to him, she jumped up and had all but opened the door of the cab when her mother succeeded in mastering her. As soon as she was persuaded that such had never been the intention, she was quiet. When they reached the house she was easily induced to go to bed at once.

Her mother lived in a very humble way, with one servant, a trustworthy woman. To her she confided the whole story, and with her consulted as to what had better be done. Between them they resolved to keep her, for a while at least, in retirement and silence. To this conclusion they came on the following grounds : First, the daughter's terror and the mother's own fear of Mr. Dempster ; next, it must be confessed, the resentment of both mistress and servant because of his rudeness when he came to inquire after her; third, the evident condition of the poor creature's mind; and last, the longing of the two women to have her to themselves, that they might nurse and cosset her to their hearts' content.

They were to have more of this indulgence, however, than, for her sake, they would have desired, for before morning she was very ill. She had brain fever, in fact, and they had their hands full, ~specially as they desired to take every precaution to prevent the neighbourhood from knowing there was any one but themselves in the house.

It was a severe attack, but she passed the crisis favourably, and began to recover. One morning, after a quieter night than usual, she called her mother, and told her she had had a strange dream—that she had a baby somewhere, but could not find him, and was wandering about looking for him.

" Wasn't it a curious dream, mamma ? " she said. " I wish it were a true one. I knew exactly what my baby was like, and went into house after house full of children, sure that I could pick him out of thousands. I was just going up to the door of the Foundling Hospital to look for him there when I woke."

As she ceased, a strange trouble passed like a cloud over her forehead and eyes, and her hand, worn almost transparent by the fever followed it over forehead and eyes.

She seemed trying to recall something forgotten. But her mother thought it better to say nothing.

Each of the two nights following she had the same dream.

"Three times, mother," she said. "I am not superstitious, as you know, but I can't help feeling as if it must mean something. I don't know what to make of it else—except it be that I haven't got over the fever yet. And, indeed, I am afraid my head is not quite right, for I can't be sure sometimes, such a hold has my dream of me, that I haven't got a baby somewhere about the world. Give me your hand, mother, and sing to me."

Still her mother thought it more prudent to say nothing, and do what she could to divert her thoughts; for she judged it must be better to let her brain come right, as it were, of itself.

In the middle of the next night she woke her with a cry.

"O, mother, mother! I know it all now. I am not out of my mind any more. How I came here I cannot tell—but I know I have a husband and a baby at Hackney—and— oh, such a horrible roll of butcher's bills!"

"Yes, yes, my dear! I know all about it," answered her mother. "But never mind; you can pay them all yourself now, for I heard only yesterday that your aunt Lucy is dead, and has left you the hundred pounds she promised you twenty years ago."

"Oh, bless her!" cried Mrs. Dempster, springing out of bed, much to the dismay of her mother, who boded a return of the fever. "I must go home to my baby at once. But tell me all about it, mamma. How did I come here? I seem to remember being in a carriage with you, and that is the last I know."

Then, upon condition that she got into bed at once, and promised not to move until she gave her leave, her mother consented to tell her all she knew. She listened in silence, with face flushed and eyes glowing, but drank a cooling draught, lay down again, and at daybreak was fast asleep. When she awoke she was herself again.

CHAPTER V.

WHAT CAME OF IT.

MEANTIME, things were going, as they should, in rather a dull fashion with Duncan Dempster. His chariot wheels were gone, and he drove heavily. The weather was good; he seldom failed of the box-seat on the omnibus; a ray of light, the first he had ever seen there, visited his table, reflected from a new window on the opposite side of a court into the heart of his dismal back office; and best of all, business was better than usual. Yet was

Dempster not cheerful. He was not, indeed, a man an acquaintance would ever have thought of calling cheerful; but in grays there are gradations; and however differently a man's barometer may be set from those of other people, it has its ups and downs, its fair weather and foul. But not yet had he an idea how much his mental equilibrium had been dependent upon the dim consciousness of having that quiet uninterested wife in the comfortable house at Hackney. It had been stronger than it seemed, the spidery, invisible line connecting that office and that house, along which had run twice a day the hard dumpling that dwelt in Mr. Dempster's bosom. Vaguely connected with that home after all must have been that endless careful gathering of treasure in the city; for now, though he could no more stop making money than he could stop breathing, it had not the same interest as formerly. Indeed, he had less interest than before in keeping his lungs themselves going. But he kept on doing everything as usual.

Not one of the men he met ever said a word to him about his wife. The general impression was that she had left him for preferable society, and no one wondered at her throwing aside such " a dry old stick," whom even the devoted slaves of business contemned as having nothing in him but business.

A further change was, however, in progress within him. The first sign of it was that he began to doubt whether his wife had indeed been false to him—had forsaken him in any other company than that of Death. But there was one great difficulty in the way of the conclusion. It was impossible for him to imagine suicide as proceeding from any cause but insanity, and what could have produced the disorder in one who had no cares or anxieties, everything she wanted, and nothing to trouble her, a devoted husband, and a happy home? Yet the mere idea made him think more pitifully, and so more tenderly of her than before. It had not yet occurred to him to consider whether he might not have had something to do with her conduct or condition. Blame was a thing he had never made acquaintance with—least of all in the form of self-blame. To himself he was simply all right—the poised centre of things capable of righteous judgment on every one else. But it must not be forgotten how little he knew about his own affairs at all; his was a very different condition from that of one who had closed his eyes and hardened his heart to suspicions concerning himself. His eyes had never yet been opened to anything but the order of things in the money world—its laws, its penalties, its rewards—those he did understand. But apparently he was worth troubling. A slow dissatisfaction was now preying upon him—a sense of want—of not having something he once had, a vague discomfort, growing restless. This feeling was no doubt the worse that the birth of the child had brought such a sudden rush of fresh interest into his occupation, which doubt concerning that birth had again so suddenly checked; but even if the child should prove after all his own, a supposition he was now willing to admit as possibly a true one, he could never without his mother feel any enthusiasm about him, even such enthusiasm as might be allowed to a man who knew money from moonshine, and common sense from hysterics. Yet once and again, about this time, the nurse coming into the room after a few minutes' absence, found him bending over the sleeping infant, and, as she described him, "looking as if he would have cried if he had only known how."

One frosty evening in late autumn the forsaken husband came from London — I doubt if he would now have said "home" — as usual, on the top of the omnibus. His was a tough nature physically, as well as morally, and if he had found himself inside an omnibus he would have thought he was going to die. The sun was down. A green hue rose from the horizon half-way to the zenith, but a pale yellow lingered over the vanished sun, like the gold at the bottom of a chrysolite. The stars were twinkling small and sharp in the azure overhead. A cold wind blew in little gusts, now from this side, now from that, as they went

steadily along. The horses' hoofs rang loud
on the hard road. The night got hold of
him : it was at this season, and on nights
like these, that he had haunted the house
of Lucy's father, doing his best to persuade
her to make him, as he said, a happy man.
It now seemed as if then, and then only, he
had been a happy man. Certainly, of all
his life, it was the time when he came
nearest to having a peep out of the upper
windows of the house of life. He had been
a dweller in the lower regions, a hewer of
wood to the god of the cellar; and after his
marriage, he had gone straight down again
to the temple of the earthy god—to a
worship whose god and temple and treasure
caves will one day drop suddenly from under
the votary's feet, and leave him dangling in
the air without even a pocket about him—
without even his banker's book to show for
his respectability.

The night, I say, recalled the lovely season
of his courtship, and again, in the mirror of
loss, he caught a glimpse of things beyond
him. Ah, if only that time and its hopes
had remained with him! How different
things would have been now! If Lucy had
proved what he thought her!—remained
what she seemed—the gentle, complaisant,
yielding lady he imagined her, promising
him a life of bliss! Alas, she would not
even keep account of five pounds a week
to please him! He never thought whether

he, on his part, might not have, in some
measure, come short of her expectations in a
husband; whether she, the more lovely in
inward design and outward fashion, might
not have indulged yet more exquisite dreams
of bliss which, by devotion to his ideal of
life, he had done his part in disappointing.
He only thought what a foolishness it all
was; that thus it would go on to the end of
the book; that youth after youth would have
his turn of such a wooing, and such a disappointment. Sunsets, indeed! The suns of
man's happiness never did anything but set!
Out of money even—and who could say
there was any poetry in that?—there was
not half the satisfaction to be got that one
expected. It was all a mess of expectations
and disappointments mashed up together—
nothing more. That was the world—on a
fair judgment.

Such were his reflections till the driver
pulled up for him to get down at his own
gate. As he got down the said driver
glanced up curiously at the row of windows
on the first floor, and as soon as Mr. Dempster's back was turned, pointed to them with
the butt-end of his whip, and nodded queerly
to the gentleman who sat on his other side.

"That's more'n I've seen this six weeks,"
he said. "There's something more'n common
up this evenin', sir."

There was light in the drawing-room—
that was all the wonder; but at those

windows Mr. Dempster himself looked so fixedly that he had nearly stumbled up his own door-steps.

He carried a latch-key now, for he did not care to stand at the door till the boy answered the bell; people's eyes, as they passed, seemed to burn holes in the back of his coat.

He opened the street door quietly, and went straight up the stair to the drawing-room. Perhaps he thought to detect some liberty taken by his servants. He was a little earlier than usual. He opened that door, took two steps into the room, and stood arrested, motionless. With his shabby hat on his head, his shabby greatcoat on his back—for he grudged every penny spent on his clothes —his arms hanging down by his sides, and his knees bent, ready to tremble, he looked not a little out of keeping in the soft-lighted, dainty, delicate-hued drawing-room. Could he believe his eyes? The light of a large lamp was centred upon a gracious figure in white—his wife, just as he used to see her before he married her! That was the way her hair would break loose as she ran down the stair to meet him!—only then there was no baby in her lap for it to fall over like a torrent of unlighted water over a white stone! It was a lovely sight.

He had stood but a moment when she looked up and saw him. She started, but gave no cry louder than a little moan.

Instantly she rose. Turning, she laid the baby on the sofa, and flitted to him like a wraith. Arrived where he stood yet motionless, she fell upon her knees and clasped his. He was far too bewildered now to ask himself what husbands did in such circumstances, and stood like a block.

" Husband! husband!" she cried, "forgive me." With one hand she hid her face, although it was bent to the ground, and with the other held up to him a bit of paper. He took it from the thin white fingers; it might explain something—help him out of this bewilderment, half nightmare, half heavenly vision. He opened it. Nothing but a hundred-pound note! The familiar sight of bank paper, however, seemed to restore his speech.

" What does this mean, Lucy? Upon my word! Permit me to say——"

He was growing angry.

" It is to pay the butcher," she said, with a faltering voice.

" Damn the butcher!" he cried. "I hope you've got something else to say to me! Where have you been all this time?"

" At my mother's. I've had a brain fever, and been out of my mind. It was all about the butcher's bill."

Dempster stared. Perhaps he could not understand how a woman who would not keep accounts should be to such a degree troubled at the result of her neglect.

"Look at me, if you don't believe me," she cried, and as she spoke she rose and lifted her face to his.

He gazed at it for a moment—pale, thin, and worn; and out of it shone the beautiful eyes, larger than before, but shimmering uncertain like the stars of a humid night, although they looked straight into his.

Something queer was suddenly the matter with his throat—something he had never felt before—a constriction such as, had he been superstitious, he might have taken for the prologue to a rope. Then the thought came—what a brute he must be that his wife should have been afraid to tell him her trouble! Thereupon he tried to speak, but his throat was irresponsive to his will. Eve's apple kept sliding up and down in it, and would not let the words out. He had never been so served by members of his own body in his life before! It was positive rebellion, and would get him into trouble with his wife. There it was! Didn't he say so?

"Can't you forgive me, Mr. Dempster?" she said, and the voice was so sweet and so sad! "It is my own money. Aunt Lucy is dead, and left it me. I think it will be enough to pay all my debts; and I promise you—I do promise you that I will set down every halfpenny after this. Do try me once again—for baby's sake."

This last was a sudden thought. She turned and ran to the sofa. Dempster stood where he was, fighting the strange uncomfortable feeling in his throat. It would not yield a jot. Was he going to die suddenly of choking? Was it a judgment upon him? Diphtheria, perhaps! It was much about in the City!

She was back, and holding up to him their sleeping child.

The poor fellow was not half the brute he looked—only he could *not* tell what to do with that confounded lump in his throat! He dared not try to speak, for it only choked him the more. He put his arms round them both, and pressed them to his bosom. Then the lump in his throat melted and ran out at his eyes, and all doubt vanished like a mist before the sun. But he never knew that he had wept. His wife did, and that was enough.

The next morning, for the first time in his life, he lost the eight o'clock omnibus.

The following Monday morning she brought her week's account to him. He turned from it testily, but she insisted on his going over it. There was not the mistake of a halfpenny. He went to town with a smile in his heart, and that night brought her home a cheque for ten pounds instead of five.

One day, in the middle of the same week, he came upon her sitting over the little blue-and-red-ruled book with a troubled countenance. She took no notice of his entrance.

" Do leave those accounts," he said, " and attend to me."

She shook her head impatiently, and made him no other answer. One moment more, however, and she started up, threw her arms about his neck, and cried triumphantly,

"It's buttons !—fourpence-halfpenny I paid for buttons ! "

PORT IN A STORM.

"PAPA," said my sister Effie, one evening as
we all sat about the drawing-room fire. One
after another, as nothing followed, we turned
our eyes upon her. There she sat, still silent,
embroidering the corner of a cambric hand-
kerchief, apparently unaware that she had
spoken.

It was a very cold night in the beginning
of winter. My father had come home early,
and we had dined early that we might have
a long evening together, for it was my
father's and mother's wedding-day, and we
always kept it as the homeliest of holidays.
My father was seated in an easy-chair by the
chimney corner, with a jug of Burgundy near
him, and my mother sat by his side, now and
then taking a sip out of his glass.

Effie was now nearly nineteen; the rest of
us were younger. What she was thinking
about we did not know then, though we
could all guess now. Suddenly she looked
up, and seeing all eyes fixed upon her, became either aware or suspicious, and blushed
rosy red.

"You spoke to me, Effie. What was it, my dear?"

"O yes, papa. I wanted to ask you whether you wouldn't tell us, to-night, the story about how you——"

"Well, my love?"

"—About how you——"

"I am listening, my dear."

"I mean, about mamma and you."

"Yes, yes. About how I got your mamma for a mother to you. Yes. I paid a dozen of port for her."

We all and each exclaimed *Papa!* and my mother laughed.

"Tell us all about it," was the general cry.

"Well, I will," answered my father. "I must begin at the beginning, though."

And, filling his glass with Burgundy, he began.

"As far back as I can remember, I lived with my father in an old manor-house in the country. It did not belong to my father, but to an elder brother of his, who at that time was captain of a seventy-four. He loved the sea more than his life; and, as yet apparently, had loved his ship better than any woman. At least he was not married.

"My mother had been dead for some years, and my father was now in very delicate health. He had never been strong, and since my mother's death, I believe, though I was too young to notice it, he had pined away. I am not going to tell you anything about him just now, because it does not belong to my story. When I was about five years old, as nearly as I can judge, the doctors advised him to leave England. The house was put into the hands of an agent to let—at least, so I suppose; and he took me with him to Madeira, where he died. I was brought home by his servant, and by my uncle's directions, sent to a boarding-school; from there to Eton, and from there to Oxford.

"Before I had finished my studies, my uncle had been an admiral for some time. The year before I left Oxford, he married Lady Georgiana Thornbury, a widow lady, with one daughter. Thereupon he bade farewell to the sea, though I dare say he did not like the parting, and retired with his bride to the house where he was born—the same house I told you I was born in, which had been in the family for many generations, and which your cousin now lives in.

"It was late in the autumn when they arrived at Culverwood. They were no sooner settled than my uncle wrote to me, inviting me to spend Christmas-tide with them at the old place. And here you may see that my story has arrived at its beginning.

"It was with strange feelings that I entered the house. It looked so old-fashioned, and stately, and grand, to eyes which had been accustomed to all the modern commonplaces!

Yet the shadowy recollections which hung about it gave an air of homeliness to the place, which, along with the grandeur, occasioned a sense of rare delight. For what can be better than to feel that you are in stately company, and at the same time perfectly at home in it? I am grateful to this day for the lesson I had from the sense of which I have spoken—that of mingled awe and tenderness in the aspect of the old hall as I entered it for the first time after fifteen years, having left it a mere child.

" I was cordially received by my old uncle and my new aunt. But the moment Kate Thornbury entered I lost my heart, and have never found it again to this day. I get on wonderfully well without it, though, for I have got the loan of a far better one till I find my own, which, therefore, I hope I never shall."

My father glanced at my mother as he said this, and she returned his look in a way which I can now interpret as a quiet satisfied confidence. But the tears came in Effie's eyes. She had trouble before long, poor girl! But it is not her story I have to tell.—My father went on:

" Your mother was prettier then than she is now, but not so beautiful; beautiful enough, though, to make me think there never had been or could again be anything so beautiful. She met me kindly, and I met her awkwardly."

" You made me feel that I had no business there," said my mother, speaking for the first time in the course of the story.

" See there, girls," said my father. " You are always so confident in first impressions, and instinctive judgment! I was awkward because, as I said, I fell in love with your mother the moment I saw her; and she thought I regarded her as an intruder into the old family precincts.

" I will not follow the story of the days. I was very happy, except when I felt too keenly how unworthy I was of Kate Thornbury; not that she meant to make me feel it, for she was never other than kind; but she was such that I could not help feeling it. I gathered courage, however, and before three days were over, I began to tell her all my slowly reviving memories of the place, with my childish adventures associated with this and that room or outhouse or spot in the grounds; for the longer I was in the place the more my old associations with it revived, till I was quite astonished to find how much of my history in connection with Culverwood had been thoroughly imprinted on my memory. She never showed, at least, that she was weary of my stories; which, however interesting to me, must have been tiresome to any one who did not sympathize with what I felt towards my old nest. From room to room we rambled, talking or silent; and nothing could have given me a better chance, I believe, with a heart like your mother's. I think it was not long before she began to like me, at least, and liking had every opportunity of growing into something stronger, if only she too did not come to the conclusion that I was unworthy of her.

"My uncle received me like the jolly old tar that he was—welcomed me to the old ship—hoped we should make many a voyage together—and that I would take the run of the craft—all but in one thing.

"'You see, my boy,' he said, 'I married above my station, and I don't want my wife's friends to say that I laid alongside of her to get hold of her daughter's fortune. No, no, my boy; your old uncle has too much salt water in him to do a dog's trick like that. So you take care of yourself—that's all. She might turn the head of a wiser man than ever came out of our family.'

"I did not tell my uncle that his advice was already too late; for that, though it was not an hour since I had first seen her, my head was so far turned already, that the only way to get it right again, was to go on turning it in the same direction; though, no doubt, there was a danger of overhauling the screw. The old gentleman never referred to the matter again, nor took any notice of our increasing intimacy; so that I sometimes doubt even now if he could have been in earnest in the very simple warning he gave

P

me. Fortunately, Lady Georgiana liked me
—at least I thought she did, and that gave
me courage."

"That's all nonsense, my dear," said
my mother. "Mamma was nearly as fond
of you as I was; but you never wanted
courage."

"I knew better than to show my cowardice,
I dare say," returned my father. "But," he
continued, "things grew worse and worse,
till I was certain I should kill myself, or
go straight out of my mind, if your mother
would not have me. So it went on for a few
days, and Christmas was at hand.

"The admiral had invited several old friends
to come and spend the Christmas week with
him. Now you must remember that, although you look on me as an old-fashioned
fogie—— "

"Oh, papa!" we all interrupted; but he
went on.

"Yet my old uncle was an older-fashioned
fogie, and his friends were much the same as
himself. Now, *I* am fond of a glass of port,
though I dare not take it, and must content
myself with Burgundy. Uncle Bob would
have called Burgundy pig-wash. *He* could
not do without his port, though he was a
moderate enough man, as customs were.
Fancy, then, his dismay when, on questioning his butler, an old coxen of his own,
and after going down to inspect in person,
he found that there was scarcely more than

a dozen of port in the wine-cellar. He turned white with dismay, and, till he had brought the blood back to his countenance by swearing, he was something awful to behold in the dim light of the tallow candle old Jacob held in his tattooed fist. I will not repeat the words he used ; fortunately, they are out of fashion amongst gentlemen, although ladies, I understand, are beginning to revive the custom, now old, and always ugly. Jacob reminded his honour that he would not have more put down till he had got a proper cellar built, for the one there was, he had said, was not fit to put anything but dead men in. Thereupon, after abusing Jacob for not reminding him of the necessities of the coming season, he turned to me, and began, certainly not to swear at his own father, but to expostulate sideways with the absent shade for not having provided a decent cellar before his departure from this world of dinners and wine, hinting that it was somewhat selfish, and very inconsiderate of the welfare of those who were to come after him. Having a little exhausted his indignation, he came up, and wrote the most peremptory order to his wine-merchant, in Liverpool, to let him have thirty dozen of port before Christmas Day, even if he had to send it by post-chaise. I took the letter to the post myself, for the old man would trust nobody but me, and indeed would have preferred taking it himself; but in winter he was always lame from the effects of a bruise he had received from a falling spar in the battle of Aboukir.

"That night I remember well. I lay in bed wondering whether I might venture to say a word, or even to give a hint to your mother that there was a word that pined to be said if it might. All at once I heard a whine of the wind in the old chimney. How well I knew that whine! For my kind aunt had taken the trouble to find out from me what room I had occupied as a boy, and, by the third night I spent there, she had got it ready for me. I jumped out of bed, and found that the snow was falling fast and thick. I jumped into bed again, and began wondering what my uncle would do if the port did not arrive. And then I thought that, if the snow went on falling as it did, and if the wind rose any higher, it might turn out that the roads through the hilly part of Yorkshire in which Culverwood lay, might very well be blocked up.

> "The north wind doth blow,
>   And we shall have snow,
> And what will my uncle do then, poor thing?
>   He'll run for his port,
>   But he will run short,
> And have too much water to drink, poor thing!

"With the influences of the chamber of my childhood crowding upon me, I kept repeating the travestied rhyme to myself, till I fell asleep.

"Now, boys and girls, if I were writing a novel, I should like to make you, somehow or other, put together the facts—that I was in the room I have mentioned; that I had been in the cellar with my uncle for the first time that evening; that I had seen my uncle's distress, and heard his reflections upon his father. I may add that I was not myself, even then, so indifferent to the merits of a good glass of port as to be unable to enter into my uncle's dismay, and that of his guests at last, if they should find that the snow-storm had actually closed up the sweet approaches of the expected port. If I was personally indifferent to the matter, I fear it is to be attributed to your mother, and not to myself."

"Nonsense!" interposed my mother once more. "I never knew such a man for making little of himself and much of other people. You never drank a glass too much port in your life."

"That's why I'm so fond of it, my dear," returned my father. "I declare you make me quite discontented with my pig-wash here.

"That night I had a dream.

"The next day the visitors began to arrive. Before the evening after, they had all come. There were five of them—three tars and two land-crabs, as they called each other when they got jolly, which, by-the-way, they would not have done long without me.

"My uncle's anxiety visibly increased.

Each guest, as he came down to breakfast, received each morning a more constrained greeting.—I beg your pardon, ladies; I forgot to mention that my aunt had lady-visitors, of course. But the fact is, it is only the port-drinking visitors in whom my story is interested, always excepted your mother.

"These ladies my admiral uncle greeted with something even approaching to servility. I understood him well enough. He instinctively sought to make a party to protect him when the awful secret of his cellar should be found out. But for two preliminary days or so, his resources would serve; for he had plenty of excellent claret and Madeira—stuff I don't know much about—and both Jacob and himself condescended to manœuvre a little.

"The wine did not arrive. But the morning of Christmas Eve did. I was sitting in my room, trying to write a song for Kate—that's your mother, my dears——"

"I know, papa," said Effie, as if she were very knowing to know that.

"——when my uncle came into the room, looking like Sintram with Death and the Other One after him—that's the nonsense you read to me the other day, isn't it, Effie?"

"Not nonsense, dear papa," remonstrated Effie; and I loved her for saying it, for surely *that* is not nonsense.

"I didn't mean it," said my father; and turning to my mother, added: "It must be your fault, my dear, that my children are so serious that they always take a joke for earnest. However, it was no joke with my uncle. If he didn't look like Sintram he looked like t'other one.

" ' The roads are frozen—I mean snowed up,' he said. ' There's just one bottle of port left, and what Captain Calker will say—I dare say I know, but I'd rather not. Damn this weather!—God forgive me!—that's not right—but it *is* trying—ain't it, my boy ? '

" ' What will you give me for a dozen of port, uncle ? ' was all my answer.

" ' Give you ? I'll give you Culverwood, you rogue.'

" ' Done,' I cried.

" ' That is,' stammered my uncle, ' that is,' and he reddened like the funnel of one of his hated steamers, ' that is, you know, always provided, you know. It wouldn't be fair to Lady Georgiana, now, would it ? I put it to yourself—if she took the trouble, you know. You understand me, my boy ? '

" ' That's of course, uncle,' I said.

" ' Ah ! I see you're a gentleman like your father, not to trip a man when he stumbles,' said my uncle. For such was the dear old man's sense of honour, that he was actually uncomfortable about the hasty promise he had made without first specifying the exception. The exception, you know, has Culverwood at the present hour, and right welcome he is.

" ' Of course, uncle,' I said — ' between gentlemen, you know. Still, I want my joke out, too. What will you give me for a dozen of port to tide you over Christmas Day ? '

" ' Give you, my boy ? I'll give you—— '

" But here he checked himself, as one that had been burned already.

" ' Bah ! ' he said, turning his back, and going towards the door ; ' what's the use of joking about serious affairs like this ? '

" And so he left the room. And I let him go. For I had heard that the road from Liverpool was impassable, the wind and snow having continued every day since that night of which I told you. Meantime, I had never been able to summon the courage to say one word to your mother—I beg her pardon, I mean Miss Thornbury.

" Christmas Day arrived. My uncle was awful to behold. His friends were evidently anxious about him. They thought he was ill. There was such a hesitation about him, like a shark with a bait, and such a flurry, like a whale in his last agonies. He had a horrible secret which he dared not tell, and which yet *would* come out of its grave at the appointed hour.

" Down in the kitchen the roast beef and turkey were meeting their deserts. Up in the store-room—for Lady Georgiana was not above housekeeping, any more than her daughter—the ladies of the house were doing their part; and I was oscillating between my uncle and his niece, making myself amazingly useful now to one and now to the other. The turkey and the beef were on the table, nay, they had been well eaten, before I felt that my moment was come. Outside, the wind was howling, and driving the snow with soft pats against the window-panes. Eager-eyed I watched General Fortescue, who despised sherry or Madeira even during dinner, and would no more touch champagne than he would *eau sucrée*, but drank port after fish or with cheese indiscriminately— with eager eyes I watched how the last bottle dwindled out its fading life in the clear decanter. Glass after glass was supplied to General Fortescue by the fearless cockswain, who, if he might have had his choice, would rather have boarded a Frenchman than waited for what was to follow. My uncle scarcely ate at all, and the only thing that stopped his face from growing longer with the removal of every dish was that nothing but death could have made it longer than it was already. It was my interest to let matters go as far as they might up to a certain point, beyond which it was not my interest to let them go, if I could help it. At the same time I was curious to know how my uncle would announce—confess the terrible fact that in his house, on Christmas Day, having invited his oldest friends to share with him the festivities of the season, there was not one bottle more of port to had.

"I waited till the last moment—till I fancied the admiral was opening his mouth, like a fish in despair, to make his confession. He had not even dared to make a confidante of his wife in such an awful dilemma. Then I pretended to have dropped my table-napkin behind my chair, and rising to seek it, stole round behind my uncle, and whispered in his ear :

"'What will you give me for a dozen of port now, uncle ?'

"'Bah !' he said, 'I'm at the gratings ; don't torture me.'

"'I'm in earnest, uncle.'

"He looked round at me with a sudden flash of bewildered hope in his eye. In the last agony he was capable of believing in a miracle. But he made me no reply. He only stared.

"'Will you give me Kate ? I want Kate,' I whispered.

"'I will, my boy. That is, if she'll have you. That is, I mean to say, if you produce the true tawny.'

"'Of course, uncle ; honour bright—as port in a storm,' I answered, trembling in my shoes and everything else I had on, for I was not more than three parts confident in the result.

"The gentlemen beside Kate happening at the moment to be occupied, each with the lady on his other side, I went behind her, and whispered to her as I had whispered to my uncle, though not exactly in the same terms. Perhaps I had got a little courage from the champagne I had drunk; perhaps the presence of the company gave me a kind of mesmeric strength; perhaps the excitement of the whole venture kept me up; perhaps Kate herself gave me courage, like a goddess of old, in some way I did not understand. At all events I said to her:

" ' Kate,'—we had got so far even then— ' my uncle hasn't another bottle of port in his cellar. Consider what a state General Fortescue will be in soon. He'll be tipsy for want of it. Will you come and help me to find a bottle or two?'

" She rose at once, with a white-rose blush —so delicate I don't believe any one saw it but myself. But the shadow of a stray ringlet could not fall on her cheek without my seeing it.

" When we got into the hall, the wind was roaring loud, and the few lights were flickering and waving gustily with alternate light and shade across the old portraits which I had known so well as a child—for I used to think what each would say first, if he or she came down out of the frame and spoke to me.

" I stopped, and taking Kate's hand, I said—

" ' I daren't let you come farther, Kate, before I tell you another thing: my uncle has promised, if I find him a dozen of port—you must have seen what a state the poor man is in—to let me say something to you—I suppose he meant your mamma, but I prefer saying it to you, if you will let me. Will you come and help me to find the port?'

" She said nothing, but took up a candle that was on a table in the hall, and stood waiting. I ventured to look at her. Her face was now celestial rosy red, and I could not doubt that she had understood me. She looked so beautiful that I stood staring at her without moving. What the servants could have been about that not one of them crossed the hall, I can't think.

" At last Kate laughed and said—' Well?' I started, and I dare say took my turn at blushing. At least I did not know what to say. I had forgotten all about the guests inside. ' Where's the port?' said Kate. I caught hold of her hand again and kissed it."

" You needn't be quite so minute in your account, my dear," said my mother, smiling.

" I will be more careful in future, my love," returned my father.

" ' What do you want me to do?' said Kate.

" ' Only to hold the candle for me,' I answered, restored to my seven senses at last; and, taking it from her, I led the way, and she followed, till we had passed through the kitchen and reached the cellar-stairs.

These were steep and awkward, and she let me help her down."

" Now, Edward!" said my mother.

" Yes, yes, my love, I understand," returned my father.

" Up to this time your mother had asked no questions; but when we stood in a vast, low cellar, which we had made several turns to reach, and I gave her the candle, and took up a great crowbar which lay on the floor, she said at last—

" ' Edward, are you going to bury me alive? or what *are* you going to do?'

" ' I'm going to dig you out,' I said, for I was nearly beside myself with joy, as I struck the crowbar like a battering-ram into the wall. You can fancy, John, that I didn't work the worse that Kate was holding the candle for me.

" Very soon, though with great effort, I had dislodged a brick, and the next blow I gave into the hole sent back a dull echo. I was right!

" I worked now like a madman, and, in a very few minutes more, I had dislodged the whole of the brick-thick wall which filled up an archway of stone and curtained an ancient door in the lock of which the key now showed itself. It had been well greased, and I turned it without much difficulty.

" I took the candle from Kate, and led her into a spacious region of sawdust, cobweb, and wine-fungus.

" ' There, Kate ! ' I cried, in delight.

" ' But,' said Kate, ' will the wine be good ? '

" ' General Fortescue will answer you that,' I returned, exultantly. ' Now come, and hold the light again while I find the port-bin.'

" I soon found not one, but several well-filled port-bins. Which to choose I could not tell. I must chance that. Kate carried a bottle and the candle, and I carried two bottles very carefully. We put them down in the kitchen with orders they should not be touched. We had soon carried the dozen to the hall-table by the dining-room door.

" When at length, with Jacob chuckling and rubbing his hands behind us, we entered the dining-room, Kate and I, for Kate would not part with her share in the joyful business, loaded with a level bottle in each hand, which we carefully erected on the sideboard, I presume, from the stare of the company, that we presented a rather remarkable appearance—Kate in her white muslin, and I in my best clothes, covered with brick-dust, and cobwebs, and lime. But we could not be half so amusing to them as they were to us. There they sat with the dessert before them but no wine-decanters forthcoming. How long they had sat thus, I have no idea. If you think your mamma has, you may ask her. Captain Calker and General Fortescue looked positively white about the gills. My uncle, clinging to the last hope, despairingly,

had sat still and said nothing, and the guests
could not understand the awful delay. Even
Lady Georgiana had begun to fear a mutiny
in the kitchen, or something equally awful.
But to see the flash that passed across my
uncle's face, when he saw us appear with
ported arms! He immediately began to pretend that nothing had been the matter.

" ' What the deuce has kept you, Ned, my
boy?' he said. 'Fair Hebe,' he went on,
'I beg your pardon. Jacob, you can go on
decanting. It was very careless of you to
forget it. Meantime, Hebe, bring that bottle
to General Jupiter, there. He's got a corkscrew in the tail of his robe, or I'm mistaken.'

" Out came General Fortescue's corkscrew.
I was trembling once more with anxiety.
The cork gave the genuine plop; the bottle
was lowered; glug, glug, glug, came from
its beneficent throat, and out flowed something tawny as a lion's mane. The general
lifted it lazily to his lips, saluting his nose on
the way.

" ' Fifteen! by Gyeove!' he cried. ' Well,
Admiral, this *was* worth waiting for! Take
care how you decant that, Jacob—on peril of
your life.'

" My uncle was triumphant. He winked
hard at me not to tell. Kate and I retired,
she to change her dress, I to get mine well
brushed, and my hands washed. By the time
I returned to the dining-room, no one had
any questions to ask. For Kate, the ladies

had gone to the drawing-room before she **was** ready, and I believe she had some difficulty in keeping my uncle's counsel. But she did. —Need I say that was the happiest Christmas I ever spent?"

"But how did you find the cellar, papa?" asked Effie.

"Where are your brains, Effie? Don't you remember I told you that I had a dream?"

"Yes. But you don't mean to say the existence of that wine-cellar was revealed to you in a dream?"

"But I do, indeed. I had seen the wine-cellar built up just before we left for Madeira. It was my father's plan for securing the wine when the house was let. And very well it turned out for the wine, and me too. I had forgotten all about it. Everything had conspired to bring it to my memory, but had just failed of success. I had fallen asleep under all the influences I told you of— influences from the region of my childhood. They operated still when I was asleep, and, all other distracting influences being removed, at length roused in my sleeping brain the memory of what I had seen. In the morning I remembered not my dream only, but the event of which my dream was a reproduction. Still, I was under considerable doubt about the place, and in this I followed the dream only, as near as I could judge.

"The admiral kept his word, and interposed no difficulties between Kate and me.
Not that, to tell the truth, I was ever very
anxious about that rock ahead ; but it was
very possible that his fastidious honour or
pride might have occasioned a considerable
interference with our happiness for a time.
As it turned out, he could not leave me
Culverwood, and I regretted the fact as little
as he did himself. His gratitude to me was,
however, excessive, assuming occasionally
ludicrous outbursts of thankfulness. I do not
believe he could have been more grateful if
I had saved his ship and its whole crew.
For his hospitality was at stake. Kind old
man ! "

Here ended my father's story, with a
light sigh, a gaze into the bright coals, a kiss
of my mother's hand which he held in his,
and another glass of Burgundy.

IF I HAD A FATHER.

A DRAMA.

ACT I.

SCENE.—*A Sculptor's studio.* ARTHUR GER-VAISE *working at a clay figure and humming a tune. A knock.*

Ger. Come in. (*Throws a wet cloth over the clay. Enter* WARREN *by the door communicating with the house.*) Ah, Warren! How do you do?

War. How are you, Gervaise? I'm delighted to see you once more. I have but just heard of your return.

Ger. I've been home but a fortnight. I was just thinking of you.

War. I was certain I should find you at work.

Ger. You see my work can go on by any light. It is more independent than yours.

War. I wish it weren't, then.

Ger. Why?

War. Because there would be a chance of our getting you out of your den sometimes.

Ger. Like any other wild beast when the dark falls—eh ?

War. Just so.

Ger. And where the good ?

War. Why shouldn't you roar a little now and then like other honest lions ?

Ger. I doubt if the roaring lions do much beyond roaring.

War. And I doubt whether the lion that won't even whisk his tail, will get food enough shoved through his bars to make it worth his while to keep a cage in London.

Ger. I certainly shall not make use of myself to recommend my work.

War. What is it now ?

Ger. Oh, nothing !—only a little fancy of my own.

War. There again !   The moment I set foot in your study, you throw the sheet over your clay, and when I ask you what you are working at—"Oh—a little fancy of my own!"

Ger. I couldn't tell it was you coming.

War. Let me see what you've been doing, then.

Ger. Oh, she's a mere Lot's-wife as yet !

War. (*approaching the figure*). Of course, of course !   I understand all that.

Ger. (*laying his hand on his arm*). Excuse me : I would rather not show it.

War. I beg your pardon.—I couldn't believe you really meant it.

Ger. I'll show you the mould if you like.

War. I don't know what you mean by

that : you would never throw a wet sheet over a cast! (GER. *lifts a painting from the floor and sets it on an easel.* WAR. *regards it for a few moments in silence.*) Ah! by Jove, Gervaise! some one sent you down the wrong turn : you ought to have been a painter. What a sky! And what a sea! Those blues and greens—rich as a peacock's feather-eyes! Superb! A tropical night! The dolphin at its last gasp in the west, and all above, an abyss of blue, at the bottom of which the stars lie like gems in the mine-shaft of the darkness!

Ger. *You* seem to have taken the wrong turn, Warren! *You* ought to have been a poet.

War. Such a thing as that puts the slang out of a fellow's head.

Ger. I'm glad you like it. I do myself, though it falls short of my intent sadly enough.

War. But I don't for the life of me see what *this* has to do with *that*. You said something about a mould.

Ger. I will tell you what I meant. Every individual aspect of nature looks to me as if about to give birth to a human form, embodying that of which itself only dreams. In this way landscape-painting is, in my eyes, the mother of sculpture. That Apollo is of the summer dawn; that Aphrodite of the moonlit sea; this picture represents the mother of my Psyche.

War. Under the sheet there?

Ger. Yes. You shall see her some day; but to show your work too soon, is to uncork your champagne before dinner.

War. Well, you've spoiled my picture. I shall go home and scrape my canvas to the bone.

Ger. On second thoughts, I *will* show you my Psyche. (*Uncovers the clay.* WAR. *stands in admiration. Enter* WATERFIELD *by same door.*)

Wat. Ah, Warren! here you are before me! Mr. Gervaise, I hope I see you well.

War. Mr. Waterfield—an old friend of yours, Gervaise, I believe.

Ger. I cannot appropriate the honour.

Wat. I was twice in your studio at Rome, but it's six months ago, Mr. Gervaise. Ha! (*using his eye-glass*) What a charming figure! A Psyche! Wings suggested by—— Very skilful! Contour lovely! Altogether antique in pose and expression!—Is she a commission?

Ger. No.

Wat. Then I beg you will consider her one.

Ger. Excuse me; I never work on commission—at least never in this kind. A bust or two I have done.

Wat. By Jove!—I *should* like to see your model!—This is perfect. Are you going to carve her?

Ger. Possibly.

Wat. Uncommissioned?

Ger. If at all.

Wat. Well, I can't call it running any risk. What lines!—You will let me drop in some day when you've got your model here?

Ger. Impossible.

Wat. You don't mean——?

Ger. I had no model.

Wat. No model? Ha! ha!—You must excuse me! (GER. *takes up the wet sheet.*) I understand. Reasons. A little mystery enhances—eh?—is convenient too—balks intrusion—throws the drapery over the mignonette. I understand. (GER. *covers the clay.*) Oh! pray don't carry out my figure. That *is* a damper now!

Ger. I am not fond of acting the showman. You must excuse me : I am busy.

Wat. Ah well!—some other time—when you've got on with her a bit. Good morning. Ta, ta, Warren.

Ger. Good morning. This way, if you please. (*Shows him out by the door to the street.*) How did the fellow find his way here?

War. I am the culprit, I'm sorry to say. He asked me for your address, and I gave it him.

Ger. How long have you known him?

War. A month or two.

Ger. Don't bring him here again.

War. Don't say I *brought* him. I didn't do that. But I'm afraid you've not seen the last of him.

Ger. Oh yes, I have! Old Martha would let in anybody, but I've got a man now.— William!

Enter COL. GERVAISE *dressed as a servant.*

You didn't see the gentleman just gone, I'm afraid, William?

Col. G. No, sir.

Ger. Don't let in any one calling himself *Waterfield.*

Col. G. No, sir.

Ger. I'm going out with Mr. Warren. I shall be back shortly.

Col. G. Very well, sir. *Exit into the house.*

Ger. (*to* WAR.) I can't touch clay again till I get that fellow out of my head.

War. Come along, then.

Exeunt GER, *and* WAR.

Re-enter COL. G. *polishing a boot. Regards it with dissatisfaction.*

Col. G. Confound the thing! I wish it were a scabbard. When I think I'm getting it all right—one rub more and it's gone dull again!

The house-door opens slowly, and THOMAS *peeps cautiously in.*

Th. What sort of a plaze be this, maister?

Col. G. You ought to have asked that outside. How did you get in?

Th. By th' dur-hole. Iv yo leave th' **dur** oppen, th' dogs'll coom in.

Col. G. I must speak to Martha again. She *will* leave the street-door open!—Well, you needn't look so frightened. It ain't a robbers' cave.

Th. That be more'n aw knaw—not for sartin sure, maister. Nobory mun keawnt upon nobory up to Lonnon, they tells mo. But iv a gentleman axes mo into his heawse, aw'm noan beawn to be afeard. Aw'll coom in, for mayhap yo can help mo. It be a coorous plaze. What dun yo mak here?

Col. G. What would you think now?

Th. It looks to mo like a mason's shed—a greight one.

Col. G. You're not so far wrong.

Th. (*advancing*). It do look a queer plaze. Aw be noan so sure abeawt it. But they wonnot coot mo throat beout warnin'. Aw'll bother noan. (*Sits down on the dais and wipes his face.*) Well, aw be a'most weary.

Col. G. Is there anything I can do for you?

Th. Nay, aw donnot know; but beout aw get somebory to help mo, aw dunnot think aw'll coom to th' end in haste. Aw're a lookin' for summut aw've lost, mon.

Col. G. Did you come all the way from Lancashire to look for it?

Th. Eh, lad! aw thowt thae'rt beawn to know wheer aw coom fro!

Col. G. Anybody could tell that, the first word you spoke. I mean no offence

Th. (*looking disappointed*). Well, noan's ta'en. But thae dunnot say thae's ne'er been to Lancashire thisel'?

Col. G. No, I don't say that: I've been to Lancashire several times.

Th. Wheer to?

Col. G. Why, Manchester.

Th. That's noan ov it.

Col. G. And Lancaster.

Th. Tut! tut! That's noan of it, nayther.

Col. G. And Liverpool. I was once there for a whole week.

Th. Nay, nay. Noather o' those plazes. Fur away off 'em.

Col. G. But what does it matter where I have or haven't been?

Th. Mun aw tell tho again? Aw've lost summut, aw tell tho. Didsto ne'er hear tell ov th' owd woman 'at lost her shillin'? Hoo couldn't sit her deawn beawt hoo feawnd it! Yon's me. (*Hides his face in his hands.*)

Col. G. Ah! now I begin to guess! (*aside*). —You don't mean you've lost your——

Th. (*starting up and grasping his stick with both hands*). Aw *do* mane aw've lost mo yung lass; and aw dunnot say thae's feawnd her, but aw do say thae knows wheer hoo is. Aw do. Theighur! Nea then!

Col. G. What on earth makes you think that? I don't know what you're after.

Th. Thae knows well enough. Thae knowed what aw'd lost afoor aw tou'd tho

Yo' be denyin' your own name. Thae knows. Aw'll tay tho afore the police, beout thou gie her oop. Aw wull.

Col. G. What story have you to tell the police then? They'll want to know.

Th. Story saysto? The dule's i' th' mon! Didn't aw seigh th' mon 'at stealed her away goo into this heawse not mich over hauve an hour ago?—Aw seigh him wi' mo own eighes.

Col. G. Why didn't you speak to him?

Th. He poppit in at th' same dur, and there aw've been a-watching ever since. Aw've not took my eighes off ov it. He's somewheeres now in this same heawse.

Col. G. He *may* have been out in the morning (*aside*).—But you see there are more doors than one to the place. There is a back door; and there is a door out into the street.

Th. Eigh! eigh! Th' t'one has to do wi' th' t'other—have it? Three dur-holes to one shed! That looks bad!

Col. G. He's not here, whoever it was. There's not a man but myself in the place.

Th. Hea am aw to know yo're not playin' a marlock wi' mo? He'll be oop i' th' heawse theer. Aw mun go look (*going*).

Col. G. (*preventing him*). And how am *I* to know you're not a housebreaker?

Th. Dun yo think an owd mon like mosel' would be of mich use for sich wark as that, mon?

Col. G. The more fit for a spy, though, to see what might be made of it.

Th. Eh, mon! Dun they do sich things as yon? But aw'm seechin' nothin', man nor meawse, that donnot belung me. Aw tell yo true. Gie mo mo Mattie, and aw'll trouble yo no moor. Aw winnot—if yo'll give mo back mo Mattie. (*Comes close up to him and lays his hand on his arm.*) Be yo a feyther, mon?

Col. G. Yes.

Th. Ov a pratty yung lass?

Col. G. Well, no. I have but a son.

Th. Then thae winnot help mo?

Col. G. I shall be very glad to help you, if you will tell me how.

Th. Tell yor maister 'at Mattie's owd feyther's coom a' the gait fro Rachda to fot her whoam, and aw'll be much obleeged to him iv he'll let her goo beout lunger delay, for her mother wants her to whoam: hoo's but poorly. Tell yor maister that.

Col. G. But I don't believe my master knows anything about her.

Th. Aw're tellin' tho, aw seigh' th' mon goo into this heawse but a feow minutes agoo?

Col. G. You've mistaken somebody for him.

Th. Well, aw'm beawn to tell tho moore. Twothre days ago, aw seigh mo chylt coom eawt ov this same dur—aw mane th' heawse-dur, yon.

Col. G. Are you sure of that?

Th. Sure as death. Aw seigh her back.

Col. G. Her back! Who could be sure of a back?

Th. By th' maskins! dosto think I dunnot know mo Mattie's back? I seign her coom eawt o' that dur, aw tell tho!

Col. G. Why didn't you speak to her?

Th. Aw co'd.

Col. G. And she didn't answer?

Th. Aw didn't co' leawd. Aw're not willin' to have ony mak ov a din.

Col. G. But you followed her surely?

Th. Aw did; but aw're noan so good at walkin' as aw wur when aw coom; th' stwons ha' blistered mo fet. An it're the edge o' dark like. Aw connot seigh weel at neet, wi o' th' lamps; an afoor aw geet oop wi' her, hoo's reawnd th' nook, and gwon fro mo seet.

Col. G. There are ten thousands girls in London you might take for your own under such circumstances—not seeing more than the backs of them.

Th. Ten theawsand girls like mo Mattie, saysto?—wi'her greight eighes and her lung yure?—Puh!

Col. G. But you've just said you didn't see her face!

Th. Dunnot aw know what th' face ov mo chylt be like, beout seein' ov it? Aw'm noan ov a lump-yed. Nobory as seigh her once wouldn't know her again.

Col. G. (*aside*). He's a lunatic!—I don't see what I can do for you, old fellow.

Th. (*rising*). And aw met ha' known it beout axin'! O'reet! Aw're a greight foo'!

But aw're beawn to coom in : aw lung'd to goo through th' same dur wi' mo Mattie. Good day, sir. It be like maister, like mon ! God's curse upon o' sich ! (*Turns his back. After a moment turns again.*) Noa. Aw winnot say that; for mo Mattie's sake aw winnot say that. God forgie you ! (*going by the house*).

Col. G. This way, please ! (*opening the street-door*).

Th. Aw see. Aw'm not to have a chance ov seein' oather Mattie or th' mon. *Exit.*

COL. G. *resumes his boot absently.* *Re-enter* THOMAS, *shaking his fist.*

Th. But aw tell tho, aw'll stick to th' place day and neet, aw wull. Aw wull. Aw wull.

Col. G. Come back to-morrow.

Th. Coom back, saysto ? Aw'll not goo away (*growing fierce*). Wilto gie mo mo Mattie ? Aw'm noan beawn to ston here so mich lunger. Wilto gie mo mo Mattie ?

Col. G. I cannot give you what I haven't got.

Th. Aw'll break thi yed, thou villain ! (*threatening him with his stick*). Eh, Mattie ! Mattie ! to loe sich a mon's maister more'n me ! I would dey fur thee, Mattie. *Exit.*

Col. G. It's all a mistake, of course. There are plenty of young men—but my Arthur's none of such. I cannot believe it of him. The daughter ! If I could find *her*, *she* would

settle the question. (*It begins to grow dark.*)
I must help the old man to find her. He's
sure to come back. Arthur does *not* look the
least like it. But—(*polishes vigorously*). I
can*not* get this boot to look like a gentleman's. I wish I had taken a lesson or two
first. I'll get hold of a shoeblack, and make
him come for a morning or two. No, he
does *not* look like it. There he comes. (*Goes
on polishing.*)

Enter GER.

Ger. William !
Col. G. (*turning*). Yes, sir.
Ger. Light the gas. Any one called ?
Col. G. Yes, sir.
Ger. Who ?
Col. G. I don't know, sir. (*Lighting the
gas.*)
Ger. You should have asked his name.
(*Stands before the clay, contemplating it.*)
Col. G. I'm sorry I forgot, sir. It was
only an old man from the country—after his
daughter, he said.
Ger. Came to offer his daughter, or him-
self perhaps. (*Begins to work at the figure.*)
Col. G. (*watching him stealthily*). He
looked a respectable old party—from Lan-
cashire, he said.
Ger. I dare say. You will have many
such callers. Take the address. Models, you
know.
Col. G. If he calls again, sir ?

Ger. Ask him to leave his address, I say.

Col. G. But he told me you knew her.

Ger. Possibly. I had a good many models before I left. But it's of no consequence; I don't want any at present.

Col. G. He seemed in a great way, sir— and swore. I couldn't make him out.

Ger. Ah! hm!

Col. G. He says he saw her come out of the house.

Ger. *Has* there been any girl here? Have you seen any about?

Col. G. No, sir.

Ger. My aunt had a dressmaker to meet her here the other evening. I have had no model since I came back.

Col. G. The man was in a sad taking about her, sir. I didn't know what to make of it. There seemed some truth—something suspicious.

Ger. Perhaps my aunt can throw some light upon it. (Col. G. *lingers.*) That will do. (*Exit* Col. G.) How oddly the man behaves! A sun-stroke in India, perhaps. Or he may have had a knock on the head. I must keep my eye on him. (*Stops working, steps backward, and gazes at the Psyche.*) She is growing very like some one! Who can it be? She knows she is puzzling me, the beauty! See how she is keeping back a smile! She knows if she lets one smile out, her whole face will follow it through the clay. How strange the half-lights of memory

are! You know and you don't know—both
at once. Like a bat in the twilight you are
sure of it, and the same moment it is nowhere. Who *is* my Psyche like ?—The forehead above the eyebrow, and round by the
temple ? The half-playful, half-sorrowful
curve of the lip? The hope in the lifted
eyelid ? There is more there than ever I
put there. Some power has been shaping my
ends. By heaven, I have it !—No—yes—it
is—it is Constance—momently dawning out
of the clay! What *does* this mean ? *She*
never gave me a sitting—at least, she has
not done so for the last ten years—yet here
she is—she, and no other ! I never thought
she was beautiful. When she came with my
aunt the other day though, I did fancy I saw
a new soul dawning through the lovely face.
Here it is—the same soul breaking through
the clay of my Psyche !—I will give just one
touch to the corner of the mouth.

> *Gives a few touches, then st ps back again
> and contemplates the figure. Turns
> away and walks up and down. The
> light darkens to slow plaintive music,
> which lasts for a minute. Then the
> morning begins to dawn, gleaming blue
> upon the statues and casts, and reveal-
> ing* GER. *seated before his Psyche,
> gazing at her. He rises, and exit.
> Enter* COL. G. *and looks about.*

Col. G. I don't know what to make of it !
Or rather I'm afraid I do know what to make

of it! It looks bad. He's not been in bed all night. But it shows he has some conscience left--and that's a comfort.

Enter Mrs. CLIFFORD, *peeping round cautiously.*

Col. G. What, Clara! you here so early!

Mrs. C. Well, you know, brother, you're so fond of mystery!

Col. G. It's very kind of you to come! But we must be very careful; I can't tell when my master may be home.

Mrs. C. Has he been out all night, then?

Col. G. Oh no; he's just gone.

Mrs. C. I never knew him such an early bird. I made sure he was safe in bed for a couple of hours yet. But I do trust, Walter, you have had enough of this fooling, and are prepared to act like a rational man and a gentleman.

Col. G. On the contrary, Clara, with my usual obstinacy, I am more determined than ever that my boy shall not know me, until, as I told you, I have rendered him such service as may prove me not altogether unworthy to be his father. Twenty years of neglect will be hard to surmount.

Mrs. C. But mere menial service cannot discharge the least portion of your obligations. As his father alone can you really serve him.

Col. G. You persist in misunderstanding me. This is not the service I mean. I scorn

R

the fancy.   This is only the means, as I told you plainly before, of finding out *how* I may serve him—of learning what he really needs —or most desires.   If I fail in discovering how to recommend myself to him, I shall go back to India, and content myself with leaving him a tolerable fortune.

Mrs. C. How ever a hair-brained fellow like you, Walter, could have made such a soldier!—Why don't you tell your boy you love him, and have done with it?

Col. G. I will, as soon as I have proof to back the assertion.

Mrs. C. I tell you it is rank pride.

Col. G. It may be pride, sister; but it is the pride of a repentant thief who puts off his confession until he has the money in his hand to prove the genuineness of his sorrow.

Mrs. C. It never *was* of any use to argue with *you*, Walter; you know that, or at least I know it.   So I give up.—I trust you have got over your prejudice against his profession.   It is not my fault.

Col. G. In truth, I had forgotten the profession—as you call it—in watching the professor.

Mrs. C. And has it not once occurred to you to ask how he may take such watching?

Col. G. By the time he is aware of it, he will be ready to understand it.

Mrs. C. But suppose he should discover you before you have thus established your position?

Col. G. I must run the risk.

Mrs. C. Suppose then you should thus find out something he would not have you know?

Col. G. (*hurriedly*). Do you imagine his servant might know a thing he would hide from his father?

Mrs. C. I do not, Walter. I can trust him. But he might well resent the espionage of even his father. You cannot get rid of the vile look of the thing.

Col. G. Again I say, my boy shall be my judge, and my love shall be my plea. In any case I shall have to ask his forgiveness. But there is his key in the lock! Run into the house.

Exit MRS. C. *Enter* GER., *and goes straight to the Psyche.*

Col. G. Breakfast is waiting, sir.

Ger. By and by, William.

Col. G. You haven't been in bed, sir!

Ger. Well? What of that?

Col. G. I hope you're not ill, sir.

Ger. Not in the least: I work all night sometimes.—You can go. (COL. G. *lingers, with a searching gaze at the Psyche.*)—I don't want anything.

Col. G. Pardon me, sir, but I am sure you are ill. You've done *no* work since last night.

Ger. (*with displeasure*). I am quite well, and wish to be alone.

Col. G. Mayn't I go and fetch a doctor, sir? It is better to take things in time.

Ger. You are troublesome. (*Exit* COL. G.)
—What can the fellow mean? He looked at
me so strangely too! He's officious—that's
all, I dare say. A good sort of man, I do
think! William!—What is it in the man's
face?—(*Enter Col. G.*) Is the breakfast
ready?

Col. G. Quite ready, sir.

Ger. I'm sorry I spoke to you so hastily.
The fact is——

Col. G. Don't mention it, sir. Speak as
you will to me; I shan't mind it. When
there's anything on a man's conscience—I—I
—I mean on a man's mind——

Ger. What *do* you mean?

Col. G. I mean, when there is anything
there, he can't well help his temper, sir.

Ger. I don't understand you; but, anyhow,
you—go too far, William.

Col. G. I beg your pardon, sir: I forgot
myself. I do humbly beg your pardon.
Shall I make some fresh coffee, sir? It's
not cold—only it's stood too long.

Ger. The coffee will do well enough. (*Exit*
COL. G.)—*Is* she so beautiful? (*turning to the
Psyche*)—Is there a likeness?—I see it.—
Nonsense! A mere chance confluence of the
ideal and the actual.—Even then the chance
must mean something. Such a *mere* chance
would indeed be a strange one!

Enter CONSTANCE.

Oh, my heart! here she comes! my Psyche herself!—Well, Constance!

Con. Oh, Arthur, I am *so* glad I've found you! I want to talk to you about something. I know you don't care much about me now, but I *must* tell you, for it would be wrong not.

Ger. (*aside*). How beautiful she is! What *can* she have to tell me about? It cannot be —it *shall* not be—. Sit down, won't you? (*offering her a chair.*)

Con. No. *You* sit there (*pointing to the dais*), and I will sit here (*placing herself on the lower step*). It was here I used to sit so often when I was a little girl. Why can't one keep little? I was always with you then! (*Sighs.*)

Ger. It is not my fault, Constance.

Con. Oh no! I suppose it can't be. Only I don't see why. Oh, Arthur, where should I be but for you! I saw the old place yesterday. How dreadful and yet how dear it was!

Ger. Who took you there?

Con. Nobody. I went alone.

Ger. It was hardly safe.—I don't like your going out alone, Constance.

Con. Why, Arthur! I used to know every court and alley about Shoreditch better than I know Berkeley Square now!

Ger. But what made you go there?

Con. I went to find a dressmaker who has been working for my aunt, and lost my way. And—would you believe it?—I was actually frightened!

Ger. No wonder! There are rough people about there.

Con. I never used to think them rough when I lived among them with my father and mother. There must be just as good people there as anywhere else. Yet I could not help shuddering at the thought of living there again!—How strange it made me feel! You have been my angel, Arthur. What would have become of me if you hadn't taken me, I dare not think.

Ger. I have had my reward, Constance : you are happy.

Con. Not quite. There's something I want to tell you.

Ger. Tell on, child.

Con. Oh, thank you!—that is how you used to talk to me. (*Hesitates.*)

Ger. (*with foreboding*) Well, what is it?

Con. (*pulling the fingers of her gloves*) A gentleman—you know him—has been—calling upon aunt—and me. We have seen a good deal of him.

Ger. Who is he?

Con. Mr. Waterfield. (*Keeps her eyes on the floor.*)

Ger. Well?

Con. He says—he—he—he wants me to marry him.—Aunt likes him.

Ger. And you?

Con. I like him too. I don't think I like him enough—I dare say I shall. It is *so* good of him to take poor me! He is *very* rich, they say.

Ger. Have you accepted him?

Con. I am afraid he thinks so.—Ye—e—s. —I hardly know.

Ger. Haven't you—been rather—in a hurry—Constance?

Con. No, indeed! I haven't been in a hurry at all. He has been a long time trying to make me like him. I have been too long a burden to Mrs. Clifford.

Ger. So! it is her doing, then!

Con. You were away, you know.

Ger. (*bitterly*) Yes; too far—chipping stones and making mud-pies!

Con. I don't know what you mean by that, Arthur.

Ger. Oh—nothing. I mean that—that— Of course if you are engaged to him, then—

Con. I'm afraid I've done very wrong, Arthur. If I had thought you would care!— I knew aunt would be pleased!—she wanted me to have him, I knew.—I ought to do what I can to please her,—ought I not? I have no right to——

Ger. Surely, surely. Yes, yes; I understand. It was not your fault. Only you mustn't marry him, if you——. Thank you for telling me.

Con. I ought to have told you before—

before I let him speak to me again. But I didn't think you would care—not much.

Ger. Yes, yes.

Con. (*looking up with anxiety*) Ah! you *are* vexed with me, Arthur! I see how wrong it was now. I never saw you look like that. I am very, very sorry. (*Bursts into tears.*)

Ger. No, no, child! Only it is rather sudden, and I want to think about it. Shall I send William home with you?

Con. No, thank you. I have a cab waiting. You're not angry with your little beggar, Arthur?

Ger. What is there to be angry about, child?

Con. That I—did anything without asking you first.

Ger. Nonsense! You couldn't help it. *You*'re not to blame one bit.

Con. Oh, yes, I am! I ought to have asked you first. But indeed I did not know you would care. Good-bye.—Shall I go at once?

Ger. Good-bye. (*Exit* CON., *looking back troubled.*) Come at last! Oh fool! fool! fool! In love with her at last!—and too late! For three years I haven't seen her—have not once written to her! Since I came back I've seen her just twice,—and now in the very hell of love! The ragged little darling that used to lie coiled up there in that corner! If it were my sister, it would be hard to lose her so! And to such a fellow as that!—not

even a gentleman! How *could* she take him
for one! That does perplex me! Ah, well!
I suppose men *have* borne such things before,
and men will bear them again! I must work!
Nothing but work will save me. (*Approaches
the Psyche, but turns from it with a look of despair and disgust.*) What a fool I have been!
—Constance! Constance!—A brute like that
to touch one of her fingers! God in heaven!
It will drive me mad. (*Rushes out, leaving
the door open.*)

Enter COL. GERVAISE.

Col. G. Gone again! and without his
breakfast! My poor boy! There's something very wrong with you! It's that girl!
It must be! But there's conscience in him
yet!—It is all my fault. If I had been a
father to him, this would never have happened.—If he were to marry the girl now?—
Only, who can tell but *she* led *him* astray?
I have known such a thing. (*Sits down and
buries his face in his hands.*)

Enter WATERFIELD.

Wat. Is Mr. Gervaise in?
Col. G. (*rising*) No, sir.
Wat. Tell him I called, will you? [*Exit.*
Col. G. Yes, sir.—Forgot again. Young
man;—gentleman or cad?—don't know;
think the latter.

Enter THOMAS.

Th. Han yo heard speyk ov mo chylt yet, sir ?

Col. G. (*starting up*). In the name of God, I know nothing of your child ; but bring her here, and I will give you a hundred pounds —in golden sovereigns.

Th. Hea am aw to fot her yere, when I dunnot know wheer hoo be, sir ?

Col. G. That's your business. Bring her, and there will be your money.

Th. Dun yo think, sir, o' the gouden suverings i' th' Bank ov England would put a sharper edge on mo oud eighes when they look for mo lass ? Eh, mon ! Yo dunnot know the heart ov a feyther—ov the feyther ov a lass-barn, sir. Han yo kilt and buried her, and nea be yo sorry for't ? I' hoo be dead and gwoan, tell mo, sir, and aw'll goo whoam again, for mo oud lass be main lonesome beout mo, and we'll wait till we goo to her, for hoo winnot coom no moor to us.

Col. G. For anything I know, your daughter is alive and well. Bring her here, I say, and I will make you happy.

Th. Aw shannot want thee or thi suverings either to mak mo happy then, maister. Iv aw hed a houd o' mo lass, it's noan o' yere aw'd be a coomin' wi' her. It's reet streight whoam to her mother we'd be gooin', aw'll

be beawn. Nay, nay, mon!—aw'm noan sich
a greight foo as yo tak mo for.

Exit. Col. G. *follows him. Enter.* Ger.
*Sits down before the Psyche, but without
looking at her.*

Ger. Oh those fingers! They are striking
terrible chords on my heart! I *will* conquer
it. But I *will* love her. The spear shall fill
its own wound. To draw it out and die,
would be no victory. "I'll but lie down and
bleed awhile, and then I'll rise and fight
again." Brave old Sir Andrew!

Enter Col. G.

Col. G. I beg your pardon, sir—a young
man called while you were out.

Ger. (*listlessly*). Very well, William.

Col. G. Is there any message, if he calls
again, sir? He said he would.

Ger. No. (Col. G. *lingers.*) You can go.

Col. G. I hope you feel better, sir?

Ger. Quite well.

Col. G. Can I get you anything, sir?

Ger. No, thank you; I want nothing.—
Why do you stay?

Col. G. Can't you think of something I
can do for you, sir?

Ger. Fetch that red cloth.

Col. G. Yes, sir.

Ger. Throw it over that ——

Col. G. This, sir?

Ger. No, no—the clay there. Thank you.
(*A knock at the door.*) See who that is.

Col. G. Are you at home, sir?

Ger. That depends. Not to Mr. Water-field. Oh, my head! my head! [*Exit* COL. G.

Enter CONSTANCE. GER. *starts, but keeps his head leaning on his hand.*

Con. I forgot to say to you, Arthur,——. But you are ill! What is the matter, dear Arthur?

Ger. (*without looking up*) Nothing—only a headache.

Con. Do come home with me, and let aunt and me nurse you. Don't be vexed with me any more. I will do whatever you like. I couldn't go home without seeing you again. And now I find you ill!

Ger. Not a bit. I am only dreadfully busy. I must go out of town. I am so busy! I can't stay in it a moment longer. I have so many things to do.

Con. Mayn't I come and see you while you work? I never used to interrupt you. I want so to sit once more in my old place. (*Draws a stool towards him.*)

Ger. No, no—not—not there! Constance used to sit there. William!

Con. You frighten me, Arthur!

Enter COL. G.

Ger. Bring a chair, William.
Constance sits down like a chidden child.
   Exit COL. G.

Con. I must have offended you more than I thought, Arthur! What *can* I say? It is so stupid to be always saying *I am sorry*.

Ger. No, no. But some one may call.

Con. You mean more than that. Will you not let me understand?

Ger. Your friend Mr. Waterfield called a few minutes ago. He will be here again presently, I dare say.

Con. (*indifferently*). Indeed!

Ger. I suppose you appointed—expected—to meet him here.

Con. Arthur! Do you think I would come to you to meet *him?* I saw him this morning; I don't want to see him again. I wish you knew him.

Ger. Why should you want me to know him?

Con. Because you would do him good.

Ger. What good does he want done him?

Con. He has got beautiful things in him—talks well—in bits—arms and feet and faces —never anything like—(*turning to the Psyche*) Why have you——? Has *she* been naughty too?

Ger. Is it *only* naughty things that must be put out of sight, Constance?

Con. Dear Arthur! you spoke like your own self then.

Ger. (*rising hurriedly*). Excuse me. I must go. It is very rude, but—William!

Enter Col. G.

Col. G. Yes, sir.

Ger. Fetch a hansom directly.

Col. G. Yes, sir.   *Exit.*

Con. You do frighten me, Arthur! I am
sure you are ill.

Ger. Not at all. I have an engagement.

Con. I must go then—must I?

Ger. Do not think me unkind?

Con. I will not think anything you would
not have me think.

Re-enter Col. G.

Col. G. The cab is at the door, sir.

Ger. Thank you. Then show Miss Lacordère out. Stay. I will open the door for
her myself.   *Exeunt* Ger. *and* Con.

Col. G. He speaks like one in despair,
forcing every word! If he should die! Oh,
my God!

Re-enter Ger.   *Walks up and down the room.*

Col. G. Ain't you going, sir?

Ger. No. I have sent the lady in the cab.

Col. G. Then hadn't you better lie down,
sir?

Ger. Lie down! What do you mean? I'm
not in the way of lying down except to
sleep.

Col. G. And let me go for the doctor, sir?

Ger. The doctor! Ha! ha ha!—You are a soldier, you say?

Col. G. Yes, sir.

Ger. Right. We're all soldiers—or ought to be. I will put you to your catechism. What is a soldier's first duty?

Col. G. Obedience, sir.

[GER. *sits down and leans his head on his hands.* COL. G. *watches him.*

Ger. Ah! obedience, is it? Then turn those women out. They will hurt you—may kill you; but you must not mind that. They burn, they blister, and they blast, for as white as they look! The hottest is the white fire. But duty, old soldier!—obedience, you know!—Ha! ha! Oh, my head! my head! I believe I am losing my senses, William. I was in a bad part of the town this morning. I went to see a place I knew long ago. It had gone to hell—but the black edges of it were left. There was a smell—and I can't get it out of me. Oh, William! William! take hold of me. Don't let them come near me. Psyche is laughing at me. I told you to throw the red cloth over her.

Col. G. My poor boy!

Ger. Don't fancy you're my father, though! I wish you were. But I cannot allow that.— Why the devil didn't you throw the red cloth over that butterfly? She's sucking the blood from my heart.

Col. G. You said the Psyche, sir! The red cloth *is* over the Psyche, sir. Look.

Ger. Yes. Yes. I beg your pardon. Take it off. It is too red. It will scorch her wings. It burns my brain. Take it off, I say! (COL. G. *uncovers the Psyche.*) There! I told you! She's laughing at me! Ungrateful child! *I*'m not her Cupid. Cover her up. Not the red cloth again. It's too hot, I say. I won't torture *her*. I am a man and I can bear it. She's a woman and she shan't bear it.

Sinks back in his chair. COL. G. *lays him on the dais, and sits down beside him.*

Col. G. His heart's all right! And when a fellow's miserable over his faults, there must be some way out of them.—But the consequences?—Ah! there's the rub.

Ger. What's the matter? Where am I?

Col. G. I must fetch a doctor, sir. You've been in a faint.

Ger. Why couldn't I keep in it? It was very nice : you know nothing—and that's the nicest thing of all. Why is it we can't stop, William?

Col. G. I don't understand you, sir.

Ger. Stop living, I mean. It's no use killing yourself, for you don't stop then. At least they say you go on living all the same. If I thought it did mean stopping, William—

Gol. C. Do come to your room, sir.

Ger. I won't. I'll stop here. How hot it is! Don't let anybody in.

Stretches out his hand. COL. G. *holds it. He falls asleep.*

Col. G. What *shall* I do? If he married her, he'd be miserable, and make her miserable too. I'll take her away somewhere. I'll be a father to her; I'll tend her as if she were his widow. But what confusions would follow! Alas! alas! one crime is the mother of a thousand miseries! And now he's in for a fever—typhus, perhaps!—I *must* find this girl!—What a sweet creature that Miss Lacordère is! If only he might have *her!* I don't care what she was.

Ger. Don't let them near me, William! They will drive me mad. They think I shall love them. I *will* not. If she comes one step nearer, I shall strike her. You Diana! Hecate! Hell-cat!—Fire-hearted Chaos is burning me to ashes! My brain is a cinder! Some water, William!

Col. G. Here it is, sir.

Ger. But just look to Psyche there. Ah. she's off! There she goes! melting away in the blue, like a dissolving vapour. Bring me my field-glass, William. I may catch a glimpse of her yet. Make haste.

Col. G. Pray don't talk so, sir. Do be quiet, or you will make yourself very ill. Think what will become of me if——

Ger. What worse would *you* be, William? You are a soldier. I must talk. You are all wrong about it : it keeps me quiet (*holding his head with both hands*). I should go raving mad else (*wildly*). Give me some water. (*He drinks eagerly, then looks slowly round*

s

the room.) Now they *are* gone, and I do believe they won't come again! I see everything—and your face, William. You are very good to me—very patient! I should die if it weren't for you.

Col. G. I would die for you, sir.

Ger. Would you? But perhaps you don't care much for your life. Anybody might have *my* life for the asking. I dare say it's just as good to be dead.—Ah! there is a toad —a toad with a tail! No; it's a toad with a slow-worm after him. Take them away, William!—Thank you.—I used to think life pleasant, but now—somehow there's nothing in it. She told me the truth about it—Constance did. Don't let those women come back. What if I *should* love them, William!—love and hate them both at once! William! William! (*A knock at the door.*) See who that is. Mind you don't let *them* in.

Col. G. Martha is there, sir.

Ger. She's but an old woman; she can't keep them out. They would walk over her. All the goddesses have such long legs! You go and look. You'll easily know them: if they've got no irises to their eyes, don't let them in, for the love of God, William! Real women have irises to their eyes: those have none—those frightful snowy beauties.—And yet snow is very nice! And I'm so hot! *There* they come again!   *Exit* Col. G.

Enter MRS. CLIFFORD.

Ger. Aunt! aunt! help me! There they come!

Mrs. C. What is it, my Arthur? They shan't hurt you. I am here. I will take care of you.

Ger. Yes, yes, you will! I am not a bit afraid of them now. Do you know them, aunt? I'll tell you a secret: they are Juno and Diana and Venus.—They hate sculptors. But I never wronged them. Three white women — only, between their fingers and behind their knees they are purple—and inside their lips. when they smile—and in the hollows of their eyes—ugh! They want me to love them; and they say you are all— all of you women—no better than they are. I *know* that is a lie; for they have no eyelids and no irises to their eyes.

Mrs. C. Dear boy, they shan't come near you. Shall I sing to you, and drive them away?

Ger. No, don't. I can't bear birds in my brain.

Mrs. C. How long have you had this headache? (*laying her hand on his forehead.*)

Ger. Only a year or two—since the white woman came—that woman (*pointing to the Psyche*). She's been buried for ages, and won't grow brown.

Mrs. C. There's no woman there, Arthur.

Ger. Of course not. It was an old story

that bothered me.   Oh, my head! my head!
—There's my father standing behind the
door and won't come in!—*He* could help
me now, if he would.   William! show my
father in.   But he isn't in the story—so he
can't.

Mrs. C. Do try to keep yourself quiet,
Arthur.   The doctor will be here in a few
minutes.

Ger. He shan't come here!   He would
put the white woman out.   She does smell
earthy, but I won't part with her. (*A knock.*)
What a devil of a noise!   Why don't they
use the knocker?   What's the use of taking
a sledge-hammer?

Mrs. C. It's that stupid James!

Enter CONSTANCE.   MRS. C. *goes to meet her.*

Mrs. C. Constance, you go and hurry the
doctor.   I will stay with Arthur.

Con. Is he *very* ill, aunt?

Mrs. C. I'm afraid he is.

Ger. (*sitting up*). Constance! Constance!

Con. Here I am! (*running to him*).

Ger. Oh, my head!   I wish I could find
somewhere to lay it!—Sit by me, Constance,
and let me lay my head on your shoulder—
for one minute—only one minute.   It aches
so! (*She sits down by him.   His head sinks on
her shoulder.   MRS. C. looks annoyed, and exit.*)

Con. Thank you, thank you, dear Arthur!
(*sobbing*).   You used to like me!   I could not

believe you hated me now. You *have* for-given me? Dear head!

He closes his eyes. Slow plaintive music.

Ger. (*half waking*). I can't read. When I get to the bottom of the page, I wonder what it was all about. I shall never get to Garibaldi! and if I don't, I shall never get farther. If I could but keep that one line away! It drives me mad, mad. "He took her by the lily-white hand."—I could strangle myself 'for thinking of such things, but they *will* come!—I *won't* go mad. I should never get to Garibaldi, and never be rid of this red-hot ploughshare ploughing up my heart. I will *not* go mad! I will die like a man.

Con. Arthur! Arthur!

Ger. God in heaven! she is there! And the others are behind her!—Psyche! Psyche! Don't speak to those women! Come alone, and I will tear my heart out and give it you. —It is Psyche herself now, and the rest are gone! Psyche—listen.

Con. It's only me, Arthur! your own little Constance! If aunt would but let me stay and nurse you! But I don't know what's come to her: she's not like herself at all.

Ger. Who's that behind you?

Con. Behind me? (*looking round*). There's nobody behind me.

Ger. I thought there was somebody behind you. William!—What can have become of William?

Con. I dare say aunt has sent him some-where.

Ger. Then he's gone! he's gone!

Con. You're not afraid of being left alone with me, Arthur?

Ger. Oh no! of course not?—What *can* have become of William? Don't you know they sent him—not those women, but the dead people—to look after me? He's a good fellow. He said he would die for me. Ha! ha! ha! Not much in that—is there?

Con. Don't laugh so, dear Arthur.

Ger. Well, I won't. I have something to tell you, Constance. I will try to keep my senses till I've told you.

Con. Do tell me. I hope I haven't done anything more to vex you. Indeed I am sorry. I won't speak to that man again, if you like. I would rather not—if you wish it.

Ger. What right have I to dictate to you, my child?

Con. Every right. I am yours. I belong to you. Nobody owned me when you took me.

Ger. Don't talk like that; you will drive me mad.

Con. Arthur! Arthur!

Ger. Listen to me, Constance. I am going to Garibaldi. He wants soldiers. I must not live an idle life any longer.—We must part, Constance.—Good-bye, my darling!

Con. No, no; not yet; we'll talk about it by-and-by. You see I shall have ever so

many things to make for you before you can
go! (*smiling*).

Ger. Garibaldi can't wait, Constance—and
I can't wait. I shall die if I stop here.

Con. Oh, Arthur, you are in some trouble,
and you won't tell me what it is, so I can't
help you!

Ger. I shall be killed, I know. I mean to
be. Will you think of me sometimes? Give
me one kiss. I may have a last kiss.

Con. (*weeping.*) My heart will break if you
talk like that, Arthur. I will do anything
you please. There's something wrong, dreadfully wrong! And it must be my fault!—
Oh! there's that man! (*starting up.*) He
shall *not* come here.

[*Runs to the house-door, and stands listening,
with her hand on the key.*

END OF ACT I.

ACT II.

SCENE.—*A street in Mayfair.* MRS. CLIF-
FORD'S *house.   A pastrycook's shop.   Boys
looking in at the window.*

Bill. I say, Jim, ain't it a lot o' grub ?   If
I wos a pig now,——

Jack. I likes to hear Bill a supposin' of
hisself.   Go it, Bill !—There ain't nothink *he*
can't suppose hisself, Jim.—Bein' as you ain't
a pig, Bill, you've got yer own trotters, an'
yer own tater-trap.

Bill. Vereupon blue Bobby eccosts me
with the remark, " I wants you, Bill ; " and
seein' me too parerlyzed to bolt, he pops me
in that 'ere jug vithout e'er a handle.

Jack. Mother kep' a pig once.

Jim. What was he like, Jack ?

Jack. As like any other pig as ever he
could look ; accep' that where other pigs is
black he wor white, an' where other pigs is
white he wor black.

Jim. Did you have the milk in your tea,
Jack ?

Jack. Pigs ain't got no milk, Jim, you
stupe !

Bill. Pigs *has* milk, Jack, only they don't

give it to coves.—I wish I wos the Lord
Mayor!

Jack. Go it again, Bill. He ought ha' been
a beak, Bill ought. What 'ud you do, Bill,
supposin' as how you wos the Lord Mayor?

Bill. I'd take all the beaks, an' all the
peelers, an' put their own bracelets on 'em,
an' feed 'em once a day on scraps o' wittles to
bring out the hunger : a cove can't be hungry
upon nuffin at all.

Jim. He gets **what** mother calls the
squeamishes.

Jack. Well, Bill?

Bill. Well, the werry moment their bellies
was as long an' as loose as a o'-clo'-bag of
a winter's mornin', I'd bring 'em all up to
this 'ere winder, five or six at a time—with
the darbies on, mind ye——

Jim. And I'm to be there to see, Bill—
ain't I?

Bill. If you're good, Jim, an' don't forget
yer prayers.

Jack. My eye! it's as good as a penny
gaff! Go it, Bill.

Bill. Then I up an' addresses 'em : " My
Lords an' Gen'lemen, 'cos as how ye're all
good boys, an' goes to church, an' don't eat
too many wittles, an' don't take off your bracelets when you goes to bed, you shall obswerve
me eat."

Jim. Go it, Bill! I likes you, Bill.

Bill. No, Jim ; I must close. The imagination is a 'ungry gift, as the cock said when

he bolted the pebbles. Let's sojourn the meetin'.

Jack. Yes; come along. 'Tain't a comf'able corner this yere : the wind cuts round uncommon sharp. Them pies ain't good—leastways not to look at.

Bill. They ain't disgestible. But look ye here, Jack and Jim—hearkee, my kids. (*Puts an arm round the neck of each, and whispers first to one and then to the other.*)

Enter MATTIE *and* SUSAN.

Sus. Now, Mattie, we're close to the house, an' I don't want to be seen with you, for she's mad at *me*.

Mat. You must have made her mad, then, Sue.

Sus. She madded me first: what else when she wouldn't believe a word I said ? She'd ha' sworn on the gospel book, we sent the parcel up the spout. But she'll believe *you*, an' give you something, and then we'll have a chop !

Mat. How can you expect that, Sue, when the work's lost ?

Sus. Never mind ; you go and see.

Mat. I shan't take it, Susan. I couldn't.

Sus. Stuff and nonsense ! I'll wait you round the corner : I don't like the smell o' them pastry things.

Exit. MATTIE *walks past the window.*

Mat. I don't like going. It makes me feel a thief to be suspected.

Bill. Lor! it's our Mattie! There's our Mattie!—Mattie! Mattie!

Mat. Ah, Bill! you're there—are you?

Bill. Yes, Mattie. It's a tart-show. You walks up and takes yer chice;—leastways, you makes it: somebody else takes it.

Mat. Wouldn't you like to *take* your choice sometimes, Bill?

Bill. In course I would.

Mat. Then why don't you work, and better yourself a bit?

Bill. Bless you, Mattie! myself is werry comf'able. He never complains.

Mat. You're hungry sometimes, — ain't you?

Bill. Most remarkable 'ungry, Mattie—this werry moment. Odd you should ask now—ain't it?

Mat. You would get plenty to eat if you would work.

Bill. Thank you—I'd rayther not. Them as ain't 'ungry never enj'ys their damaged tarts. If I'm 'appy, vere's the odds? as the cat said to the mouse as wanted to be let off the engagement. Why should I work more'n any other gen'leman?

Mat. A gentleman that don't work is a curse to his neighbours, Bill.

Bill. Bless you, Mattie! I ain't a curse—nohow to nobody. I don't see as you've got any call to say that, Mattie. I don't go fakin' clies, or crackin' cribs—nothin' o' the sort. An' I don't mind doin' of a odd job, if it *is* a odd one. Don't go for to say that again, Mattie.

Mat. I won't, then, Bill. But just look at yourself!—You're all in rags.

Bill. Rags is the hairier, as the Skye terrier said to the black-an'-tan.—I shouldn't object to a new pair of old trousers, though.

Mat. Why don't you have a pair of real new ones? If you would only sweep a crossing——

Bill. There ain't a crossin' but what's took. Besides, my legs ain't put together for one place all day long. It ain't to be done, Mattie. They can't do it.

Mat. There's the shoe-black business, then.

Bill. That ain't so bad, acause you can shoulder your box and trudge. But if it's all the same to you, Mattie, I'd rayther enj'y life : they say it's short.

Mat. But it ain't the same to me. It's so bad for you to be idle, Bill!

Bill. Not as I knows on. I'm tollable jolly, so long's I gets the browns for my bed.

Mat. Wouldn't you like a bed with a blanket to it?

Bill. Well, yes—if it was guv to me. But I don't go in for knocking of yourself about, to sleep warm.

Mat. Well, look here, Bill. It's all Susan and I can do to pay for our room, and get a bit of bread and a cup of tea. It ain't enough.—If you were to earn a few pence now————

Bill. Oh golly! I never thought o' that. What a hass I wur, to be sure! I'll go a shoe-blackin' to-morrow—I will.

Mat. Did you ever black a shoe, Bill?

Bill. I tried a boot oncet—when Jim wor a blackin' for a day or two. But I made nothink on it—nothink worth mentionin'. The blackin' or som'at was wrong. The gen'leman said it wur coal-dust, an' he'd slog me, an' adwised me to go an' learn my trade.

Mat. And what did you say to that?

Bill. Holler'd out "Shine yer boots!" as loud as I could holler.

Mat. You must try my boots next time you come.

Bill. This wery night, Mattie. I'll make 'em shine like plate glass—see then if I don't. But where'll I get a box and brushes?

Mat. You shall have our brushes and my footstool.

Bill. I see! Turn the stool upside down, put the brushes in, and carry it by one leg—as drunken Moll does her kid.—Here you are, sir! Black your boots, sir?—Shine your trotters, sir? (*bawling.*)

Mat. That'll do; that'll do, Bill! Famous! You needn't do it again (*holding her ears*). Would you like a tart?

Bill. Just wouldn't I, then!—Shine your boooooots!

Mat. (*laughing*). Do hold your tongue, Bill. There's a penny for a tart.

Bill. Thank you, Mattie. Thank you.
Exit into the shop.
Jack and Jim (*touching their supposed caps*). Please, ma'am! Please, ma'am! I likes 'em too. I likes 'em more 'n Bill.

Mat. I'm very sorry, but—(*feeling in her pocket*) I've got a ha'penny, I believe. No—there's a penny! You must share it, you know. (*Gives it to Jack. Knocks at Mrs. Clifford's door.*)

Jack and Jim. Thank you, ma'am. Thank you, ma'am.
Exit MATTIE *into* MRS. CLIFFORD'S.

Jim. Now, Jack, what's it to be?

Jack. I believe I shall spend it in St. Martin's Lane.

Jim. A ha'p'orth on it's mine, you know, Jack.

Jack. Well, you do put the stunners on me!

Jim. She said we wos to divide it—she did.

Jack. 'Taint possible. It beats my ivories. (*He pretends to bite it.* JIM *flies at him in a rage.*)

Re-enter BILL, *with his mouth full.*

Bill. Now what are you two a squabblin' over? Oh! Jack's got a yennep, and Jim's lookin' shirty.

Jim. She told him to divide it, and he won't.

Bill. Who told him?

Jim. Mattie.

Bill. You dare, Jack ? Hand over.

Jack. Be hanged if I do.

Bill. Then do and be hanged. (*A struggle.*) There, Jim ! Now you go and buy what you like.

Jim. Am I to give Jack the half?

Bill. Yes, if our Mattie said it.

Jim. All right, Bill. (*Goes into the shop.*)

Jack. I owe you one for that, Bill.

Bill. Owe it me then, Jack. I do like fair play—always did (*eating*).

Jack. You ain't a sharin' of *your* yennep, Bill.

Bill. Mattie didn't say I was to. She knowed one wouldn't break up into three nohow. 'Tain't in natur', Jack.

Jack. You might ha' guv me a bite, anyhow, Bill.

Bill. It ain't desirable, Jack—size o' trap dooly considered. Here comes your share.

Re-enter JIM. *Gives a bun to* JACK.

Jim. I tell you what, Bill—she ain't *your* Mattie. She ain't nobody's Mattie ; she's a hangel.

Bill. No, Jim, she ain't a hangel; she 'ain't got no wings, leastways outside her clo'es, and she 'ain't got clo'es enough to hide 'em. I wish I wos a hangel !

Jack. At it again, Bill ! I *do* like to hear Bill a wishin' of hisself ! Why, Bill ?

Bill. Acause they're never 'ungry.

Jack. How do you know they ain't?

Bill. You never sees 'em loafin' about nowheres.

Jim. Is Mattie your sister, Bill?

Bill. No, Jim; I ain't good 'nough to have a sister like she.

Jack. Your sweetheart, Bill? Ha! ha! ha!

Bill. Dry up, Jack.

Jim. Tell me about her, Bill. *I* didn't jaw you.

Bill. She lives in our court, Jim. Makes shirts and things.

Jack. Oh! ho!

Bill *hits* Jack. Jack *doubles himself up.*

Bill. Jim, our Mattie ain't like other gals; I never see her out afore this blessed day — upon my word and honour, Jim, never!

Jack (*wiping his nose with his sleeve*). You don't know a joke from a jemmy, Bill.

Bill. I'll joke you!—A hangel tips you a tart, and you plucks her feathers! Get on t'other side of the way, you little dirty devil, or I'll give you another smeller—cheap too. Off with you!

Jack. No, Bill; no, please. I'm wery sorry. I ain't so bad's all that comes to.

Bill. If you wants to go with Jim and me, then behave like a gen'leman.

Jim. I calls our Mattie a brick!

Bill. None o' *your* jaw, Jim! She ain't *your* Mattie.

Enter THOMAS.

Tho. Childer, dun yo know th' way to Paradise—Row, or Road, or summat?

Bill. Dunnow, sir. You axes at the Sunday-school.

Tho. Wheer's th' Sunday-school, chylt?

Bill. Second door round the corner, sir.

Tho. Second dur reawnd th' corner! Which corner, my man?

Bill. Round *any* corner. Second door 's all-ways Sunday-school. (*Takes a sight. Exeunt boys.*)

THOMAS *sits down on a door-step.*

Tho. Eh, but aw be main weary! Surely th' Lord dunnot be a forsakin' ov mo. There's that abeawt th' lost ship. Oop yon, wheer th' angels keep greight flocks ov 'em, they dunnot like to lose one ov 'em, an' they met well be helpin' ov mo to look for mo lost lamb i' this awful plaze! What has th' shepherd o' th' sheep himsel' to do, God bless him! but go look for th' lost ones and carry 'em whoam! O Lord! gie mo mo Mattie. Aw'm a silly ship mosel, a sarchin' for mo lost lamb. (*Boys begin to gather and stare.*) She's o' the world to me. O Lord, hear mo, and gie mo mo Mattie. Nea, aw'll geet oop, and go look again. (*Rises.*)

First Boy. Ain't he a cricket, Tommy?

Second Boy. Spry, ain't he? Prod him, and see him jump. (*General insult.*)

T

Tho. Why, childer, what have aw **done,** that yo cry after mo like a thief?

First Boy. Daddy Longlegs! Daddy Longlegs!

    They hustle and crowd him.   Re-enter BILL.
        THOMAS *makes a rush.   They run.   He*
        seizes BILL.   *They gather again.*

Tho. Han yo getten a mother, lad?

Bill. No, thank ye.   'Ain't got no mother. Come of a haunt, I do.

First Boy. Game!—ain't he?

Tho. Well, aw'll tak yo whoam **to** yor aunt—aw wull.

Bill. Will you now, old chap?   Wery well. (*Squats.*)

Tho. (*holding him up by the collar, and shaking his stick over him*). Tell mo wheer's yor aunt, or aw'll breyk every bone i' yor body.

Bill (*wriggling and howling and rubbing his eyes with alternate sleeves*). Let me go, I say.   Let me go and I'll tell ye.   I will indeed, sir.

Tho. (*letting go*). Wheer then, mo lad?

Bill (*starting up*). I' the church-cellar, sir—first bin over the left—feeds musty, and smells strong.   Ho! ho! ho! (*Takes a sight.*)

    THOMAS *makes a dart.*   BILL *dodges him.*

First Boy. Ain't he a cricket *now*, Tommy?

Second Boy. Got one leg too many for a cricket, Sam.

Third Boy. That's what he jerks hisself with, Tommy.

Tho. Boys, I want to be freens wi' yo.
Here's a penny.

*One of the boys knocks it out of his hand.
A scramble.*

Tho. Now, boys, dun yo know wheer's a
young woman bi th' name ov Mattie—some-
wheer abeawt Paradise Row?

First Boy. Yes, old un.

Second Boy. Lots on 'em.

Third Boy. Which on em' do you want,
Mr. Cricket?

Fourth Boy. You ain't peticlar, I s'pose,
old corner-bones?

First Boy. Don't you fret, old stilts. We'll
find you a Mattie. There's plenty on 'em—
all nice gals.

Tho. I want mo own Mattie.

First Boy. Why, you'd never tell one from
t'other on 'em!

Third Boy. All on 'em wery glad to see
old Daddy Longlegs!

Tho. Oh dear! Oh dear! What an awful
plaze this Lon'on do be! To see the childer
so bad!

Second Boy. Don't cry, gran'pa. *She'd*
chaff you worser 'n us! We're only poor
little innocent boys. We don't know nothink,
bless you! Oh no!

First Boy. You'd better let her alone, arter
all, bag o' nails.

Second Boy. *She'll* have it out on you now,
for woppin' of her when she wor a kid.

First Boy. She's a wopper herself now.

Third Boy. Mighty fine, with your shirt for a great-coat. He! he! he!

Fourth Boy. Mattie never kicks us poor innocent boys—cos we 'ain't got no mothers to take our parts. Boo hoo!

Enter JACK—*his hands in his pockets.*

Jack. What's the row, Bill?

Bill. Dunnow, Jack. Old chap collared me when I wasn't alludin' to him. He's after some Mattie or other. It can't be our Mattie. *She* wouldn't never have such a blazin' old parient as that.

Jack. Supposin' it was your Mattie, Bill, would you split, and let Scull-and-cross-bones nab her?

Bill. Would I? Would I 'and over our Mattie to her natural enemy? Did you ax it, Jack?

Jack. Natural enemy! My eye, Bill! what words you fakes!

Bill. Ain't he her natural enemy, then? Ain't it yer father as bumps yer 'ed, an' cusses ye, an' lets ye see him eat? Afore he gets our Mattie, I'll bite!

Tho. Poor lad! poor lad! Dunnot say that! Her feyther's th' best freen' hoo's getten. Th' moor's th' pity, for it's not mich he can do for her. But he would dee for her —he would.

Boys (*all together*). Go along, Daddy-devil! Pick yer own bones, an' ha' done.

Rag-raker!
Skin-cat!
Bag o' nails!
Scull-an'-cross-bones!

Old Daddy Longlegs wouldn't say his prayers—
Take him by his left leg, and throw him downstairs.

Go along! Go to hell!
We'll skin you.
Melt ye down for taller, we will.
Only he 'ain't got none, the red herrin'!
*They throw things at him. He sits down on
the door-step, and covers his head with
his arms. Enter* COL. G. *Boys run off.*
Tho. Oh, mo Mattie! mo Mattie!
Col. G. Poor old fellow! Are you hurt?
Tho. Eh! *yo* be a followin' ov mo too!
Col. G. What are you doing here?
Tom. What am aw doin' yere! Thee
knows well enough what aw're a doin' yere.
It 're o' thy fau't, mon.
Col. G. Why, you've got a blow! Your
head is cut! Poor old fellow!
Tho. Never yo mind mo yed.
Col. G. You must go home.
Tho. Goo whoam, says to! Aw goo no-
wheers but to th' grave afoor aw've feawnd
mo chylt.
Col. G. Come along with me; I will do all
I can to find her. Perhaps I can help you
after all.
Tho. Aw mak nea deawbt o' that, mon.
And thae seems a gradely chap. Aw'm

a'most spent. An' aw'm sick, sick! Dunnot let th' boys shove mo abeawt again.

Col. G. I will not. They shan't come near you. Take my arm. Poor old fellow! If you would but trust me! Hey! Cab there!
Exeunt.

Enter SUSAN, *peeping.*

Sus. I wonder whatever's come to Mattie! It's long time she was out again.

Enter MATTIE, *hurriedly.*

Mat. Oh, Susan! Susan! (*Falls.*)
Sus. Mattie! Mattie! (*Kneels beside her, and undoes her bonnet.*)

Enter POLICEMAN.

Pol. What ails her? (*Goes to lift her.*)
Sus. Leave her alone, will you? Let her head down. Get some water.
Pol. Drunk—is she?
Sus. Hold your tongue, you brute! If she'd a satin frock on, i'stead o' this here poor cotton gownd, you'd ha' showed her t'other side o' your manners! Get away with you. You're too ugly to look at.—Mattie! Mattie! Look up, child.
Pol. She mustn't lie there.
Mat. Susan!
Pol. Come, my girl.

Sus. You keep off, I tell you! Don't touch her. She's none o' your sort. Come, Mattie, dear.—Why don't you make 'em move on?

Pol. You'd better keep a civil tongue in your head, young woman.

Sus. You live lobster!

Pol. I'll have to lock you up, I see. One violent. T'other incapable.

Sus. You're another. Mattie, my dear, come along home.

Pol. That's right; be off with you.

MATTIE *rises.*

Mat. Let's go, Sue! Let's get farther off.

Sus. You can't walk, child. If I hadn't been so short o' wittles for a week, I could ha' carried you. But it's only a step to the cook-shop.

Mat. No money, Sue. (*Tries to walk.*)

Sus. O Lord! What *shall* I do! And that blue-bottle there a buzzin' an' a starin' at us like a dead codfish!—Boh!

Enter BILL.

Bill. Our Mattie! Gracious! what's the row, Susan?

Sus. She ain't well. Take her other arm, Bill, and help her out o' this. We ain't in no Christian country. Pluck up, Mattie, dear.

Bill. Come into the tart-shop. I'm a customer.

They go towards the shop. Exit POLICEMAN.

Mat. No, no, Sukey! I can't abide the

smell of it. Let me sit on the kerb for a minute. (*Sits down.*) Oh, father! father!

Bill. Never you mind, Mattie! If he wor twenty fathers, he shan't come near ye.

Mat. Oh, Bill! if you could find him for me! He would take me home.

Bill. Now who'd ha' thought o' that? Axially wantin' her own father! I'd run far enough out o' the way o' mine—an' farther if he wur a-axin' arter me.

Mat. Oh me! my side!

Sus. It's hunger, poor dear! (*Sits down beside her.*)

Bill (*aside*). This won't do, Bill! I'm ashamed o' *you*, Bill!   *Exit.*

Mat. No, Susan, it's not hunger. It's the old story, Sue.

Sus. Mattie! I never! You don't mean to go for to tell me you're a breakin' of your precious heart about *him?* It's not your gentleman sure*ly*! It's not *him* ye're turnin' sick about, this time o' day?

MATTIE *nods her head listlessly.*

Sus. What's up fresh, then? You was pretty bobbish when you left me. It's little he thinks of *you*, I'll be bound.

Mat That's true enough. It's little he ever thought of me. He *did* say he loved me, though. It's fifty times he did!

Sus. Lies, lies, Mattie—all lies!

Mat. No, Susan; it wasn't lies. He meant it—at the time. That's what made it look all right. Oh dear! Oh dear!

Sus. But what's come to you now, Mattie? What's fresh in it? You're not turned like this all at once for nothink!

Mat. I've seen him!

Sus. Seen him! Oh, my! I wish it had been me. *I*'d ha' seen him! I'd ha' torn his ugly eyes out.

Mat. They ain't ugly eyes. They're big and blue, and they sparkle so when he talks to her!

Sus. And who's *her?* Ye didn't mention a *her.* Some brazen-faced imperence!

Mat. No. The young lady at Mrs. Clifford's.

Sus. Oho! See if I do a stitch for her! —Shan't I leave a needle in *her* shimmy, just!

Mat. What *shall* I do! All the good's gone out of me! And such a pain here!

Sus. Keep in yer breath a minute, an' push yer ribs out. It's one on 'em's got a top o' the other.

Mat. Such a grand creature! And her colour coming and going like the shadows on the corn! It's no wonder he forgot poor me. But it'll burn itself out afore long.

Sus. Don't ye talk like that, Mattie; I can't abear it.

Mat. If I was dressed like her, though, and could get my colour back! But laws! I'm *such* a washed out piece o' goods beside her!

Sus. That's as I say, Matilda! It's the dress makes the differ.

Mat. No, Susan, it ain't. It's the free

look of them—and the head up—and the white hands—and the taper fingers. They're stronger than us, and they're that trained like, that all their body goes in one, like the music at a concert. *I* couldn't pick up a needle without going down on my knees after it. It's the pain in my side, Sue.— Yes, it's a fine thing to be born a lady. It's *not* the clothes, Sue. If we was dressed ever so, we couldn't come near them. It's that look,—I don't know what.

Sus. Speak for yerself, Mattie; *I'*m not a goin' to think such small beer of *my*self, *I* can tell you! I believe if I'd been took in time——

Mat. It's a big *if* that though, Sue.—And then she looked *so* good ! You'd hardly think it of me,—perhaps it's because I'm dying— but for one minute I could ha' kissed her very shoes. Oh, my side !

Sus. (*putting her arm tight round her waist*). Does that help it Mattie, dear ?—a little teeny bit ?

Mat. Yes, Sukey. It holds it together a bit. Will he break her heart too, I wonder ?

Sus. No fear o' that ! Ladies takes care o' theirselves. They're brought up to it.

Mat. It's only poor girls gentlemen don't mind hurting, I suppose.

Sus. It's the ladies' fathers and brothers, Mattie ! We've got nobody to look after us.

Mat. They may break their hearts, though, for all that.

Sus They won't forgive them like you, then, Mattie!

Mat. I dare say they're much the same as we are when it comes to that, Sue.

Sus. Don't say *me*, Mattie. *I* wouldn't forgive him—no, not if I was to die for it. But what came of it, child?

Mat. I made some noise, I suppose, and the lady started.

Sus. And then you up and spoke?

Mat. I turned sick, and fell down.

Sus. Poor dear!

Mat. She got me a glass of wine, but I couldn't swallow it, and got up and crawled out.

Sus. Did he see you?

Mat. I think he did.

Sus. You'll tell her, in course?

Mat. No, Sue; he'd hate me, and I couldn't bear that. Oh me! my side! It's so bad!

Sus. Let's try for home, Mattie. It's a long way, and there's nothing to eat when you're there; but you can lie down, and that's everything to them as can't sit up.

Mat. (*rising*). I keep fancying I'm going to meet my father.

Sus. Let's fancy it then every turn all the way home, an' that'll get us along. There, take my arm. There!—Come along. *Exeunt.*

Slow music. Twilight.

Enter BILL *with a three-legged stool, brushes, etc.*

Bill. Come! it's blackin' all over! When

gents can't no longer see their boots, 'tain't much use offerin' to shine 'em. But if I can get a penny, I will. I *must* take a tart to Mattie, or this here damaged one (*laying his hand on his stomach*) won't go to sleep this night.

Enter WATERFIELD.

Bill. Black your boots for a party, sir?

Wat. (*aside*) The very rascal I saw her speaking to! But wasn't she a brick not to split! That's what I call devotion now! There *are* some of them capable of it. I'll set her up for life. I'd give a cool thousand it hadn't happened, though. I saw her father too hanging about Gervaise's yesterday.

Bill. Clean your boots, sir? Shine 'em till they grin like a Cheshire cat eatin' cheese!

Wat. Shine away, you beggar.

Bill (*turning up his trousers*). I ain't no beggar, sir. Shine for a shiner's fair play.

Wat. Do you live in this neighbourhood?

Bill. No, sir.

Wat. Where, then?

Bill (*feeling where a pocket should be*). I don't appear to 'ave a card about me, sir, but my address is Lamb's Court, Camomile Street —leastways I do my sleepin' not far off of it. I've lived there, what livin' I *have* done, sin' ever I wor anywheres as I knows on.

Wat. Do you happen to know a girl of the name of Pearson?

Bill. No, sir. I can't say as how I rec'lect the name. Is she a old girl or a young un?

Wat. You young liar! I saw you talking to her not two hours ago!

Bill. Did ye now, sir? That's odd, ain't it? Bless you! I talks to everybody. I ain't proud, sir.

Wat. Well, do you see this? (*holding up a sovereign*).

Bill. That's one o' them things what don't require much seein', sir. There! Bright as a butterfly! T'other twin, sir!

Wat. I'll give you this, if you'll do something for me—and another to that when the thing's done.

Bill. 'Tain't stealin', sir?

Wat. No.

Bill. Cos, you see, Mattie——

Wat. Who did you say?

Bill. Old Madge as lets the beds at tuppence a short night. 'Tain't stealin', you say, sir?

Wat. What do you take me for? I want you to find out for me where the girl Pearson lives—that's all.

Bill. (*snatching the sovereign and putting it in his mouth*). Now then, sir!—What's the young woman like?

Wat. Rather tall—thin—dark hair—large dark eyes—and long white hands. Her name's Matilda—Mattie Pearson—the girl you were talking to, I tell you, on this very spot an hour or two ago.

Bill (*dropping the sovereign, and stooping to find it*). Golly! it *is* our Mattie!

Wat. Shall you know her again?

Bill. Any boy as wasn't a hass would know his own grandmother by them spots. Besides, I remember sich a gal addressin' of me this mornin'. If you say her it was, I'll detect her for ye.

Wat. There's a good boy! What's your name?

Bill. Timothy, sir.

Wat. What else?

Bill. Never had no other—leastways as I knows on.

Wat. Well, Timothy—there's the other sov.—and it's yours the moment you take me to her. Look at it.

Bill. My eye!—Is she a square Moll, sir?

Wat. What do you mean by that?

Bill. Green you are, to be sure!—She ain't one as steals, or——

Wat. Not she. She's a sempstress—a needlewoman, or something of the sort.

Bill. And where shall I find *you*, sir?

Wat. Let me see:—to-morrow night—on the steps of St. Martin's Church—ten o'clock.

Bill. But if I don't find her? It may be a week—or a month—or——

Wat. Come whether you find her or not, and let me know.

Bill. All serene, sir! There you are, sir! Brush your trousers, sir?

Wat. No; leave 'em.—Don't forget now.

Bill. Honour bright, sir ! Not if I knows it, sir !

Wat. There's that other skid, you know.

Bill. All right, sir ! Anything more, sir ?

Wat. Damn your impudence ! Get along.

Exit. BILL *watches him into* MRS. CLIF-FORD'S.

Bill. Now by all the 'ungry gums of Arabiar, 'ere's a swell arter our Mattie !—A right rig'lar swell ! I knows 'em—soverings an' red socks. What's come to our Mattie ? 'Ere's Daddy Longlegs arter her, vith his penny and his blessin' ! an' 'ere's this 'ere mighty swell vith his soverings—an' his red socks ! An' she's 'ungry, poor gal !—This 'ere yellow-boy ?—I 'ain't got no faith in swells—no more 'n in Daddy Longlegses—I 'ain't !—S'posin' he wants to marry her ?—Not if I knows it. He ain't half good 'nough for *her*. Too many quids—goin' a flingin' on 'em about like buttons ! He's been a crackin' o' cribs—*he* has. I ain't a goin' to interduce our Mattie to no sich blokes as him. No fathers or lovyers for me—says I !—But this here pebble o' Paradise !—What's to be done wi' the cherub ? I can't tell *her* a lie about it, an' who'll break it up for a cove like me, lookin' jes' as if I'd been an' tarred myself and crep' through a rag-bag ! They'd jug me. An' what 'ud Mattie say then ? I wish I 'adn't 'a' touched it. I'm blowed if I don't toss it over a bridge !—Then the gent 'ain't **got the weight on his dunop out o' me. O**

Lord! what *shall* I do with it? I wish I'd
skied it in his face! I don't believe it's a
good un; I don't! (*Bites it.*) It do taste
wery nasty. It's nothin' better 'n a gilt
fardin'! Jes' what a cove might look for
from sich a swell! (*Goes to a street lamp and
examines it.*) Lor! there's a bobby! (*Exit.
Re-enter to the lamp.*) I wish the gen'leman
'ad guv me a penny. I can't do nothin' wi'
this 'ere quid. Vere am I to put it? I 'ain't
got no pocket, an' if I was to stow it in my
'tato-trap, I couldn't wag my red rag—an'
Mother Madge 'ud soon have me by the
chops. Nor I've got noveres to plant it.—O
Lor! it's all I've got, an' Madge lets nobody
go to bed without the tuppence. It's all up
with Bill—*for* the night!—Where's the odds!
—there's a first-class hotel by the river—The
Adelphi Arches, they calls it—where they'll
take me in fast enough, and I can go to sleep
with it in my cheek. Coves is past talkin' to
you there. Nobody as sees me in that 'ere
'aunt of luxury, 'ill take me for a millionaire
vith a skid in his mouth. 'Tain't a bit cold
to-night neither (*going*).—Vy do they say a
aunt of luxury? I s'pose acause she's wife to
my uncle.   *Exit.*

    *Slow music. The night passes. A police-
        man crosses twice.* THOMAS *crosses be-
        tween. Dawn.*

Re-enter BILL.

Bill. I'm hanged if this here blasted quid

ain't a burnin' of me like a red-hot fardin'!
I'm blest if I've slep' more 'n half the night.
I woke up oncet, with it a slippin' down red
lane. I wish I had swallered it. Then nobody 'd 'a' ast me vere I got it. I don't
wonder as rich coves turn out sich a bad lot.
I believe the devil's in this 'ere!

Knocks at MRS. CLIFFORD'S *door.* JAMES
opens. Is shutting it again. BILL *shoves
in his stool.*

Bill. Hillo, Blazes! where's your manners?
Is that the way you behaves to callers on
your gov'nor's business?

James (*half opening the door*). Get about
your own business, you imperent boy!

Bill. I'm about it now, young man. I
wants to see your gov'nor.

James. *You*'ve got business with *him*, have
you, eh?

Bill. Amazin' precoxity! You've hit it!
I *have* got business with *him*, Door-post—not
in the wery smallest with *you*, Door-post!—
essep' the knife-boy's been and neglected of
your feet-bags this mornin'. (JAMES *would
slam the door.* BILL *shoves in his stool.*) Don't
you try that 'ere little game again, young
man! for if I loses my temper and takes to
hollerin', you'll wish yourself farther.

James. A humbug you are! I 'ain't got
no gov'nor, boy. The master as belongs to
me is a mis'ess.

Bill. Then that 'ere gen'lemen as comes
an' goes, ain't your master—eh?

James. What gen'leman, stoopid?

Bill. Oh! it don't matter.

James. What *have—you—got* to say to
him?

Bill. Some'at pickled : it'll keep.

James. I'll give him a message, if you
like.

Bill. Well, you may tell him the bargain's
hoff, and if he wants his money, it's a waitin'
of him round the corner.

James. You little blackguard! Do you
suppose a gen'leman's a goin' to deliver sich
a message as that! Be off, you himp! (*Makes
a dart at him.*)

Bill (*dodging him*). How d'e do, Clumsy?
Don't touch me; I ain't nice. Why, what
was you made for, Parrot? Is them calves
your own rearin' now? Is that a quid or a
fardin? Have a shot, now, Shins.

James. None o' your imperence, young
blackie! 'And me over the money, and I'll
give it to the gen'leman.

Bill. Do you see anything peticlar green
in my eye, Rainbow?

JAMES *makes a rush.* BILL *gets down before
him.* JAMES *tumbles over him.* BILL
blacks his face with his brush.

Bill (*running a little way*). Ha! ha! ha!
Bill Shoeblack—his mark! Who's blackie
now? You owes me a penny—twopence—
'twor sich a ugly job! Ain't shiny? I'll
come back and shine ye for another penny.
Good mornin', Jim Crow! Take my adwice,

and don't on no account apply your winegar
afore you've opened your hoyster. Likeways :
Butter don't melt on a cold tater.　　*Exit.*
Exit JAMES *into the house, banging the door.*

Enter WATERFIELD, *followed by* BILL.

Bill. Please, sir, I been a watchin' for you.
Wat. Go to the devil !
Bill. I'd rayther not. So there's your suv'-
ring !
Wat. Go along.　　Meet me where I told
you.
Bill. I won't.　　There's yer skid.
Wat. Be off, or I'll give you in charge.
Hey !　Policeman !　　　　　　　　　*Exit.*
Bill. Well, I'm blowed ! This quid 'll be
the hangin' o' me ! *Damn you !* (*Throws it
fiercely on the ground and stamps on it.*) Serves
me right for chaffin' the old un ! He didn't
look a bad sort—*for* a gov'nor.—Now I re-
flexes, I heerd Mattie spoony on some father
or other, afore. O Lord ! I'll get Jim and
Jack to help me look out for him. (*Enter*
THOMAS.) Lor' ha' mussy !—talk o' the old
un !—I'm wery peticlar glad as I found you,
daddy.　I been a lookin' for ye—leastways I
was a goin' to look for ye this wery moment as
you turns up. I chaffed you like a zorologicle
monkey yesterday, daddy, an' I'm wery
sorry. But you see fathers ain't nice i' this
'ere part o' the continent. (*Enter* JAMES,
in plain clothes, watching them.) They ain't

no good nohow to nobody. If *I* wos a husband and a father, I don't know as how I should be A One, myself. P'r'aps I might think it wur my turn to break arms and legs. I knowed more 'n one father as did. It's no wonder the boys is a plaguy lot, daddy.

Tho. Goo away, boy. Dosto yer, aw've seen so mich wickedness sin' aw coom to Lon'on, that aw dunnot knaw whether to breighk thi yed, or to goo wi' tho? There be thieves and there be robbers.

Bill. Never fear, daddy. You ain't worth robbin' of, I don't think.

Tho. How dosto knaw that? Aw've moore 'n I want to lose abeawt mo.

Bill. Then Mattie 'ill have som'at to eat—will she, daddy?

Tho. Som'at to eight, boy! Be mo Mattie hungry—dun yo think?

Bill. Many and many's the time, daddy.

Tho. Yigh—afore her dinner!

Bill. And after it too, daddy.

Tho. O Lord!—And what does hoo do when hoo 's hungry?

Bill. Grins and bears it. Come and see her, daddy?

Tho. O Lord! Mo Mattie, an' nothin' to eight! Goo on, boy. Aw'm beawn to follow yo. Tak mo wheer yo like. Aw'll goo.

Bill. Come along then, daddy.

James (collaring him). Hullo, young un!

You're the rascal as stole the suvering : *I* saw you!

Bill. Dunno what you're up to. I never stole nothink.

James. Oh no! of course not! What's that in yer fist now? (*Catches* BILL'S *hand, and forces it open.*) There!

BILL *drops his stool on* JAMES'S *foot, throws up the coin, catches it with his other hand, and puts it in his mouth.*

Tho. Theighur! Theighur! The like ov that! Aw're agooin wi' a thief—aw wur!

Bill. Never you mind, daddy. It wur guv to me.

James. That's what they allus says, sir.— You come along.—I'd be obliged to you, sir, if you would come too, and say you saw him.

Tho. Nay! aw connot say aw seigh him steyle it.

James. You saw it in his hand.

Tho. Yigh! aw did.

Bill. It was guv to me, I tell ye.

James. Honest boy, this one! Looks like it, don't he, sir? What do you think of yourself, you young devil, a decoying of a grey-haired old gen'leman like this? Why, sir, him an' his pals 'ud ha' taken every penny you had about you! Murdered you, they might—I've knowed as much. It's a good thing I 'appened on the spot.—Come along, you bad boy!

Bill. I didn't take it. And I won't go.

James. Come along. They'll change it for you at the lock-up.

Bill. You didn't see me steal it! You ain't never a goin' to gi' me in charge?

James. Wrong again, young un! That's percisely what I *am* a goin' to do!

Bill. Oh, sir! please, sir! I'm a honest boy. It's the Bible-truth. I'll kiss twenty books on it.

James. I won't ax you.—Why, sir, he ain't even one o' the shoe-brigade. He 'ain't got a red coat. Bless my soul! he 'ain't even got a box—nothin' but a scrubby pair o' brushes —as I'm alive! *He* ain't no shoeblack. He's a thief as purtends to black shoes, and picks pockets.

Bill. You're a liar! I never picked a pocket in my life.

James. Bad language, you see! What more would you have?

Tho. Who'd iver ha' thowt o' sich wickedness in a boy like that!

Bill. I ain't a wicked boy.

Tho. Nay, doan't thae tell mo that! Thae made gam of mo, and hurried and scurried mo, as iv aw'd been a mak ov a deevil—yo did.

James. He's one of the worst boys I know. This Timothy is one of the very worst boys in all London.

Bill (*aside*). *Timothy*, eh? I twigs! It's Rainbow, by Peter and Paul!—Look ye here, old gen'leman! This 'ere's a bad cove as is takin' adwantage o' your woolliness. *I* knows him. His master guv me the suvering. He guv it to me to tell him where your Mattie was.

James. Don't you fancy you're goin' to take in an experienced old gen'leman like that with your cock-and-bull stories! Come along, I say. Hey! Police!

Bill. Here you are! (*Takes the coin from his mouth, rubs it dry on his jacket, and offers it.*) *I* don't want it. Give it to old Hunx there.—*He* shan'+ never see his Mattie! I wur right to chivy him, arter all.

James (*taking the coin*). Now look here, Timothy. I'm a detective hofficer. But I won't never be hard on no boy as wants to make a honest livin'. So you be hoff! I'll show the old gen'leman where he wants to go to.

BILL *moves two paces, and takes a sight at him.*

Tho. The Lord be praised! Dosto know eawr Mattie then?

James. It's the dooty of a detective hofficer to know every girl in his beat.

Bill. My eye! there's a oner!

Tho. Tak mo to her, sir, an' aw'll pray for yo.

James. I will.—If I cotch you nearer than Mile End, I'll give you in charge *at oncet.*

Bill (*bolting five yards*). He's a humbug, daddy! but he'll serve *you* right. He'll melt you down for taller. He ain't no 'tective. *I* know him.

Tho. Goo away.

Bill. Good-bye, daddy! *He* don't know your Mattie. Good-bye, skelington!   *Exit.*

Tho. Eh! sech a boy!

James. Let me see. You want a girl of the name of Mattie?

Tho. Aw do, sir.

James. The name is not an oncommon one. There's Mattie Kent?

Tho. Nay; it's noan o' her.

James. Then there's Mattie Winchfield?

Tho. Nay; it's noan o' her.

James. Then there's Mattie Pearson?

Tho. Yigh, that's hoo!   That's hoo! Wheer?   Wheer?

James. Well, it's too far for a man of your age to walk. But I'll call a cab, and we'll go comfortable.

Tho. But aw connot affoord to peigh for a cab—as yo co it.

James. You don't suppose I'm a goin' to put an honest man like you to expense!

Tho. It's but raysonable I should peigh. But thae knows best.

James. Hey!   Cab there!   *Exeunt.*

Re-enter BILL, *following them.*

Bill. I'll have an eye of him, though. The swell as give me the yellow-boy—he's his master! Poor old codger! He'll believe any **cove** but the one as tells him the truth!

Exit.

Enter from the house MRS. CLIFFORD. *Enter from opposite side* COL. G.

Col. G. I was just coming to see you, Clara.

Mrs. C. And I was going to see you. How's Arthur to-day? I thought you would have come yesterday.

Col. G. My poor boy is as dependent on me as if I were *not* his father. I am very anxious about him. The fever keeps returning.

Mrs. C. Fortune seems to have favoured your mad scheme, Walter.

Col. G. Or something better than fortune.

Mrs. C. You have had rare and ample opportunity. You may end the farce when you please, and in triumph.

Col. G. On the contrary, Clara, it would be nothing but an anticlimax to end what you are pleased to call *the farce* now. As if I could make a merit of nursing my own boy! I did more for my black servant. I wish I had him here.

Mrs. C. You would like to double the watch—would you?

Col. G. Something has vexed you, Clara.

Mrs. C. I never liked the scheme, and I like it less every day.

Col. G. I have had no chance yet. He has been ill all the time. I wish you would come and see him a little oftener.

Mrs. C. He doesn't want me. You are everything now. Besides, I can't come alone.

Col. G. Why not?

Mrs. C. Constance would fancy I did not want to take her.

Col. G. Then why not take her?

Mrs. C. I have my reasons.

Col. G. What are they?

Mrs. C. Never mind.

Col. G. I insist upon knowing them.

Mrs. C. It would break my heart, Walter, to quarrel with you, but I *will* if you use such an expression.

Col. G. But why shouldn't you bring Miss Lacordère with you?

Mrs. C. He's but a boy, and it might put some nonsense in his head.

Col. G. She's a fine girl. You make a friend of her.

Mrs. C. She's a good girl, and a lady-like girl; but I don't want to meddle with the bulwarks of society. I hope to goodness they will last *my* time.

Col. G. Clara, I begin to doubt whether pride *be* a Christian virtue.

Mrs. C. I see! You'll be a radical before long. *Every*thing is going that way.

Col. G. I don't care what I am, so I do what's right. I'm sick of all that kind of thing. What I want is bare honesty. I believe I'm a tory as yet, but I should be a radical to-morrow if I thought justice lay on that side.—If a man falls in love with a woman, why shouldn't he marry her?

Mrs. C. She may be unfit for him.

Col. G. How should he fall in love with her, then? Men don't fall in love with birds.

Mrs. C. It's a risk—a great risk.

Col. G. None the greater that he pleases himself, and all the more worth taking. I wish my poor boy——

Mrs. C. Your poor boy might please himself and yet not succeed in pleasing you, brother!

Col. G. (*aside*). She *knows* something.—I must go and see about his dinner. Good-bye, sister.

Mrs. C. Good-bye, then. You *will* have your own way!

Col. G. This once, Clara. *Exeunt severally.*

END OF ACT II.

ACT III.

SCENE.—*A garret-room.* MATTIE. SUSAN.

Mat. At the worst we've got to die some day, Sue, and I don't know but hunger may be as easy a way as another.

Sus. I'd rather have a choice, though. And it's not hunger I would choose.

Mat. There are worse ways.

Sus. Never mind : we don't seem likely to be bothered wi' choosin'.

Mat. There's that button-hole done. (*Lays down her work with a sigh, and leans back in her chair.*)

Sus. I'll take it to old Nathan. It'll be a chop a-piece. It's wonderful what a chop can do to hearten you up.

Mat. I don't think we ought to buy chops, dear. We must be content with bread, I think.

Sus. Bread, indeed!

Mat. Well, it's something to eat.

Sus. Do you call it eatin' when you see a dog polishin' a bone?

Mat. Bread's very good with a cup of tea.

Sus. Tea, indeed! Fawn-colour, trimmed with sky-blue!—If you'd mentioned lobster-salad and sherry, now!

Mat. I never tasted lobster-salad.

Sus. I have, though ; and I do call lobster-salad good. You don't care about your wittles : *I* do. When I'm hungry, I'm not at all comfortable.

Mat. Poor dear Sue! There is a crust in the cupboard.

Sus. I *can't* eat crusts. I want summat nice. I ain't dyin' of 'unger. It's only I'm peckish. *Very* peckish, though. I could eat —let me see what I *could* eat :—I could eat a lobster-salad, and two dozen oysters, and a lump of cake, and a wing and a leg of a chicken—if it was a spring chicken, with watercreases round it—and a Bath-bun, and a sandwich ; and in fact I don't know what I couldn't eat, except just that crust in the cupboard. And I do believe I could drink a whole bottle of champagne.

Mat. I don't know what one of those things tastes like—scarce one ; and I don't believe you do either.

Sus. Don't I ?—I never did taste champagne, but I've seen them eating lobster-salad many a time ;—girls not half so good-lookin' as you or me, Mattie, and fine gentlemen a waitin' upon 'em. Oh dear! I *am* so hungry! Think of having your supper with a real gentleman as talks to you as if you was fit to talk to—not like them Jew-tailors, as tosses your work about as if it dirtied their fingers—and them none so clean for all their fine rings !

Mat. I saw Nathan's Joseph in a pastry-cook's last Saturday, and a very pretty girl with him, poor thing!

Sus. Oh the hussy to let that beast pay for her!

Mat. I suppose she was hungry.

Sus. I'd die before I let a snob like that treat *me*. No, Mattie! I spoke of a *real* gentleman.

Mat. Are you sure you wouldn't take Nathan's Joseph for a gentleman if he was civil to you?

Sus. Thank you, miss! I know a sham from a real gentleman the moment I set eyes on him.

Mat. What do you mean by a real gentleman, Susan?

Sus. A gentleman as makes a lady of his girl.

Mat. But what sort of lady, Sue? The poor girl may fancy herself a lady, but only till she's left in the dirt. That sort of gentleman makes fine speeches to your face, and calls you horrid names behind your back. Sue, dear, don't have a word to say to one of them—if he speaks ever so soft.

Sus. Lawks, Mattie! they ain't all one sort.

Mat. *You* won't have more than one sort to choose from. They may be rough or civil, good-natured or bad, but they're all the same in this, that not one of them cares a pin more for you than if you was a horse—no—nor half a quarter so much. Don't for God's sake have a word to say to one of them. If I die, Susan——

Sus. If you do, Matilda—if you go and do that thing, I'll take to gin—that's what I'll do. Don't say I didn't act fair, and tell you beforehand.

Mat. How can I help dying, Susan?

Sus. I say, Don't do it, Mattie. We'll fall out, if you do. Don't do it, Matilda—La! there's that lumping Bill again—*al*ways a comin' up the stair when you don't want him!

Enter BILL.

Mat. Well, Bill, how have you been getting on?

Bill. Pretty tollol, Mattie. But I can't go on so. (*Holds out his stool.*) It ain't respectable.

Mat. What ain't respectable? Everything's respectable that's honest.

Bill. Why, who ever saw a respectable shiner goin' about with a three-legged stool for a blackin' box? It ain't the thing. The rig'lars chaffs me fit to throw it at their 'eads, they does—only there's too many on 'em, an' I've got to dror it mild. A box I must have, or a feller's ockypation's gone. Look ye here! One bob, one tanner, and a joey! There! that's what comes of never condescending to an 'a'penny.

Sus. Bless us! what mighty fine **words** we've got a waitin' on us!

Bill. If I 'ave a weakness, Miss Susan, it's for the right word in the right place—as the coster said to the devil-dodger as blowed him up for purfane swearin'.—When a gen'leman hoffers me an 'a'penny, I axes him in the purlitest manner I can assume, to oblige me by givin' of it to the first beggar he may 'ave the good fort'n to meet. *Some* on 'em throws down the 'a'penny. Most on 'em makes it a penny.—But I say, Mattie, you don't want nobody arter you—do you now?

Mat. I don't know what you mean by that, Bill.

Bill. You don't want a father—do you now? Do she, Susan?

Sus. We want no father a hectorin' here, Bill. You 'ain't seen one about, have you?

Bill. I seen a rig'lar swell arter Mattie, anyhow.

Mat. What *do* you mean, Bill?

Bill. A rig'lar swell—I repeats it—a astin' arter a young woman by the name o' Mattie.

Sus. (*pulling him aside*). Hold your tongue, Bill! You'll kill her! You young viper! Hold your tongue, or I'll twist your neck. Don't you see how white she is?

Mat. What was he like? Do tell me, Bill.

Bill. A long-legged rig'lar swell, with a gold chain, and a cane with a hivory 'andle.

Sus. He's a bad man, Bill, and Mattie

can't abide him. If you tell him where she is, she'll never speak to you again.

Mat. Oh, Susan! what *shall* I do? Don't bring him here, Bill. I shall have to run away again; and I can't, for we owe a week's rent.

Sus. There, Bill!

Bill. Don't you be afeard, Mattie. He shan't touch you. Nor the old one neither.

Mat. There wasn't an old man with him? —not an old man with a long stick?

Bill. Not with *him*. Daddy was on his own hook?

Mat. It must have been my father, Susan. (*Sinks back on her chair.*)

Sus. 'Tain't the least likely.—There, Bill! I always said you was no good! You've killed her.

Bill. Mattie! Mattie! I didn't tell him where you was.

Mat. (*reviving*). Run and fetch him, Bill— there's a dear! Oh! how proud I've been! If mother did say a hard word, she didn't mean it —not for long. Run, Bill, run and fetch him.

Bill. Mattie, I was a fetchin' of him, but he wouldn't trust me. And didn't he cut up crusty, and collar me tight! He's a game old cock—he is, Mattie.

Mat. (*getting up and pacing about the room*). Oh, Susan! my heart 'll break. To think he's somewhere near and I can't get to him! Oh my side! *Don't* you know where he is, Bill?

Bill. He's someveres about, and blow me

if I don't find him!—a respectable old party
in a white pinny, an' 'peared as if he'd go on
a walkin' till he walked hisself up standin'.
A scrumptious old party!

Mat. Had he a stick, Bill?

Bill. Yes—a knobby stick—leastways a
stick wi' knobs all over it.

Mat. That's him, Susan!

Bill. I could swear to the stick. I was too
near gittin' at the taste on it not to know it
again.

Mat. When was it you saw him, Bill?

Bill. Yesterday, Mattie—jest arter you
give me the tart. I sawr him again this
mornin', but he wouldn't place no confidence
in me.

Mat. Oh dear! Why didn't you come
straight to me, Bill?

Bill. If I'd only ha' known as you wanted
him! But that was sech a *un*likely thing!
It's werry perwokin'! I uses my judgment,
an' puts my hoof in it! I *am* sorry, Mattie.
But I didn't know no better (*crying*).

Mat. Don't cry, Bill. You'll find him for
me yet—won't you?

Bill. I'm off this indentical minute. But
you see——

Sus. There! **there**!—now you mizzle. *I*
don't want no fathers here — goodness
knows; but the poor girl's took a fancy to
hers, and she'll die if she don't get him.
Run now—there's a good boy! (*Exit* BILL.)
You 'ain't forgotten who's a comin', Mattie?

Mat. No, indeed.

Sus. Well, I hope she'll be civil, or I'll just give her a bit of my mind.

Mat. Not enough to change hers, I'm afraid. That sort of thing never does any good.

Sus. And am I to go a twiddlin' of my thumbs, and sayin' *yes, ma'am,* an' *no, ma'am?* Not if I knows it, Matilda!

Mat. You will only make her the more positive in her ill opinion of us.

Sus. An' what's that to me?

Mat. Well, I don't like to be thought a thief. Besides, Mrs. Clifford has been kind to us.

Sus. She's paid us for work done; so has old Nathan.

Mat. Did old Nathan ever give you a glass of wine when you took home his slops?

Sus. Oh! that don't cost much; and besides, she takes it out in kingdom-come.

Mat. You're unfair, Susan.

Sus. Well, it's little fairness I get.

Mat. And to set that right you're unfair yourself! What you call speaking your mind, is as cheap, and as nasty, as the worst shoddy old Nathan ever got gobble-stitched into coats and trousers.

Sus. Very well, Miss Matilda! (*rising and snatching her bonnet*). The sooner we part the better! You stick by your fine friends! I don't care *that* for them! (*snapping her fingers*)—and you may tell 'em so! I can

make a livin' without them or you either.
Goodness gracious knows it ain't much of
a livin' I've made sin' I come across *you*,
Miss!   *Exit.*

Mat. (*trying to rise*). Susan! Susan!
(*Lays her head on the table*).

A tap at the door, and enter MRS. CLIFFORD,
with JAMES *behind.* MATTIE *rises.*

Mrs. C. Wait on the landing, James.

James. Yes, ma'am.

Exit JAMES, *leaving the door a little ajar.*

Mrs. C. Well, Miss Pearson! (*Mattie offers
a chair.*) No, thank you. That person is
still with you, I see!

Mat. Indeed, ma'am, she's an honest girl.

Mrs. C. She is a low creature, and capable
of anything. I advise you to get rid of her.

Mat. Was she rude on the stair, ma'am?

Mrs. C. Rude! Vulgar—quite vulgar!
Insulting!

Mat. I am very sorry. But, believe me,
ma'am, she is an honest girl, and never
pawned that work. It was done—every
stitch of it; and the loss of the money is
hard upon us too. Indeed, ma'am, she did
lose the parcel.

Mrs. C. You have only her word for it.
If you don't give *her* up, I give *you* up.

Mat. I can't, ma'am. She might go into
bad ways if I did.

Mrs. C. She can't well get into worse.

Her language! You would do ever so much better without her.

Mat. I daren't, ma'am. I should never get it off my conscience.

Mrs. C. Your conscience indeed! (*rising*). I wish you a good morning, Miss Pearson. —(*Sound of a blow, followed by scuffling.*)— What is that? I fear I have got into an improper place.

Susan *bursts in.*

Sus. Yes, ma'am, and that you have! It's a *wery* improper place for the likes o' you, ma'am—as believes all sorts o' wicked things of people as is poor. Who are you to bring your low flunkies a-listenin' at honest girls' doors! (*Turning to James in the doorway.*) Get out, will you? Let me catch you here again, and I'll mark you that the devil wouldn't know his own! You dirty Paul Pry—you! (*Falls on her knees to Mattie.*) Mattie, you angel!

Mat. (*trying to make her get up*) Never mind. It's all right between you and me, Susan.

Mrs. C. I see! I thought as much!

Sus. (*starting up*) As much as what, then, my lady? Oh, *I* know you and your sort— well enough! We're the dirt under your feet—lucky if we stick to your shoes! But this room's mine.

Mrs. C. That linen was mine, young woman, I believe.

Sus. An' it's for that miserable parcel you come a-talkin', an' abusin' as no lady ought to! How dare you look that angel in the face there an' say she stole it—which you're not fit to lace her boots for her! There!

Mat. Susan! Susan! do be quiet.

Sus. It's all very well for the likes o' me (*courtesying spitefully*)—which I'm no better'n I should be, and a great deal worse, if I'm on my oath to your ladyship—that's neither here nor there!—but *she's* better'n a van-load o' sich ladies as you, pryin' into other people's houses, with yer bibles, an' yer religion, an' yer flunkies! *I* know ye! I *do!*

Mat. Don't, Susan.

Sus. Why don't ye go an' pay twopence a week to somebody to learn ye good manners? I been better brought up myself.

Mrs. C. I see I was wrong: I ought at once to have handed the matter over to the police.

Sus. The perlice, indeed!—You get out of this, ma'am, or I'll make you!—you and your cowardly man-pup there, as is afraid to look me in the face through the crack o' the door! Get out, I say, with your—*in-solence*—that's your word!

Exit MRS. CLIFFORD.

Mat. Susan! Susan! what is to become of us?

Sus. She daren't do it—the old scrooge! But just let her try it on! See if I don't show her up afore the magistrate! Mattie!

I'll work my fingers to the bone for you. I would do worse, only you won't let me. I'll go to the court, and tell the magistrate you're a-dyin' of hunger, which it's as true as gospel.

Mat. They'd send me to the workhouse, Sukey.

Sus. There *must* be some good people somewheres, Mattie.

Mat. Yes; if we could get at them. But we can live till we die, Sukey.

Sus. I'll go and list for a soldier, I will. Women ha' done it afore. It's quite respectable, so long as they don't find you out —and they shouldn't me. There's ne'er a one o' the redcoats 'ill cut up rougher 'n I shall—barrin' the beard, and *that* don't go for much now-a-days.

Mat. And what should I do without you, Susan ?

Sus. Do you care to have me, then ?

Mat. That I do, indeed. But you shouldn't have talked like that to Mrs. Clifford. Ladies ain't used to such words. They sound worse than they are—quite dreadful, to them. She don't know your kind heart as I do. Besides, the *look* of things is against us. Ain't it now ? Say yourself.

Sus. (*starting up*) I'll go and beg her pardon. I'll go direckly—I will. I swear I will. I can't abear her, but I'll do it. I believe hunger has nigh drove me mad.

Mat. It takes all the madness out of me,—

No, Susan; we must bear it now. Come along. We can be miserable just as well working. There's your sleeve. I'll thread your needle for you. Don't cry—there's a dear!

Sus. I *will* cry. It's all I ever could do to my own mind, and it's all as is left me. But if I could get my claws on that lovyer o' yours, I wouldn't cry then. *He's* at the bottom of it! I don't see myself what's the use of fallin' in love. One man's as much of a fool as another to me. But you must go to bed. You ain't fit. You'll be easier when you've got your frock off. There! Why, child, you're all of a tremble!—And no wonder, wi' nothing on her blessed body but her frock and her shimmy!

Mat. Don't take off my frock, Sue. I must get on with my work.

Sus. Lie down a bit, anyhow. I'll lie at your back, and you'll soon be as warm's a toast. (MAT. *lies down.*) O Lord! she's dead! Her heart's stopped beatin'. (*Runs out of the room.*)

    A moment of silence. A tap at the door. CONSTANCE *peeps in, then enters, with a basket.*

Con. Miss Pearson!—She's asleep. (*Goes near.*) Good heavens! (*Lays her hand on her.*) No. (*Takes a bottle from her basket, finds a cup, and pours into it.*) Take this,

Miss Pearson; it will do you good. There now! You'll find something else in the basket.

Mat. I don't want anything. I had so nearly got away! Why did you bring me back?

Con. Life is good!

Mat. It is *not* good. How dare you do it? Why keep a miserable creature alive? Life ain't to us what it is to you. The grave is the only place *we* have any right to.

Con. If I could make your life worth something to you——

Mat. *You* make my life worth to me! You don't know what you're saying, miss. (*Sitting up.*)

Con. I think I do.

Mat. I will *not* owe my life to you. I *could* love you, though—your hands are so white, and your look so brave. That's what comes of being born a lady. *We* never have a chance.

Cow. Miss Pearson—Mattie, I would call you, if you wouldn't be offended——

Mat. Me offended, miss!—I've not got life enough for it. I only want my father and my mother, and a long sleep.—If I had been born rich——

Con. You might have been miserable all the same. Listen, Mattie. I will tell you *my* story—I was once as badly off as you— worse in some ways—ran about the streets without shoes to my feet, and hardly a frock to cover me.

Mat. La, miss! you don't say so! It's not possible! Look at you!

Con. Indeed, I tell you the truth. I know what hunger is too—-well enough. My father was a silkweaver in Spitalfields. When he died, I didn't know where to go. But a gentleman—

Mat. Oh! a gentleman!—(*Fiercely.*) Why couldn't you be content with *one*, then?

Con. I don't understand you.

Mat. I dare say not! There! take your basket. I'll die afore a morsel passes *my* lips. There! Go away, miss.

Con. (*aside*). Poor girl! she is delirious. I must ask William to fetch a doctor.   *Exit.*

Mat. I wish my hands were as white as hers.

Enter SUSAN, *followed by* COL. G. CONSTANCE *behind.*

Sus. Mattie! dear Mattie! this gentleman —don't be vexed—I couldn't help him bein' a gentleman; I was cryin' that bad, and I didn't see no one come up to me, and when he spoke to me, it made me jump, and I couldn't help answerin' of him—he spoke so civil and soft like, and me nigh mad! I thought you was dead, Mattie. He says he'll see us righted, Mattie.

Col. G. I'll do what I can, if you will tell me what's amiss.

Sus. Oh, everything's amiss—everything!

—Who was that went out, Mattie—this
minute—as we come in ?

Mat. Miss Lacordère.

Sus. Her imperence! Well! I should die
of shame if I was her.

Mat. She's an angel, Susan. There's her
basket. I told her to take it away, but she
would leave it.

Sus. (*peeping into the basket*). Oh, my!
Ain't this nice? You *must* have a bit,
Mattie.

Mat. Not one mouthful. You wouldn't
have me, Susan !

Sus. *I* ain't so peticlar (*eating a great
mouthful*). You really must, Mattie. (*Goes
on eating.*)

Col. G. Don't tease her. We'll get something for her presently. And don't you eat
too much—all at once.

Sus. I think she'd like a chop, sir.—
There's that boy, Bill, again !—Always when
he ain't wanted !

Enter BILL.

Bill (*aside to Susan*). What's the row ?
What's that 'ere gent up to? I've been an'
had enough o' gents. They're a bad lot. I
been too much for one on 'em, though. I ha'
run *him* down.—And, Mattie, I've found the
old gen'leman.

Mat. My father, Bill ?

Bill. That's it percisely ! Right as a
trivet—he is !

Mat. Susan! take hold of me. My heart's going again.

Bill. Lord! what's up wi' Mattie? She *do* look dreadful.

Sus. You been an' upset her, you clumsy boy! Here—run and fetch a sausage or two, and a——

Col. G. No, no! That will never do.

Sus. Them's for Bill and me, sir. I was a goin' on, sir.—And, Bill, a chop—a nice chop. But Lord! how are we to cook it, with never a fryin'-pan, or a bit o' fire to set it on!

Col. G. You'd never think of doing a chop for an invalid in the frying-pan?

Sus. Certainly not, sir—we 'ain't got one. Everything's up the spout an' over the top. Run, Bill. A bit of cold chicken, and two pints o' bottled stout. There's the money the gen'leman give me.—'T 'ain't no Miss Lackodare's, Mattie.

Bill. I'll trouble no gen'leman to perwide for *my* family—obleeged all the same, sir. Mattie never wos a dab at dewourin', but I'll get her some'at toothsome. I favours grub myself.

Col. G. I'll go with you, Bill. I want to talk to you.

Bill. Well, I 'ain't no objection—so be you wants to talk friendly, sir.

Col. G. Good night. I'll come and see you to-morrow.

Sus. God bless you, sir. You've saved both on our lives. I *was* a goin' to drown myself, Mattie—I really was this time. Wasn't I, sir?

Col. G. Well, you looked like it—that is all I can say. You shall do it next time—so far as I'm concerned.

Sus. I won't never no more again, sir—not if Mattie don't drive me to it.

Con. (*to* Col. G.). Come back for me in a little while.

Col. G. Yes, miss. Come, Bill. *Exit.*

Bill. All right, sir. I'm a follerin', as the cat said to the pigeon. *Exit.*

Sus. I'll just go and get you a cup o' tea. Mrs. Jones's kettle's sure to be a bilin'. That's what you would like.

Exit. Constance steps aside, and Susan passes without seeing her.

Mat. Oh! to be a baby again in my mother's arms! But it'll soon be over now.

CONSTANCE *comes forward.*

Con. I hope you're a little better now?

Mat. You're very kind, miss; and I beg your pardon for speaking to you as I did.

Con. Don't say a word about it. You didn't quite know what you were saying. I'm in trouble myself. I don't know how soon I may be worse off than you.

Mat. Why, miss, I thought you were going to be married!

Con. No, I am not.

Mat. Why, miss, what's happened. He's never going to play *you* false—is he ?

Con. I don't mean ever to speak to him again ?

Mat. What has he done to offend you, miss ?

Con. Nothing.   Only I know now I don't like him.   To tell you the truth, Mattie, he's not a gentleman.

Mat. Not a gentleman, miss !   How dare you say so ?

Con. Do *you* know anything about him ? Did you ever see him ?

Mat. Yes.

Con. Where ?

Mat. Once at your house.

Con. Oh ! I remember—that time ! I begin to—— It couldn't be at the sight of him you fainted, Mattie ?—You knew him ?   Tell me ! tell me !   Make me sure of it.

Mat. To give you your revenge ! No. It's a mean spite to say he ain't a gentleman.

Con. Perhaps you and I have different ideas of what goes to make a gentleman.

Mat. Very likely.

Con. Oh ! don't be vexed, Mattie.   I didn't mean to hurt you.

Mat. Oh ! I dare say !

Con. If you talk to me like that, I must go.

Mat. I never asked you to come.

Con. Well, I did want to be friendly with you.   I wouldn't hurt you for the world.

Mat. (*bursting into tears*)   I beg your pardon, miss.   I'm behaving like a brute.

But you must forgive me; my heart is breaking.

Con. Poor dear! (*kissing her*) So is mine almost. Let us be friends. Where's Susan gone?

Mat. To fetch me a cup of tea. She'll be back directly.

Con. Don't let her say bad words: I can't bear them. I think it's because I was so used to them once—in the streets, I mean—not at home—never at home.

Mat. She don't often, miss. She's a good-hearted creature. It's only when hunger makes her cross. She don't like to be hungry.

Con. I should think not, poor girl!

Mat. Don't mind what she says, please. If you say nothing, she'll come all right. When she's spoken her mind, she feels better. Here she comes!

Re-enter SUSAN. *It begins to grow dark.*

Sus. Well, and who have we got here?

Mat. Miss Lacordère, Sukey.

Sus. There's no lack o' dare about *her*, to come here!

Mat. It's very kind of her to come, Susan.

Sus. I tell you what, miss: that parcel was stole. It *was* stole, miss!—stole from me—an' that angel there a dyin' in the street!

Con. I'm quite sure of it, Susan. I never thought anything else.

Sus. Not but I allow it was a pity, miss!—
I'm very sorry. But, bless you! (*lighting a
candle*)—with all *your* fine clothes——! My!
you look like a theayter-queen—you do, miss!
If you was to send *them* up the spout now!—
My! what a lot they'd let you have on that
silk!

Con. The shawl is worth a good deal, I
believe. It's an Indian one—all needlework.

Sus. And the bee-utiful silk! Laws, miss!
just shouldn't I like to wear a frock like that!
I *should* be hard up before I pledged *that!*
But the shawl! If I was you, miss, I would
send 'most everything up before that!—
things inside, you know, miss—where it don't
matter so much.

Con. (*laughing*) The shawl would be the
first thing I should part with. I would
rather be nice inside than out.

Sus. Lawk, miss! I shouldn't wonder if
that was one of the differs now! Well, I
never! It ain't seen! It *must* be one o' the
differs!

Con. What differs? I don't understand
you.

Sus. The differs 'tween girls an' ladies—
girls like me an' real ladies like you.

Con. Oh, I see! But how dark it has got!
What can be keeping William? I must go
at once, or what will my aunt say! Would
you mind going with me a little bit, Susan?

Sus. I'll go with pleasure, miss.

Con Just a little way, I mean, till we get

to the wide streets. You couldn't lend me an old cloak, could you ?

Sus. I 'ain't got one stitch, miss, but what I stand up in—'cep' it be a hodd glove an' 'alf a pocket-'an'kercher. Nobody 'ill know you.

Con. But I oughtn't to be out dressed like this.

Sus. You've only got to turn up your skirt over your head, miss.

Con. (*drawing up her skirt*) I never thought of that!

Sus. Well, I never!

Con. What's the matter ?

Sus. Only the whiteness o' the linin' as took my breath away, miss. It ain't no use turnin' of *it* up: you'll look like a lady whatever you do to hide it. But never mind: that ain't no disgrace so long as you don't look down on the rest of us. There, miss! There you are—fit for a play! Come along; I'll take care of you. Lawks! I'm as good as a man—*I* am!

Con. Good-bye then, Mattie.

Mat. Good-bye, miss. God bless you.

Exeunt.

END OF ACT III.

Y

ACT IV.

SCENE.—*The Studio.*

Enter COL. G.   *Walks about restless and eager.*

Col. G. Thank heaven!   If Bill has found
Mr. Warren now,——   *Exit.*

Enter WARREN.

War. What can the fellow be up to?
There's something odd about him—something
I don't like—but it can't mean mischief when
he sends for me.   Where could Gervaise have
picked him up?—Nobody here?

Re-enter COL. G. *and hurries to him with outstretched hand.*

Col. G. My dear sir!   I am greatly obliged
to you.   This is very kind.
War. (*stepping back*) Excuse me.—I do
not understand.
Col. G. I beg your pardon.   I ought to
have explained.
War. I believe something of the sort *is*
necessary.
Col. G. You are my master's friend.

War. I should be proud of the honour. Can I be of any service to him?

Col. G. I believe I can trust you. I *will* trust you—I am his father.

War. Whose father? Belzebub's?

Col. G. Arthur's—your friend Gervaise's. I am Sir Walter Gervaise. You must help me to help him.

WARREN *regards him for a moment.*

War. (*stiffly*) Sir Walter, I owe your son much—you nothing yet. I am *his* friend.

Col. G. There is not a moment to lose. Listen. An old man came about the place a few weeks ago, looking for his daughter. He has been got out of the way, but I have learned where he is: I want you to bring him.

War. I would serve your son blindfold: *you* must excuse me if I wish to understand first.

Col. G. Arthur is in trouble. He has a secret.—God forgive me!—I feared it was a bad one.

War. You don't know him as I do!

Col. G. I know him now—and can help him. Only I can't *prove* anything yet. I must have the old man. I've found his daughter, and suspect the villain: if I can bring the three together, all will come out, sure enough. The boy I sent for you will take you to the father. He will trust you, and come. (*Bell rings.*) I must go to Arthur now. *Exit.*

War. What a strange old fellow! **An** officer—and disguise himself!

Enter BILL.

Bill. Here you are, sir!

War. No vast amount of information **in** that statement, my boy!

Bill. Well, sir—here *I* are, sir.

War. That *is* a trifle more to the point, though scarcely requiring mention.

Bill. Then, here *we* are, sir.

War. That'll do—if you know what **comes** next?

Bill. I do, sir.

War. Go on, then.

Bill. Here goes! Come along, sir. You'll have to take a bobby, though.

War. We'll see about that. You go on.

Exeunt.

Enter GERVAISE, *followed by* COL. G.

Ger. What a time you have been, William!

Col. G. I'm sorry, sir. Did you want anything?

Ger. No. But I don't like to be left. You are the only friend I have.

Col. G. Thank you, sir. A man *must* do his duty, but it's a comfort when his colonel takes notice of it.

Ger. Is it *all* from duty, William? Yet why should I look for more? There was **a**

little girl I tried to do my duty by once——
My head's rather queer still, William.

Col. G. Is there nothing to be done, sir?

Ger. No; it's here—(*putting his hand to his head*)—inside.

Col. G. I meant about the little girl, sir.—
I can keep dark as well as another.—When there's anything on a man's mind, sir—good *or* bad—it's a relief to mention it. If you *could* trust me—— (*A pause.*) Men *have* trusted their servants and not repented it.

Ger. No doubt—no doubt. But there is no help for me.

Col. G. You cannot be sure of that, sir.

Ger. You would help me if you could, I believe.

Col. G. God knows I would, sir—to the last drop of my blood.

Ger. That's saying much, William. A son couldn't say more—no, nor a father either.

Col. G. Oh! yes, he could, sir.

Ger. And mean it?

Col. G. Yes.

Ger. If I had a father, William, I would tell him all about it. I was but two years old when he left me.

Col. G. Then you don't remember him, sir?

Ger. I often dream about him, and then I seem to remember him.

Col. G. What is he like, sir?—in your dreams, I mean.

Ger. I never see him distinctly: I try

hard sometimes, but it's no use.   If he would but come home!   I feel as if I could bear anything then.—But I'm talking like a girl!

Col. G. Where is your father, sir?

Ger. In India.

Col. G. A soldier, sir?

Ger. Yes.   Colonel Gervaise — you must have heard of him.   Sir Walter he is now.

Col. G. I've heard of *him*, sir—away in the north parts he's been, mostly.

Ger. Yes.   How I wish he would come home!   I would do everything to please him. I have it, William!   I'll go to India.   I did think of going to Garibaldi— but I won't— I'll go to India.   I *must* find my father.   Will you go with me?

Col. G. Willingly, sir.

Ger. Is there any fighting there now?

Col. G. Not at present, I believe.

Ger. That's a pity.   I would have listed in my father's regiment, and then—that is, by the time he found me out—he wouldn't be ashamed of me.   I've done nothing yet.   I'm nobody yet, and what could he do with a son that was nobody—a great man like him!   A fine son *I* should be!   A son ought to be worthy of his father.   Don't you think so, William?

Col. G. That wouldn't be difficult, sir!—I mean with most fathers.

Ger. Ah! but *mine*, you know, William! —Are you good at the cut and thrust?

Col. G. Pretty good, sir, I believe.

Ger. Then we'll have a bout or two. I've got rusty.—Have I said anything odd—or·—or—— I mean since I've been ill?

Col. G. Nothing you need mind, sir.

Ger. I'm glad of that.—I feel as if—(*putting his hand to his head*). William! what could you do for a man—if he was your friend?—no, I mean, if he was your enemy?

Col. G. I daren't say, sir.

Ger. Is the sun shining?

Col. G. Yes, s.⁻ It's a lovely day.

Ger. What a desert the sky is!—so dreary and wide and waste!—Ah! if I might but creep into a hole in a tree, and feel it closing about me! How comfortable those toads must feel!

Col. G. (*aside*). He's getting light-headed again! I must send for the doctor.   *Exit.*

Ger. But the tree would rot, and the walls grow thin, and the light come through. It is crumbling now! And I shall have to meet *her!* And then the wedding! Oh my God! (*Starts up and paces about the room.*)—It *is* the only way! My pistols, I think—yes.—(*Goes to a table, finds his keys, and unlocks a case.*)—There they are! I may as well have a passport at hand! (*Loading one.*)—The delicate thunder-tube! (*Turns it over lovingly.*) Solitude and silence! One roar and then rest! No — no rest! — still the demon to fight! But no eyes to meet and brave!—Who is that in the street?—She is at the door—with him!

Enter COL. G. *and seizes his arm.*

Ger. (*with a cry*). You've killed my
Psyche! (*Goes to the clay, and lifts the cloth.*)
There's the bullet-hole through her heart!

Col. G. It might have been worse, sir.

Ger. Worse! I've killed her! See where
she flies! She's gone! She's gone! (*Bursts
into tears.* COL. G. *leads him to the couch.*)
Thank you, William. I couldn't help it.
That man was with her. I meant it for
myself.

Col. G. Who did you say was with her?

Ger. You mustn't heed what I say. I am
mad. (*A knock. He starts up.*) Don't let
them in, William. I shall rave if you do.

COL. G. *catches up the pistols and exit
hurriedly.* GER. *throws himself on the
couch.*

Re-enter COL. G.

Col. G. (*aside*). He *is* in love with her!
Everything proves it. My boy! My boy!

Ger. Father! father!—Oh, William! I
was dreaming, and took you for my father!
I *must* die, William—somehow. There must
be some way out of this! The doors can't *all*
be locked.

Col. G. There's generally a chance to be
had, sir. There's always a right and a wrong
fighting it out somewhere. There's Garibaldi

in the field again! Die by the hand of an enemy—if you *will* die, sir.

Ger. (*smiling*) That I couldn't, William: the man that killed me would be my best friend.—Yes—Garibaldi!—I don't deserve it, though: he fights for his country; I should fight but for death. Only a man doesn't stop when he dies—does he, William?

Col. G. I trust not, sir. But he may hope to be quieter—that is, if he dies honestly. It's grand for a soldier! He sweeps on the roaring billows of war into a soundless haven! Think of that, sir!

Ger. Why, William! how you talk!—Yes! it would be grand! On the crest of the war-cataract—heading a cavalry charge!—To-morrow, William. I shall be getting stronger all the way. We'll start to-morrow.

Col. G. Where for, sir?

Ger. For Italy—for Garibaldi. You'll go with me?

Col. G. To the death, sir.

Ger. Yes; that's it — that's where I'm going. But not to-day. Look at my arm: it wouldn't kill a rat!—You saved my life, but I'm not grateful. If I was dead, I might be watching her—out of the lovely silence!— My poor Psyche!

Col. G. She's none the worse, sir. The pistol didn't go off.

Ger. Ah!—She ought to have fallen to pieces—long ago! You've been seeking to keep her shroud wet. But it's no matter.

Let her go. Earth to earth, and dust to dust!—the law of Nature—and Art too.

Exit into the house.

Col. G. (*following him*) I mustn't lose sight of him.—Here he comes again, thank God!

Catches up a coat, and begins brushing it.

Re-enter GER.

Ger. I don't like to see you doing that.

Col. G. Why shouldn't I serve my own— superior, sir? Anything's better than serving yourself. And that's what every one does who won't serve other people.

Ger. You are right. And it's so cheap.

Col. G. And so nasty!

Ger. Right again, William!—Right indeed!—You're a gentleman! If there's anything I could help you in—anything gone wrong,—any friends offended—I'm not altogether without influence.

Col. G. (*aside*) He will vanquish me with my own weapons!

Ger. But you *will* go to Garibaldi with me?

Col. G. I will, sir.

Ger. And ride by my side?

Col. G. Of course.

Ger. If you ride by me, you will have to ride far.

Col. G. I know, sir. But if you would be fit for fighting, you must come and have something to eat and drink.

Ger. All right. A soldier must obey: I shall begin by obeying you. Only mind you keep up with me. *Exit, leaning on* COL. G.

Enter THOMAS.

Tho. Th' dule a mon be yere! Aw're main troubled to get shut ov they reyvers! Aw'm olez i' trouble! Mine's a gradely yed! it be!—Hoy!—Nobory yere! 'T seems to me, honest men be scarce i' Lonnon. Aw'm beawn to believe nobory but mo own heighes, and mo own oud lass. *Exit.*

Re-enter GERVAISE, *followed by* COL. G.

Ger. No, William; I won't lie down. I feel much better. Let's have a bout with the foils.

Col. G. Very well, sir. (*Aside.*) A little of that will go far, I know. (*Gets down the foils.*)

Ger. And, William, you must set a block up here. I shall have a cut or two at it to-morrow. There's a good cavalry weapon up there—next that cast of Davis's arm.

Col. G. Suppose your father were to arrive just after you had started!

Ger. I shouldn't mind. I don't want to see him yet. I'm such a poor creature! The heart seems to have gone out of me. You see, William——

Enter Mrs. Clifford.

Ger. Ah! How do you do, aunt?

Mrs. C. What's this nonsense about Garibaldi, Arthur?

Ger. Who told you?

Mrs. C. You don't mean it's true?

Ger. Quite true, aunt.

Mrs. C. Really, Arthur, you are more of a scatterbrain than I took you for!

Ger. Don't say that, aunt. I only take after my father.

Mrs. C. Don't talk to me of your father! I have no patience with him. A careless hard-hearted fellow—not worthy the name of a father! (*She glares at* Sir Walter.)

Ger. You may go, William. (Col. G. *retires slowly.*)

Ger. Aunt, you have been a mother to me; but were you really my mother, I must not listen to such words of my father. He has good reasons for what he does, though I admit there is something in it we don't understand. (*Aside.*) If I could but understand how Constance——

Mrs. C. What do you say? What was that about Constance?

Ger. Oh, nothing, aunt. I was only thinking how difficult it is to understand people.

Mrs. C. If you mean Constance, I agree with you. She is a most provoking girl.

Ger. (*smiling*) I am sorry to hear that, aunt.

Mrs. C. I'm very glad you were never so silly as take a fancy to the girl. She would have led you a pretty dance! If you saw how she treats that unfortunate Waterfield! But what's bred in the bone won't out of the flesh.

Ger. There's nothing bred in her I would have out, aunt.

Mrs. C. Perhaps she originated her vulgarity. That is a shade worse.

Ger. *Vulgarity*, aunt! I cannot remember the meaning of the word when I think of *her*.

Mrs. C. If you choose to insult me, Arthur—— *Exit.*

Ger. It is high time I were gone! If I should be called in now to settle matters between—— William! William!—William!

Enter Col. G.

Ger. To-morrow, William. Not a word. If you will go with me, I shall be glad. If you will not, I shall go without you. *Exit.*

Col. G. Yes, sir.—I wish Warren were here with the old man. I don't know what to do till he comes.

Enter Constance.

Con. I thought my aunt was here, William.

Col. G. No, miss. She was here, but she's gone again.

Con. Could I see **Mr.** Gervaise for **a** moment ?

Col. G. Certainly, miss. I'll tell him.

Con. Is he still determined **on** going, William ?

Col. G. Yes, miss ;—to-morrow, he says.

Con. To-morrow !

Col. G. Yes, miss. I think **he** means **to** start for Dover in the morning.

Con. What *am* I to do ?

Col. G. What's the matter, miss ?

Con. What *can* I do ? I know he is angry with me. I don't quite know why. I wish I had never—— I can't help it now. My heart will break. (*Weeps.*)

Col. G. Don't let him go to Dover to-morrow, miss.

Con. He would have listened to me once. He won't now. It's all so different ! Everything has gone wrong somehow.

Col. G. Do try to keep him from going, miss.

Con. He would but think me forward. I could bear anything better than have him think ill of me.

Col. G. No fear of that, miss. The danger is all the other way.

Con. What other way, William ?

Col. G. He thinks you don't care **a bit** about him.

Exit. CONSTANCE *drops on the dais, nearly under the veiled Psyche.*

Enter GER. *and stands a moment regarding her.*

Ger. Constance.

Con. (*starting up, and flying to him with her hands clasped*) Arthur! Arthur! don't go. I can't bear you to go. It's all my fault, but do forgive me! Oh, do, do—*dear* Arthur! Don't go to-morrow. I shall be miserable if you do.

Ger. But why, my——why, Constance?

Con. I *was* your Constance once.

Ger. But why should I not go? Nobody wants me here.

Con. Oh, Arthur! how can you be so cruel? Can it be that——? Do say something. If you won't say anything, how can I know what you are thinking—what you wish? Perhaps you don't like—— I would —I have — I won't — Oh, Arthur! do say something.

Ger. I have nothing to say, Constance.

Con. Then I *have* lost you—altogether! I dare say I deserve it. I hardly know. God help me! What can I have done so very wicked? Oh! why did you take me out of the streets? I should have been used to them by this time! They are terrible to me now. No, no, Arthur! I thank you—thank you—with my very soul! What might I not have been by this time! But I used to lie in that corner, and I daren't now!

Enter COL. G. *behind.*

It was a happy time, for I had not offended you then.   Good-bye.   Won't you say one word to me?—You will never see me again.

She pauses a moment; then exit weeping—by the back door, behind the Psyche. COL. G. *follows her.*

Ger. How *could* she love that fellow? (*Looking up.*)   Gone? gone!   My Constance! My Psyche!   I've driven her into the wild street!   O my God!   William!   William! Constance!   Which door?   I won't go, Constance—I won't.   I will do anything you ask me.   What was that she said?—*Good-bye!* God in heaven!—William! you idiot! where are you?   William!

He rushes out by the front door.   Re-enter COL. G. *by the back door.*

Col. G. It was lucky I met Bill!   He's after her like the wind.   That message will bring her back, I think.   I could trust that boy with anything!   But where is he? (*Enter* THOMAS.)   What, friend! here at last! Thank God!   Just sit down a moment, will you?   (*Peeps into the room off the study.*) He's not there!   I heard him calling this moment!   Perhaps he's in the house.—Did *you* leave the door open, sir?

Tho. Nay.   Th' dur wur oppen.   Aw seigh sombory run eawt as aw coom oop.

Col. G. My boy! my boy!   It will kill

him!—Stop here till I come back. (*Rushes out.*)

Tho. Aw connot stop. Aw'm tired enough, God knows, to stop anywheeres; mo yed goes reawnd and reawnd, an' aw'd fain lie mo deawn. But aw mun be gooin'. Nobory can tell what may be coomin to mo Mattie. Aw mun go look, go look! Ha! ha! they couldn't keep mo, owd mon as aw wur! But aw wish aw hed a word wi' th' mon first.

Enter WARREN.

War. (*aside*) This must be the old fellow himself! Here he is after all! (*Peeps into the room.*)

Tho. Theer be nobory theer, sir. Th' maister's run eawt, and th' mon after him.

War. Run out!

Tho. Aw niver says what aw donnot mane. An' aw'm glad yo're theer, sir; for William he towd mo to stay till he coom back; but aw've not geet so mich time to spare; and so be's yo're a friend ov th' maister's, yo'll mebbe mind th' shop a smo' bit. Aw mun goo (*going*).

War. I say, old man—your name's Thomas Pearson—ain't it?

Tho. Yigh. Aw yer. But hea cooms to to knaw mo name?

War. I know all about you.

Tho. Ivvery body knaws ivvery body yere! Aw connot stur a fut fur folks as knaws mo, and knaws mo name, and knaws what aw be

z

after. Lonnon is a dreedfu' plaze. Aw mun geet mo lass to whoam. Yo'll mind th' shop till th' maister cooms back. Good neet (*going*).

War. (*stopping him*) They want you here a bit. You'd better stop. The man will be back directly. You're too suspicious.

Tho. Nea, maister, thae'rt wrung theer. Aw've trusted too mich—a theawsand times too mich.

War. You trusted the wrong people, then.

Tho. It taks no mak o' a warlock to tell mo that, maister. It's smo' comfort, noather.

War. Well now, you give me a turn, and hear what I've got to say.

Tho. Yo're o' tarred wi' th' same stick. Ivvery body maks gam ov th' poor owd mon! Let me goo, maister. Aw want mo chylt, mo Mattie!

War. You must wait till Mr. Gervaise's man comes back.

Tho. (*despairingly*) O Lord   Th' peack ov sunbrunt lies they ha' been tellin' me sin' aw coom yere!—childer an o'!

War. Have patience, man. You won't repent it.

Tho. What mun be, mun. Aw connot ha' patience, but aw con stop. Aw'd rayther goo, though. Aw'm noan sorry to rest noather. (*Sits down on the dais.*)

Enter BILL.

War. Here, boy! Don't let the old man go till some one comes.   *Exit.*

Bill. All right, sir! Hillo, daddy! There you are! Thank God!

Tho. What fur, boy? Wull he gie mo mo Mattie again—dosto think?

Bill. That he will, daddy! You come along, an' you'll know a honest boy next time. —I can't till I see Mr. William, though.

Tho. Iv thae manes th' maister's mon yere, he's run eawt. An' aw connot goo witho. Aw'm keepin' th' shop till he coom back. An' aw dunnot mich care to goo witho. Aw dunnot mich trust tho. Th' Lord have a care ov mo! Aw dunnot knaw which to trust, and which not to trust. But aw *mun* wait for maister William, as yo co' him.

Bill. All right, daddy!—Don't you stir from here till I come back—not for nobody— no, not for Joseph!

Tho. Aw dunnot knaw no Joseph.

Bill. I'll soon let you see I'm a honest boy! As you can't go to Mattie, I'll bring Mattie to you: see if I don't! An' if she ain't the right un, I'll take her back, and charge ye nuffin for carriage. Can't say fairer than that, daddy!

Tho. Bless tho, mo boy! Dosto mane it true?

Bill. Yes—an' that you'll see, afore you're an 'alf an hour older, daddy. When Mr. William comes, you say to him, "Bill's been. —All right."

Tho. Aw dunnot like secrets, lad. What don yo mane? Ivvery body seems to mane something, and nobory to say it.

Bill. Never you mind, daddy! "Bill's been.—All right." That's your ticket. I'm off. *Exit.*

Thomas *gets up, and walks about, murmuring to himself. A knock at the door.*

Tho. Somebory after mo again! Aw'll geet eawt ov th' way. (*Goes behind the Psyche.*)

Enter WATERFIELD.

Wat. Nobody here! I *am* unlucky. "Not at home," said the rascal,—and grinned, by Jove! I'll be at the bottom of this. There's no harm in Gervaise. He's a decent fellow. (*Knocks at the door of* GER.'s *room.*) I won't leave the place till I've set things right—not if I've got to give him a post-obit for five thousand—I won't!—Nobody there? (*Looks in.*) No. Then I'll go in and wait. *Exit.*

Tho. (*peeping from behind the Psyche*). That's the villain! Lord o' mercy! that's the villain! If aw're as strung as aw'm owd, aw'd scrunch his yed—aw would! Aw'm sure it's th' mon. He kep eawt ov mo way—but aw seigh him once. O Lord, keep mo hands off ov him. Aw met kill him. Aw'm sartin sure ov him when aw see him. Aw'll not goo nigh him till somebory cooms—cep' he roons away. Aw'm noan fleyed ov him, but aw met not be able to keep mo howd ov him. Oh, mo Mattie! mo Mattie! to leave thi owd faither for sich a mak ov a mon as yon! But yere cooms somebory moor. (*Goes behind the Psyche.*)

Enter MRS. CLIFFORD.

Mrs. C. No one here? She can never be in his room with him! (*Opens the door.*) Oh! Mr. Waterfield! You're here—are you?

Wat. (*coming to the door*). Mrs. Clifford! This is indeed an unexpected pleasure!

Mrs. C. Have you got Constance with you there?

Wat. I've no such good fortune.

Mrs. C. Where is she, then?

Wat. At home, I presume.

Mrs. C. Indeed she is not. I must speak to Arthur.

Wat. He's not here.

Mrs. C. Where's my—his man, then?

Wat. Taken himself off to the public-house, I suppose. There's nobody about. Odd—ain't it?

Mrs. C. I'll go and see. *Exit into the house.*

Wat. What can be the row! there is some row. *Exit into the room.*

Enter GER., *supported by* COL. G.

Col. G. Thank God! Thank God!

Ger. But where is she? I shall go mad if you've told me a lie.

Col. G. I saw her, and sent a messenger after her. We shall have news of her presently. Do have a little patience, sir.

Ger. How can I have patience? I'm a brute—a mean, selfish devil! If that fellow Waterfield was to horse-whip me—I should let him.

Tho. (*coming forward*). Theer wur that yung chap yere a while agoo, and he said aw wur to say to Maister William—what wur it aw're to say?—Yigh—it wur—"Bill's been. O'reet."

Col. G. There, sir! I told you so. Do sit down. I'll go after her.

Ger. I will. I will. Only make haste. (*Stands staring at the Psyche.*)

Tho. Th' boy said he'd be yere direckly.

Col. G. You sit down. I'll be with you presently.

Tho. (*retiring behind the Psyche*). Aw're noan likely to goo, maister.

Enter Mrs. C. *Crosses to room door. Enter* Waterfield. *They talk.*

Ger. William! I don't want them. (*Retreats towards the Psyche.*)

Col. G. Sit here one moment, sir. (*Leads him to the dais. Advances to* Mrs. C.)

Mrs. C. (*trying to pass him*). Arthur, what can—— ?

Col. G. (*intercepting her*). Let him rest a bit, ma'am, if you please. He's been out for the first time.

Mrs. C. At night! and in a fog! A pretty nurse you are! Poor boy!

Col. G. Mr. Waterfield, sir, would you mind stepping into the room again for a moment? (*Exit* WAT.) Mrs. Clifford, ma'am, would you please get a glass of wine for master? *Exit* MRS. C. *into the house.*

Ger. William! William!

Col. G. Yes, sir.

Ger. Send him away. Don't let him stop there. I have nothing to say to him.

Col. G. He shan't trouble you, sir. I'll take care of that. (*Goes behind the Psyche to* THOMAS, *but keeps watching the door of the room.*)—Did you see the man that went in there just now?

Tho. (*with anxiety*). He winnot joomp eawt ov th' window, dosto thenk, lad?

Re-enter MRS. C. *with wine.* GER. *drinks.*

Col. G. Why should he do that? Do you know anything about him?

Tho. Aw do.

Col. G. Has he seen you here?

Tho. No. Aw're afeard he'd roon away, and aw keepet snoog.

Col. G. I needn't ask who it is, then?

Tho. Yo needn't, lad.

Enter WATERFIELD.

Tho. Mo conscience! he'll pike eawt afoor aw geet howd on him! (*Rushes out and seizes* WAT.)

Enter MATTIE *and* BILL.

Tho. Thae'rt a domned villain! Wheer's mo Mattie?

WATERFIELD *knocks* THOMAS *down.*

Bill. O Lord! the swell's murdered old daddy!

All but GER. *rush together.* COLONEL GERVAISE *seizes* WATERFIELD. MATTIE *throws herself on her knees beside* THOMAS *and lifts his head.*

Mat. Father! father! Look at me! It's Mattie!—your own wicked Mattie! Look at her once, father dear! (*Lays down his head in despair, and rises.*) Who struck the good old man?

Bill. He did—the swell as give me the gold sov.

Mat. Mr. Watkins!——

Wat. I haven't the honour of the gentleman's acquaintance. I'm not Mr. Watkins. Am I now? (*to* COL. G.). Ha! ha!—Let go, I say. I'm not the man. It's all a mistake, you see.

Col. G. In good time. I might make a worse. Watkins mayn't be your name, but Watkins is your nature.

Wat. Damn your insolence! Let me go, I tell you! (*Struggles threatening.*)

Col. G. Gently, gently, young man!—If I give your neckcloth a twist now——!

Mat. Yes, there *is* a mistake—and a sad

one for me ! A wretch that would strike an old man ! Indeed you are not what I took you for.

Wat. You hear the young woman ! She says it's all a mistake.—My good girl, I'm sorry for the old gentleman ; but he oughtn't to behave like a ruffian. Really, now, you know, a fellow can't stand that sort of thing ! A downright assault ! I'm sorry I struck him, though—devilish sorry ! I'll pay the damage with pleasure. (*Puts his hand in his pocket.*)

Mat. (*turning away*) And not a gentleman ! (*Kneels by* THOMAS *and weeps.*)

Tho. (*feebly*). Dunnot greight, Mattie, mo chylt. Aw'm o' reet. Let th' mon goo. What's *he* to tho or mo ?—By th' mass ! aw'm strung enough to lick him yet (*trying to rise, but falling back*). Eigh ! eigh ! mo owd boans 'ud rayther not. It's noan blame sure to an owd mon to fo' tired o' feightin !

Mat. (*taking his head on her lap*). Father ! father ! forgive me ! I'm all yours.—I'll go home with you, and work for you till I drop. O father ! how could I leave *you* for *him?* I don't care one bit for him now—I don't indeed. You'll forgive me — won't you, father ? (*Sobs.*)

Tho. Aw wull, aw do, mo Mattie. Coom whoam—coom whoam.

Mat. Will mother forgive me, father ?

Tho. Thi mother, chylt ? Hoo's forgiven tho lung afoor—ivver so lung agoo, chylt !

Thi mother may talk leawd, but her heart is as soft as parritch. — Thae knows it, Mattie.

Wat. All this is very interesting,—only you see it's the wrong man, and I can't say he enjoys it. Take your hand off my collar—will you? I'm *not* the man, I tell you!

Bill. All I says is—it's the same swell as guv me the skid to find her. I'll kiss the book on that!

Ger. (*coming forward*). Mr. Waterfield, on your honour, do you know this girl?

Wat. Come! you ain't goin' to put me to my catechism!

Ger. You must allow appearances are against you.

Wat. Damn your appearances! What do I care?

Ger. If you will not answer my question, I must beg you to leave the place.

Wat. My own desire! Will you oblige me by ordering this bull-dog of yours to take his paws off me? What the devil is he keeping me here for?

Col. G. I've a great mind to give you in charge.

Wat. The old codger assaulted me first.

Col. G. True; but the whole affair would come to light. That's what I would have. Miss Pearson, what am I to do with this man?

Enter SUSAN *at the back door. Behind her,*
CONSTANCE *peeps in.*

Mat. Let him go. — Father! Father!
(*Kisses him.*)

Sus. That can never be Mattie's gentleman, sure-ly! Hm! I don't think much of
him. I knew he had ugly eyes! I told you
so, Mattie! I wouldn't break my heart for
him—no, nor for twenty of him—I wouldn't!
He looks like a drowned cat.

Wat. What the devil have *you* got to do
with it?

Sus. Nothing. You shut up.

Wat. Well, I'm damned if I know whether
I'm on my head or my heels.

Sus. 'Tain't no count which.

Bill (*aside to* COL. G.). She's at the back
door, Mr. William.

Col. G. Who is, Bill? Miss Lacordère?

Bill. Right you air!

Col. G. hastens to the door. CON. *peeps in
and draws back.* COL. G. *follows her.*
WATERFIELD *approaches* MATTIE.

Wat. Miss Pearson, if that's——

Mat. I don't know you—don't even know
your name.

Wat. (*looking round*). You hear her say it!
She don't know me!

Mat. Could you try and rise, father? I
want to get out of this. There's a lady here
says I'm a thief!

Tho. Nea, that she connot say, Mattie! Thae cooms ov honest folk. Aw'll geet oop direckly. (*Attempts to rise.*) Eigh! eigh! aw connot! aw connot!

Mrs. C. If I have been unjust to you, Miss Pearson, I shall not fail to make amends.

Sus. It's time you did then, ma'am. You've murdered her, and all but murdered me. That's how your little bill stands.

Ger. (*to* WAT.) Leave the place, Mr. Waterfield.

Wat. You shall answer for this, Gervaise.

Ger. Leave the study at once.

Wat. Tut! tut! I'll make it up to them. A bank note's a good plaster.

Bill. Pleasir, shall I run and fetch a bobby? I likes to see a swell wanted.

Ger. You hold your tongue. (*Retires to the dais and sits down.* MRS. C. *follows him.*)

Wat. (*taking out his pocket-book, and approaching* MATTIE). I didn't think you'd have served me so, Mattie! Indeed I didn't! It's not kind after what's been between you and me. (MATTIE *rises and stands staring at him.*) You've ruined my prospects—you have! But I don't want to bear malice : take that.—Old times, you know!—Take it. You're welcome. (*Forces the note on her. She steps back. It drops.*)

Mat. This *is* a humiliation! Will nobody take him away?

Sus. (*rushing at him*). You be off! An' them goggle eyes o' yours, or *I*'ll goggle 'em! I can't bear the sight on 'em. *I* should never ha' taken you for a gentleman. You don't look it. You slope, I say! (*Hustles him.*)

WATERFIELD *picks up the note, and exit.*

Mat. (*bursting into tears*) Father! father! don't hate me; don't despise me.

THOMAS *tries to get up, but falls back.*

Bill. Don't be in no hurry, Daddy. There's none but friends here now—'cep' the old lady;—she do look glum.

Sus. I'll soon settle her hash!

Mat. Susie! Susie! Don't—there's a dear!

Sus. What business has she here then! She's not a doin' of nothink.

Mat. Don't you see she's looking after the poor gentleman there?

Ger. William!—William!—Gone again! What a fellow he is! The best servant in the world, but always vanishing! Call your James—will you, aunt? We must have the old man put to bed. But the poor girl looks the worse of the two! She can have the spare room, and William can sleep on the sofa in mine.

Mrs. C. I'll see to it.

Exit. GER. *goes towards* THOMAS.

Tho. Coom whoam—coom whoam, Mattie! Thi mother, hoo's cryin' her eighes eawt to whoam.

Mat. I'll run for a doctor first, father.

Tho. No, no, chylt! Aw're only a bit

stonned, like. Aw'll be o' reet in a smo' bit.
Aw dunnot want no doctor. Aw'm a coomin'
reawnd.

Ger. Neither of you shall stir to-night.
Your rooms will be ready in a few minutes.

Mat. Thank you, sir! I don't know what
I should have done with him.—Susan, you
wouldn't mind going home without me?
You know Miss Lacordère——

Ger. Miss Lacordère! What do you know
of her?

Mat. Oh, dear! Oh, dear! I oughtn't to
have mentioned her. But my poor head!——

Ger. What of Miss Lacordère? For God's
sake, tell me.

Enter Mrs. C. *with* James.

Sus. Oh, nothing, sir! nothing at all!
Only Miss Lacordère has been good to us—
which it's more than can be said for everybody! (*Scowls at* Mrs. C. James *proceeds to
lift* Thomas. *She flies at him.*) Put the old
gentleman down, you sneakin' reptile! How
many doors have you been a hearkenin' at
since mornin'—eh, putty-lump? You touch
the old man again, and I'll mark you!
Here, Bill! I'll take his head — you take
his feet. We'll carry him between us like a
feather.

Mat. O Susan! do hold your tongue.

Sus. It's my only weapon, my dear. If I
was a man—see if I'd talk then.

James. It's a providence you ain't a man, young woman!

Sus. Right you are! Them's my werry motives. I ain't a makin' of no complaint on that score, young Plush! I wouldn't be a man for—no, not for—not even for sich a pair o' calves as yourn!

Sus. *and* Bill *carry* Tho. *out.* Mat. *follows.* Ger. *is going after them.*

Mrs. C. Don't you go, Arthur. They can manage quite well. I will go if you like.

Ger. They know something about Constance.

Mrs. C. Pray give yourself no anxiety about her.

Ger. What do you mean, aunt?

Mrs. C. I will be responsible for her.

Ger. Where is she then? (*Exit* Mrs. C.) William!—If he doesn't come in one minute more, I'll go after her myself. Those girls know where she is. I am as strong as a giant.—O God! All but married to that infamous fellow!—That he should ever have touched the tip of one of her fingers! What a sunrise of hope! Psyche may yet fold her wings to my prayer! William! William! —Where *can* the fellow be?

Enter Col. G. *in uniform and star, leading* Constance.

Ger. (*hurrying to meet them*). Constance! Constance! forgive me. Oh my God! You will when you know all.

Col. G. She knows enough for that already, my boy, or she wouldn't be here. Take her —and me for her sake.

Ger. What! who——? Constance!—What does it all mean?—It must be—can it be— my father?—William—It *is* William!— William my father!—O father! father! (*throwing his arms about him*) it *was* you all the time then!

Col. G. My boy! my boy! There!—take Constance, and let me go. I did want to do something for you—but —— There! I'm too much ashamed to look at you in my own person.

Ger. (*kneeling*). Father! father! don't talk like that! O father! *my* father!

Col. G. (*raising him*). My boy! my boy! I wanted to do something for you—tried hard —and was foiled.—I doubly deserved it. I doubted as well as neglected you. But God is good. He has shamed me, and saved you.

Ger. By your hand, father.

Col. G. No—by his own. It would all have come right without me. I was un- worthy of the honour, my boy. But I was allowed to try; and for that I am grateful.— Arthur, I come to you empty-handed — a beggar for your love.

Ger. How dare you say that, father?— Empty-handed—bringing me her and your- self—all I ever longed for!—my father and my Psyche! Father, *thank* you. The poor word must do its best. I thank you with my

very soul.—How *shall* I bear my happiness!
—Constance, it was my father all the time!
Did you know it? Serving me like a slave!
—humouring all my whims!—watching me
night and day!—and then bringing me——

Con. Your own little girl, Arthur. But
why did you not tell me?

Ger. Tell you what, darling?

Con. That—that—that you—— Oh! you
know what, Arthur!

Ger. How could I, my child, with that——!
—Shall I tell you now?

Con. No, no! I am too happy to listen
—even to you, Arthur! But *he* should never
have—— I did find him out at last. If
I had but known you did not like him!
(*hiding her face.*)

Ger. (*embracing his father*) Father! father!
I cannot hold my happiness! And it is *all*
your doing!

Col. G. No, I tell you, my boy! I was but
a straw on the tide of things. I will serve
you yet though. I will be your father yet.

Bill (*aside*). Fathers ain't *all* bad coves!
Here's two on 'em—good sort of old Jacobs
—both on 'em. Shouldn't mind much if I
had a father o' my own arter all!

GERVAISE *turns to* CONSTANCE—*then glances
at the Psyche.* COL. GERVAISE *removes
the sheet.* GERVAISE *leads* CONSTANCE
*to the chair on the dais—turns from her
to the Psyche, and begins to work on the
clay, glancing from the one to the other*

2 A

—the next moment leaves the Psyche, and seats himself on the dais at CONSTANCE'S *feet, looking up in her face.* COL. GERVAISE *stands regarding them fixedly. Slow distant music.* BILL *is stealing away.*

Curtain falls.

THE END.